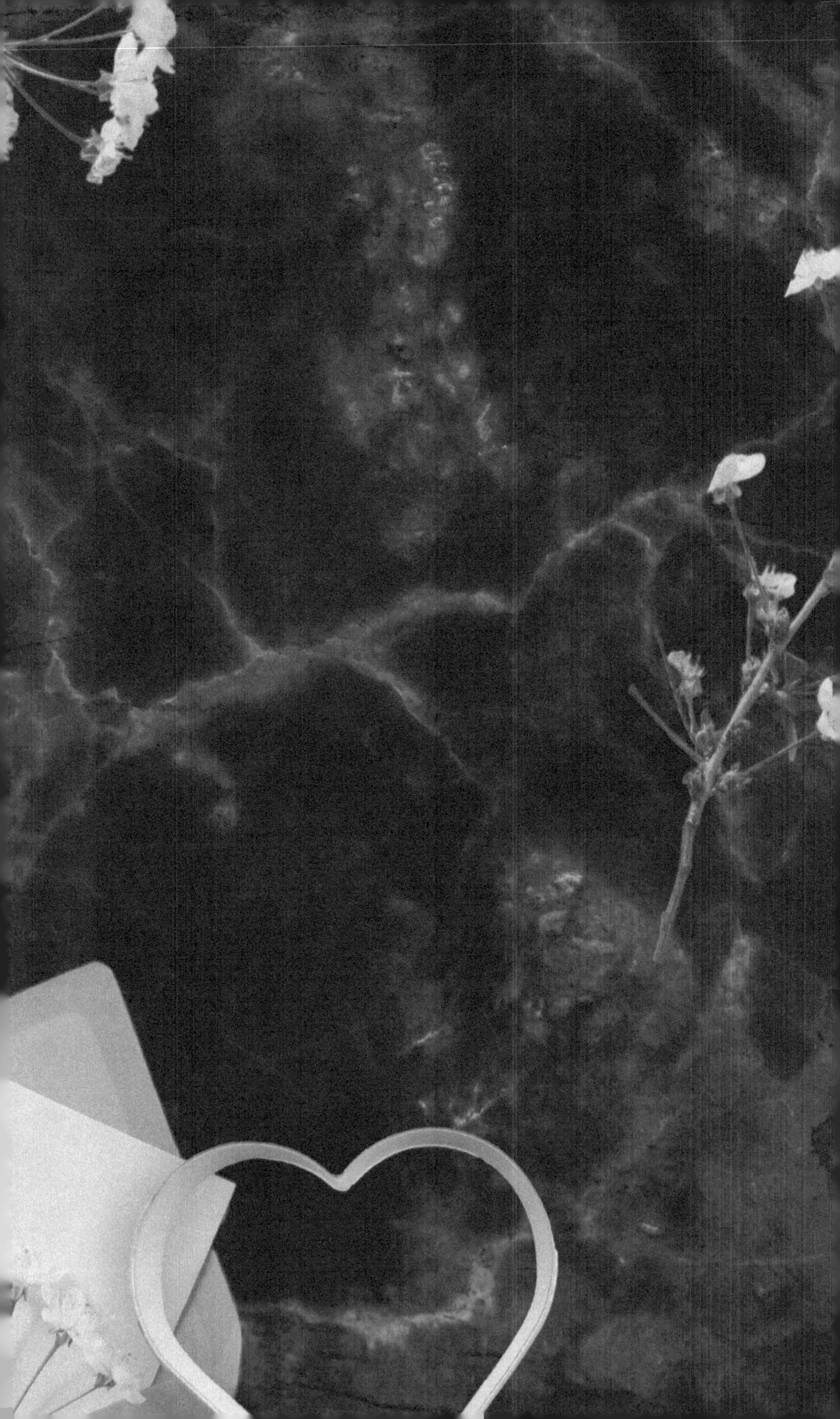

Sugar Coated Secrets

Carmen Rosales

Carmen Rosales
Erotic Quill Publishing, LLC
www.carmenrosales.com
carmen@carmenrosales.com

3020 NE 41st Terrace STE 9 #243
Homestead, Fl. 33033

Cover design and interior art by TRC Designs
Dark Edition cover by Jay Aheer

ISBN 978-1-959888-47-5

Manufactured in the United States of America
First Edition September 2024

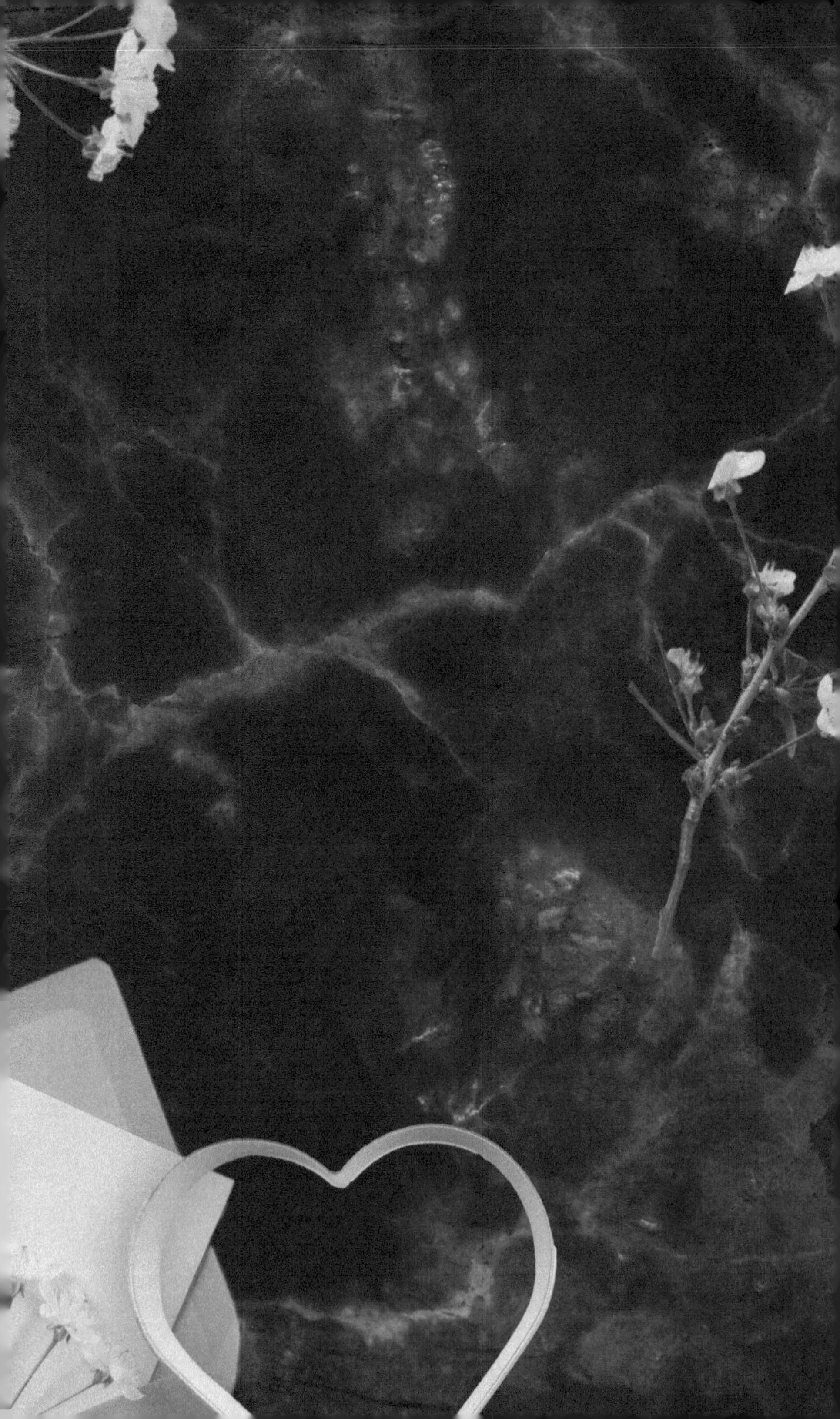

To my husband, Junior.
Another one.

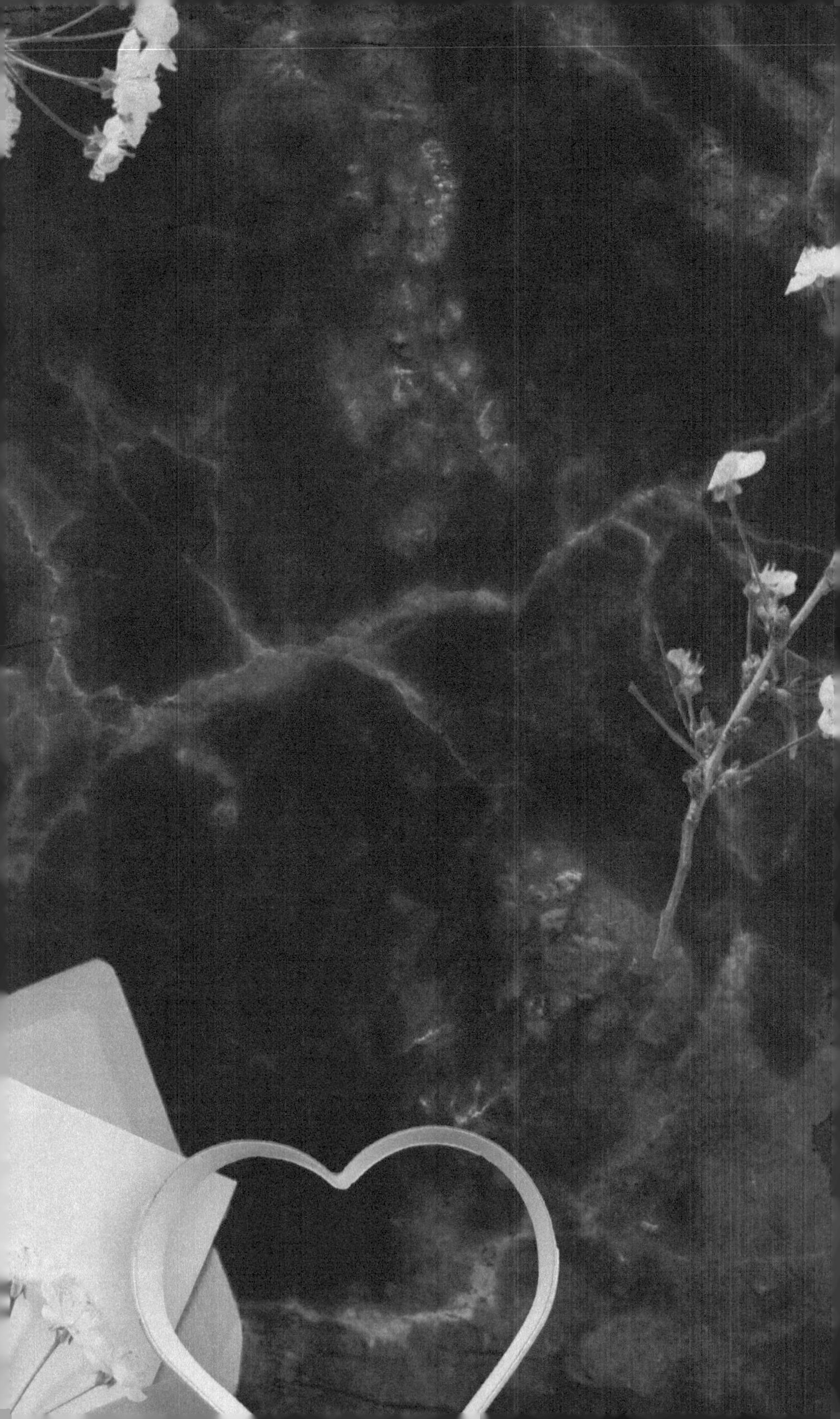

Thank you for downloading Sugar Coated Secrets.

If you are interested in reading more of my books or would like to purchase signed books and special edition book boxes with swag. You can purchase them on my website by clicking here—> https://carmenrosales.com/ or on my TikTok shop here—> @carmenrosalesbook

CLICK BELOW TO SIGN UP FOR MY NEWSLETTER FOR UPCOMING RELEASES, DEALS, SALES, SPECIAL EDITION, AND SIGN UP EVENTS.

CLICK HERE TO SIGNUP NEWSLETTER

FOR DARK ROMANCE READERS,

CARMEN ROSALES ALSO WRITES HORROR X WITH LOTS OF SPICE UNDER DELILAH CROWW. BOOKS CAN ALSO BE FOUND ON TIKTOK SHOP AND THE WEBSITE.

ALSO BY
CARMEN ROSALES

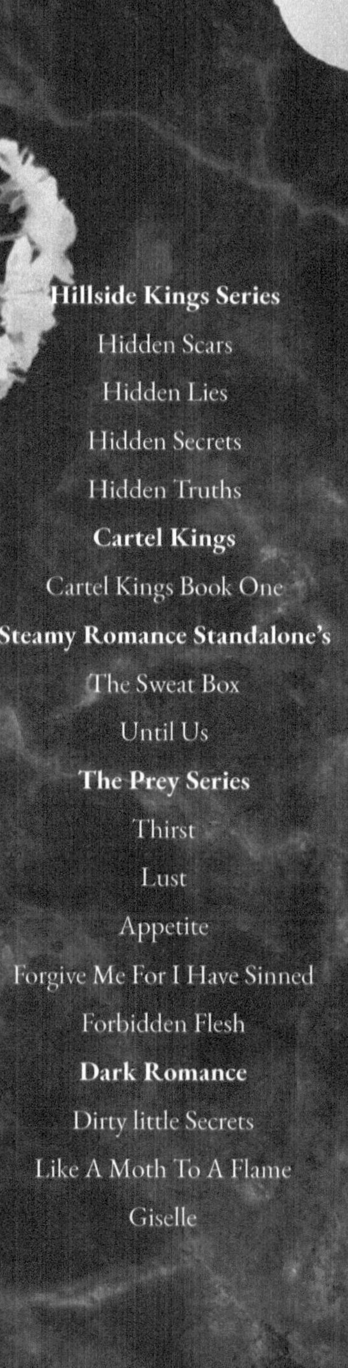

Hillside Kings Series

Hidden Scars

Hidden Lies

Hidden Secrets

Hidden Truths

Cartel Kings

Cartel Kings Book One

Steamy Romance Standalone's

The Sweat Box

Until Us

The Prey Series

Thirst

Lust

Appetite

Forgive Me For I Have Sinned

Forbidden Flesh

Dark Romance

Dirty little Secrets

Like A Moth To A Flame

Giselle

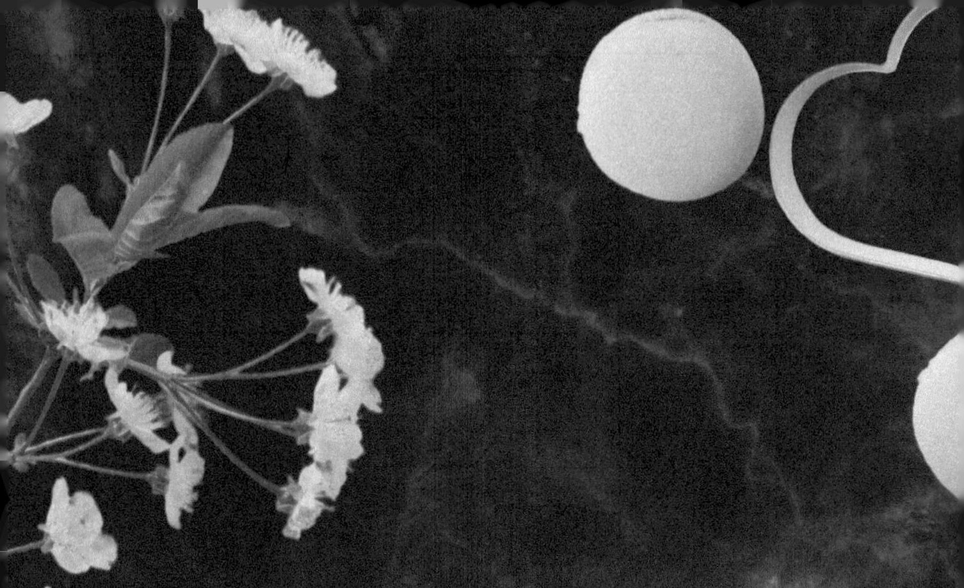

SOME SECRETS ARE ROTTEN INSIDE.
ESPECIALLY IF THEY MUST BE KEPT.

DULCE

Throughout high school, I was invisible, silently hoping Ford Keller, the quintessential bad boy everyone adored, would notice me. When he asked me out, last minute to prom, I thought my prayers had been answered.
It turned out to be a cruel joke, one that nearly broke me completely.
I smile.
I pretend everything is fine, running my grandmother's bakery.
I act like I don't remember him from school, but I remember most of the things they did that fateful night.
In a town with every reason to lie, there is no one I can trust.
Not him.
Not them.
I need to get the hell out of this town, but I can't, not yet.
To survive, I have no choice but to play their game.

IF HE'LL LET ME GO.

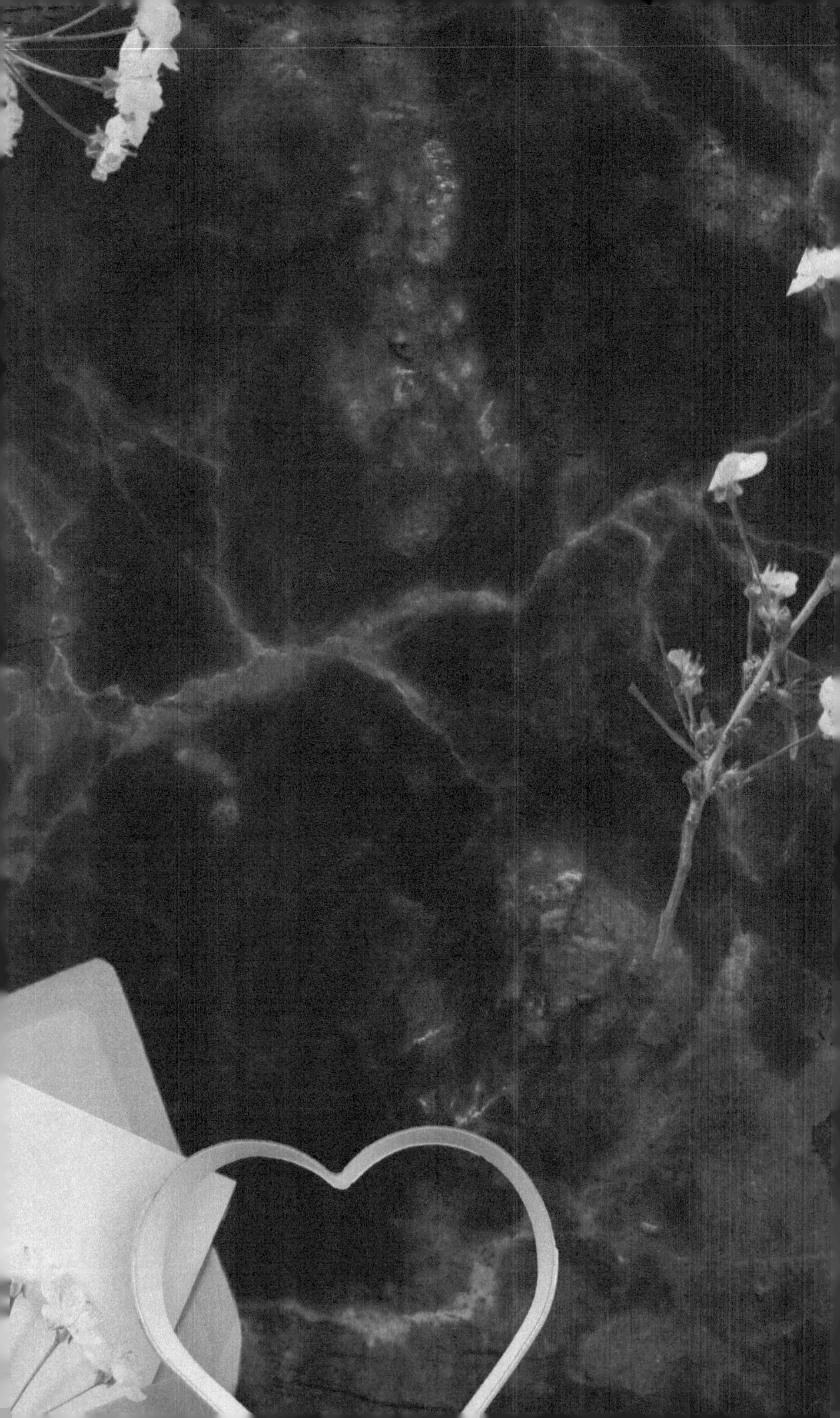

Sugar Coated Secrets

Carmen Rosales

My eyes slide open. I wait a minute for the fog to clear and my eyes to refocus. My head pounds like someone repeatedly beats a drum. The light from the sun shines across the ceiling in ripples like the morning tide. The hotel room smells like alcohol, stale perfume, and sex.

I close my eyes for a second before I look over at the bottled blonde sleeping on the bed with her mouth open and last night's makeup smeared across her face. I don't even like blondes. I don't remember much of anything from last night except hands, eyes, a woman's tongue, and a lot of touching. *What is her name?* I don't remember.

I don't do drugs, but I'll get drunk after I win a race or when I go out on the weekends when I'm homesick. This life is getting old, though.

After four years of traveling and racing around the world, I want to go home.

I grab my phone and check the time. There's a notification saying my flight leaves in three hours.

The nameless woman reaches out, and I quickly grab the bed sheet off the floor and wrap it around my waist. After five shots is one thing, but sobered by the harsh morning light, I want nothing more than to run away from her.

"Ford," she whines, reaching for me. "Come back to bed."

For whatever reason, the thought of her touching me pisses me off. I have to get away.

This is the part I hate. The cruel reality when I have to break it to them. They call my name like they know me and expect more, and I watch their hope fade when they realize that one night hasn't changed me.

"I have to go," I say flatly. "Call the concierge, and they can get you a ride."

She peers at me under her eyelashes, looking like a raccoon.

She doesn't know this is not my hotel room, and I actually have the penthouse on the top floor. I rent a standard room for my one-night stands.

"I didn't want to believe what they said about you." She sits up, causing her small breasts to peek out as she reaches for the scrap of fabric she calls a dress from the side of the bed. "That you were an asshole."

"Now you know."

"I thought we had something."

Here we go.

"I didn't bring you to a hotel room because you were special." I walk over to the chair where I tossed my pants and shirt last night.

She grabs her shoes with a huff. "You brought me here to fuck."

"You're catching on. Check-out is at eleven o'clock. I'm sure you know how the door works."

She walks into the bathroom and shuts the door with a thud.

I quickly dress, grab my phone and keys, and rush out of the room before she comes back. I press the button repeatedly for the elevator while I dial my manager.

He finally picks up when the elevator door opens. "Hey, man. How was your night with the blonde?"

I press the button for the penthouse, hoping she doesn't run out with her phone to snap a picture and post it to social media. It's happened before.

"Boring," I drawl. "Listen, Derek, make sure she leaves the room by eleven."

"You got it, Ford. You need anything before your flight?"

"Yeah, chocolate raisin cookies from Sugar..."

"Sugar Coated Sweets, I got it. Anything else?"

"Place a to-go order for when I get there."

"How many?"

"Twenty."

"Got it. Also, your cars will be there next week. I booked you a rental car at the airport. I'll text you the details."

The elevator doors open to the penthouse. "Alright, gotta go pack."

"The driver is already waiting downstairs. And Ford?"

"What?"

"When you get there, don't race this time. Public roads are not a racetrack in a rental car."

DULCE

A flurry of flour dusts the well-worn wooden table. With deft hands, I measure the last of the cocoa powder. The aroma of vanilla fills the kitchen after I place a few drops in the mixing bowl.

The door leading to the counter out front swings open, the hinges squeaking.

"That hot police officer is asking for you again, Dulce," Katie singsongs.

I pour the flour in. "I'm busy."

Katie started working for me part-time when she moved here from Mooresville after graduating from high school. She's been trying to set me up on dates ever since. If she only knew my history in this town.

She leans over the counter and grabs her apron from the hook on the wall. "I can see that, but you can't hide back here forever."

"I'm not hiding. We have five special orders for tomorrow, and I have to finish these for today."

She bumps into me playfully. "You could go out there and put him out of his misery and finally say yes. Go out on a date with him. Fuck him."

I almost drop the whisk in my hand. "It's not like that, Katie."

"You should see the way he looks at you."

With pity.

"I didn't notice."

I try to ignore her, whisking the batter by hand to avoid over mixing the dough.

"Has he asked?"

"Yes," I reply, adding whole milk to the mixing bowl.

"How many times?"

"Eight to be exact."

"Eight times?" she says in surprise. "Well, get out there. It looks like today is number nine."

I drop the whisk, knowing I have to go out there to see Officer Mays. The last thing I want is to turn down the only person who has been there for the past four years. He keeps the town safe and is eye candy for the ladies with his Wayfarers and straight black hair that seems to defy gravity.

"Okay, wrap this up for me," I instruct her, stepping aside. "They have to be in the oven in two hours to be fresh. Oh, and please get the macarons ready for me. They're on the baking sheet. Third rack."

She picks up the whisk. "Got it, boss."

I wipe my hands on my apron and give her a hug. "Thank you, Katie."

I hope she doesn't think I'm not grateful for her help. I know she means well, encouraging me to go out and date. But it's not that simple.

"You're welcome," she whispers, pulling me close. "If you ever want to talk, you know I'm here. I worry about you, Dulce. You're always working and taking care of your grandmother."

A pang hits my chest. "I'm just grateful she's lasted this long."

"That's because she's lucky she has a granddaughter who loves her and puts everyone first except herself."

I pull back, trying to hide the sadness in my eyes, knowing the last thing my grandmother and I have is luck.

"Oh..." She grabs an invoice and hands it to me. "Here is the pickup order for the cookies. There is a name instead of a company this time. I think it's a coincidence, but I'll let you be the judge."

I look at the name on the invoice, and my heart catapults in my throat.

"Ford Keller," I say softly. I haven't heard that name in a long time, but I could never forget it, even if I tried. "Yeah, I know him," I say faintly.

What I don't know is why he's returned.

Four Years Ago

DULCE

THE BATHROOM WAS FILLED WITH SHOUTS, ECHOES, and the sound of toilets flushing like airplanes when I walk in. Girls wasting time after they've escaped their last class of the day and are just waiting for the bell to ring so they can go home. Some are laughing and pushing up against each other, trying to use the mirror to apply makeup without getting wet from the other girl washing her hands. Others are leaning on the wall with their attention on their phones.

Before they notice me, I make a beeline for the stall at the end. I wait on the toilet until they leave, then use the bathroom and walk out. Throughout high school, I was considered the outcast by the popular kids at Airy High even though I went to school with most of the girls since second grade. I wasn't a nerd or considered an emo kid. I wasn't what they considered pretty by their standards. My dark-brown hair wasn't dyed and styled. I didn't wear clothes two sizes too small or show enough skin. I wore jeans, Crocs, and a band tee. I didn't wear a ton of makeup to impress anyone, and my parents didn't have money. My parents were dead. I lived in a small old house with my grandma on the edge of town. I helped her bake and worked at her bakery whenever I could.

And they made fun of me for it.

The stalls rattle from doors opening and closing, followed by latches sliding to lock and unlock. The water turns on and off. The whooshing sounds of a hand dryer go off like the roar of a small jet engine. Conversations bounce off the black-and-white tiled walls.

"So I heard Ford broke up with Summer and is not taking her to prom. She—"

"I heard he caught her at Trent's house—"

"I heard she broke it off with him because he was leaving—"

"She caught him with Heather like last time—"

"I heard he got Summer pregnant, and she lost it, and that's why they broke up—"

"I wonder who he's taking to prom—"

The water shuts off. The hand dryer goes silent. The bathroom door opens with a scream and then silence. They've left. All that can be heard are the distant voices of people out in the halls.

The bell rings.

Trying to beat the horde of rushing bodies, I hurry to use the bathroom, wash my hands, and skip the hand dryer. Instead, I wipe my hands on my jeans. I pull the door, the scream drowning the voices of all the bodies rushing to their lockers. I turn left to head to my own locker, hoping the rest of the senior class leaves before I make the mile-long trek home. My hopes of any of that happening disappear—like when I waved at Ford Keller while walking into English class, thinking he was waving at me, but instead, he walked past me like I was a ghost.

Standing next to my locker is the biggest asshole of Airy High —Trent Walker. He's lean and tall, has dirty-blond hair, and always smells like gas and motor oil from working on his car. Chris Ellis leans against the wall on his shoulder and watches me approach with a big smirk. According to the female populace, he's the nicer one of the three boys in a boy-next-door kind of way with his brown hair and high cheekbones. But he always has a look in his eyes that he knows something you don't.

Trent's always had a harsh mouth. He's good with a football but doesn't have the grades to get into a good college like Ford. When he looks at Ford, I'm unsure if he admires or hates him for it, but he has no problem getting girls. He's good at other things like fixing a motor or anything to do with his hands, but at times, Ford gets annoyed by the things he says.

Chris looks at Ford curiously. He admires Ford. They met in fifth grade when Ford's parents moved to Airy. Out of the three, Chris seems to be the nice one. I don't know much about him because he mostly keeps to himself, but then again, I really don't know anyone since I don't have any friends.

Ford Keller, Chris's best friend, the king, most popular, hottest guy ever created, is listening to the three girls who hate my existence. His eyes are blue like the sky, and he's the tallest of the three. With a chiseled body, he has arms that fit every shirt he wears and jeans that hang on narrow hips, hinting at the brand of underwear he wears (which is designer). He smells like he came from the men's cologne section of a department store.

I turn the dial on the lock to my locker as quickly as I can with clumsy fingers. Thankfully, it gives way with a click but catches Vicki's attention before I can block my face after opening the door.

"Hey, look. It's Betty Cocker," Vicki sneers, causing everyone to laugh.

I grab my notebook and pack of cookies I baked and slam the door closed, getting everyone else's attention. "My name is Dulce, and it's Betty Crocker," I say scathingly as I walk past them, instantly regretting the words sliding off my tongue. I shouldn't have said anything. For the most part, I don't, but it's the end of the year. I don't have to deal with them much longer.

Vicki snorts. "Yeah whatever, you stupid ugly bitch. That is why no guy has asked you to prom."

"What is she wearing?" Marissa says, giggling.

She stands next to Trent, wearing low-rise skinny jeans and a low-cut shirt with a push-up bra. Her makeup is overly done with a red shade of lipstick too bright for her complexion.

I act like her words didn't hit home. She is right; no one has asked me to prom. At this point, I can go alone and save this humiliation or disappoint my grandmother and stay home.

I turn around and ignore the way Ford looks at me, rolling his eyes at Vicki and her stupid friends.

"Let me guess, Vicki. You're going with Chris but wish it was Ford," I retort, watching her eyes widen. Her face turns a shade close to purple, knowing Summer is his girlfriend. "I wonder what Summer would think since you two hang out these days."

"You bitch," she says in a harsh, piercing tone while Chris raises his brows and looks between her and Ford.

I wonder what Chris sees in Vicki. She has a nice body, long dirty-blond hair, and green eyes. I don't know how he doesn't see the sultry looks she gives Ford every time they hang out or how bitter she is because, in her mind, she settled for less than who she really wanted.

I don't care what Ford thinks. I don't care what any of them think because they are all privileged assholes and bitches who deserve each other. I used to avoid them as much as possible, but I'm tired of being harassed and made fun of.

"I'm calling it like I see it," I tell her.

"Dude, did you piss yourself?" Trent says with a smirk, looking at the front of my jeans. Vicki laughs, followed by Marissa, Chris, Gwen, and then Ford.

"It's called washing your hands, Trent," I say sarcastically. "You should probably be doing it more since you keep putting yours where they don't belong."

"You're just jealous because no one but your grandma likes you," Vicki sneers. "I bet your parents died because they couldn't stand the sight of you and killed themselves." I flinch like she slapped me, taking the air from my lungs.

"Hey, knock it off, Vick," Ford chides, his eyes filled with sympathy as he looks at me.

"What?" she says in a playful little voice like she did nothing wrong, but I see the twist of fury in her eyes. "It's true."

I turn around to leave. Before I push the exit door, Trent says, "I think she likes me." His words are followed by laughter.

I'd rather die a virgin.

The sky was overcast, and I could smell the rain coming. I wanted to get home before it started, but the Crocs I wore pretty much all the time were impossible to run in.

I loved my Crocs. They were comfortable, affordable, easy to clean, and they went with all my plain outfits, including the fifties diner-style dress I wore as a uniform to work at my grandmother's bakery.

I own one fancy dress, and it was my mother's. My grandmother made the white gown for her when my father asked my mom to prom. It was the most beautiful gown my mother owned aside from her wedding dress. Both were white, and my grandmother made both.

My grandmother saved it for when it was my turn to go to prom. It's too bad she did it for nothing because I'm not going to prom tomorrow night.

Every guy or girl hopes to be asked to prom by whoever they are crushing on their senior year. I hoped, but I didn't expect it. I knew I wasn't going, and I knew just like everyone else at school that no one would ask the bakery girl they dubbed "Betty Cocker."

The clouds break in the sky, and the cold wind picks up, hitting my face as the first drops of rain fall. The blades of grass sway in the wind, picking up my hair, and the sound of leaves swaying as I pick up my pace.

The sidewalk ends, a sign that I'm a quarter of the way home. Cars speed out of the student parking lot, heading in the other direction. Their loud engines rumble as the tires kiss the pavement and horns blare. Most kids at Airy High are into racing cars on the backroads when their parents are out of town. And apparently, Ford is the best driver of all.

Ford Keller wasn't like the other boys at school. Yes, he was good-looking. Yes, he was popular. But he wasn't immature. He loved to drive his car from what I overheard at school. He raced all the popular rich kids on the backroads. It was a popular hangout, according to Summer and her friends, but what had me listening was how good he was at sex. It didn't surprise me. Ford was good at everything he did.

So good, he was accepted to some sort of prestigious racing school overseas when he got his driver's license. He was waiting to graduate from high school and make a name for himself, but he was already a celebrity in the town of Airy.

It's hard not to like him. Honestly, he hasn't made fun of me or called me names. There was never a time when my heart didn't flip or butterflies didn't swarm in my belly when I looked at him, but he didn't notice.

Sometimes I thought he noticed me, but I imagined it.

Ford only noticed me when his friends were making fun of me. He laughed along a couple of times but never said anything nasty, and those butterflies went up in ashes. Like today, he was the only one who told them to stop. I should have hated him, but I didn't.

But he never looked at me the way he looked at Summer or Heather or even Marissa. They were pretty, with nice bodies and pretty hair. All the guys liked them.

I hear a loud engine coming from behind as the rain starts to fall steadily, but I keep walking, pushing my long hair away from my face as it sticks to my skin. The tall trees sway as the wind picks up. The sound of the powerful car drowns out the wind as it stops right next to me.

I recognize the black Lamborghini Ford received for his eighteenth birthday before the dark tinted window rolls down, revealing his handsome face. I don't care if I'm getting wet, so long as I can see his handsome face when no one is around.

"Hey." He grins. "Get in. I'll give you a ride."

I shake my head out of the trance his deep blue eyes put me in and keep walking because I'm better off getting wet than taking my chances with Ford. It must be part of some prank they put him up to.

It isn't the first time. At the beginning of the year, they put a firecracker inside my locker. The year before, they locked me in the women's restroom for an entire period. At lunch one day, they switched my food with leftovers from the trash when I went to grab utensils, leaving me hungry because I was out of money.

That just brushes the surface of all the things they've done.

"I'm good," I call out. "I'm almost there." But I wasn't. I had three-quarters of a mile to go, and the cold rain coming down in sheets weighed down my clothes, making them stick to my skin. My soaking wet socks made a swooshing sound with every step I took.

"I'm not leaving you out here. It's dangerous."

I stop and face him, my wet hair sticking to my face.

"I'm fine," I snap, raising my voice over the sound of water hitting his car. Dismissing him, I keep walking, wiping the rain from my face and cursing myself for not bringing an umbrella even though the weather app on my phone that morning didn't forecast any rain.

After I take a few steps, I jump when he revs the car and pulls off the road, blocking my path. His window is still down. I can tell he's getting wet. The drops of water shine against the black interior of the door and glisten on his dark hair and face.

"Get in," he demands. "You're going to get sick or, worse, get hit"—lightning flashes and thunder rumbles above—"or you could get hit by lightning," he says with a raised brow.

"Why would I get in your car?"

"You have no reason to trust me, and I'm sorry for the way my friends treat you. But right now, I'm your best bet if you want to get where you're going without getting electrocuted or sick."

The thought of any of those scenarios is unlikely, but leaving my grandmother alone when Mary has to leave causes a panic inside my chest.

"Take me straight home, and this better not be one of your stupid pranks. I know you hang around Vicki and her stupid friends. Your girlfriend isn't any better."

"I don't have time for stupid pranks," he says. "It's dangerous for you to be out here alone. Now get in."

When another flash of lightning streaks across the sky, followed by thunder, I have no choice but to get in his car. I walk up and scan the door, looking for the handle. When I find it, I open the door, and it swings up like a bird's wing. I slide in the car, shivering from the cold air. I try not to get the inside of his car wet, but he insisted, so he kind of deserves it.

I manage to shut the door and lean back. I'm out of breath, clutching my backpack to my chest. The fact that I'm alone with Ford Keller inside his car has my stomach in knots. It smells amazing. He...smells amazing, like leather, clean ocean, and rain.

His black hair is tied back in the sexy man bun he always wears, and the bottom part of his head is shaved. His eyes are the color of a blue flame, framed by full, thick lashes that make it appear he is wearing eyeliner. He has a razor-sharp jaw, perfect straight nose, and lips so soft and symmetrical they look almost fake.

"Are you cold?"

I'm startled by his question. My hands grip my backpack, and it's not because I'm cold. My heart is beating fast, and my stomach is clenched tight, not wanting to sound stupid.

"Huh?"

"I asked if you were cold?"

"Oh, um..." *Say yes, Dulce.* "Yes," I say breathlessly.

His hand shoots out, making me jolt and causing him to freeze. "I'm just turning the heat on for you," he reassures gently.

"Oh...right."

He shakes his head and presses the button for the heat. Warm air instantly shoots out from the vent, causing goose bumps to erupt over my skin like a warm bath.

"Better?" he says softly. His voice is a caress on my skin, very different from the boy I'm used to seeing at school.

"Yes, thank you," I say shyly.

"Where are you headed?"

"Less than a mile down this road."

"Alright," he says, "but first..." He moves over me, and I freeze. My heart jumps in my throat. "I'm just trying to get to the seat belt." He pulls the belt from my right and buckles me in. I'm surprised that he cares.

He places the car in gear. My back presses into the seat as he effortlessly maneuvers the car down the curve of the road. I can't help but watch the muscles flex on his strong forearms. Chills run down my arms when he notices me staring from the corner of his eye, and his mouth lifts in a grin.

It takes him two minutes to reach the dirt road that leads to my grandmother's house because I counted. It was the best two minutes I've ever experienced in a car.

"Right here is fine," I tell him over the persistent drumming of the rain.

The car comes to a complete stop. "Here?" he asks, confused at the overhanging branches, wild grass, and clusters of bushes.

"Yes," I say nervously, my heart pounding. I point at the beat-up blue mailbox that reads Webster, with the W peeling off, and it's hammered into a slanted piece of wood. I'm glad he can't see my house from here.

"You live here?" he says, surprise laced in his words.

"Yes, right up the drive."

The windshield wipers swipe across repeatedly. He leans forward, looking at the wet, uneven patch of dirt with tall weeds growing in the center, riddled with potholes and deep ruts filled with murky water, the drops of rain creating a rhythmic patter. "Are you sure you don't need me to...?"

"No, that's okay," I say politely, pulling my long, wet strands to the side. "Thank you...for the ride."

I can feel him watching me as I unbuckle the seat belt and grip my bag.

"Why don't you wait a bit?" he says quickly.

I look up, and my wet hair slides forward as I look out the windshield, the wipers moving fast like an old clock.

"Until the rain slows down," he says, causing my heart to somersault in my chest.

It would make sense to wait a few minutes until the rain subsides. I thought he would want to get rid of me as fast as he could.

"Okay," I say softly, lowering my head.

"I hope you can accept my apology..." He swallows and then continues, "For everything."

I open my bag and reach inside for the cookies I made, and I'm glad they're still dry. I have nothing to offer him for taking me home, but maybe he would appreciate it.

"Here," I say and hand him the bag of cookies with a sticker that reads Sugar Coated Sweets with my cell phone number on it.

He gives me a side grin and takes it, looking at the label. "What are they?"

"Well, they're cookies," I rush out. "Chocolate chip raisin, to be exact. I'm not sure if you like chocolate chips or raisins. The staff at school seemed to like them when I gave out some samples today."

"Wait, you made these? Not your grandmother?"

My grandmother hasn't been able to bake in years, but I don't want to explain that to him.

"Yeah, it's an old recipe from my grandmother. I didn't use anything that contained nuts in case someone had an allergy. It's becoming more common these days, and I thought it would be good for the bakery."

I'm rambling because I'm nervous. He must think I'm a loser who only talks about baking because I can't think of anything else to say to him. We have nothing in common except that we go to the same school.

He stares at the pack of cookies for a few seconds. He's gorgeous. My heart pulses inside my chest, changing rhythm. The way the color of his eyes flicker in different shades of blue. The smooth column of his throat and the lines of hard muscle on his chest underneath his black shirt.

"Thank you, Dulce. It's very nice of you."

I smile, surprised he didn't laugh or roll down the window to throw them out. He called me by my name, not "Betty Cocker" or any of those stupid names they call me at school.

The rain slows to a drizzle. A heavy weight sits on my chest with each passing second as I look out the dark tinted window and know this is the closest I'll ever get to Ford.

"I guess it's time for me to go."

He looks out the windshield and nods. "Yeah." He holds up the bag of cookies. "Thanks for the cookies."

"The number is on the bag if you want to get some more." I could feel the heat rising in my cheeks like a wave from my neck to my face.

He looks at the sticker. "Good to know."

"Bye, Ford," I whisper.

He looks up, and I'm trapped in his blue gaze. "Bye, Dulce."

I pull the door handle.

"Wait!"

I let go. Ford jumps out of the car, walks quickly to my side, and opens my door.

My stomach flips when he holds the door so I can get out. I'm glad that the rain has ebbed almost completely. He is so tall that my forehead only reaches his chin, and I have to bend my neck to look up at him.

When I smile to thank him, the moment is ruined when a white sports car pulls up next to Ford's car, and the window rolls down. "I thought it was you," Chris calls out.

Ford turns, shuts the door, and looks over. "What's up, man?"

The passenger door to Chris's car opens, and my heart sinks when Trent gets out. Leaning over the car's roof, he looks directly at me and says, "I guess we know why he didn't make it."

"I was busy," Ford replies.

"I can tell," Trent mocks. Trent points at the bag of cookies in Ford's hand. "Can we have some?"

Ford glances at me and then at Trent. "These are mine, pussy."

Trent shakes his head. "Damn, it's like that, Ford? I thought you were too good to be slumming it."

"Go fuck yourself, Trent," Ford warns. He's half joking, but I'm not so sure. I'm confused that he is defending me for the second time today.

"Ahh, the hero," Trent mocks.

"Hey, are we going or what?" Chris snaps impatiently.

The rain comes down harder, reminding me of Mary and my grandmother.

"Thanks for the ride," I say softly before walking away, knowing there is no way Ford would ask me out to prom. I have to accept the truth like a dead weight pulling me down. Not everyone gets their wishes granted.

The private plane touches down at the small airport in Mooresville. I have been traveling in the air for thirteen hours.

I grab my bag. The rental car is already parked on the tarmac when I get off. A black convertible Porsche 911. Derek wouldn't rent me anything else so as not to upset my sponsors.

After driving for about an hour, my phone rings through the speakers as the Bluetooth picks up, and I see it's Trent. He is the only one I've kept in touch with after I decided to leave Airy after my fallout with Chris.

Chris didn't take it well when I left before prom, leaving everything and everyone behind. He didn't understand. No one did. But I had to do the right thing.

"Hey, did you just get in?"

I glance at the screen with the GPS. "I'm an hour away."

"Where are you headed first so we can catch up?"

Trent has been working to open his garage since he graduated from high school. His dream was to fix cars, and mine was to race them.

"I have to pick something up."

I didn't plan to put my name on the order at Sugar Coated Sweets when Derek placed it or pick it up myself, but I needed to see her.

"Where to?"

"Nowhere important. I'll meet you at the garage in the morning, and we can catch up. I'm jet-lagged and need some sleep."

I can hardly keep my eyes open, but I need to see her. To make sure she is okay.

"No sweat, man. I can't wait to catch up and have you around for a while. Until you get the itch to leave again anyway. See you tomorrow."

"Alright, man. Later."

I pass the welcome sign. *Town of Airy Population 15,000.* The sky is a backdrop of blue behind tall trees on the empty road. The sun blazes in the sky, and the rays on the blacktop make the surface appear like shimmering water. The air conditioner blows at full speed. I forgot how hot it can get.

I place the car in third gear, the engine emitting a deep growl. I press the accelerator and push it into fourth. The car leaps forward with the surge of power, the tires gripping the asphalt and the tress blurring.

The sudden flash of red and blue appears in the rearview mirror. A siren's wail slices through the air.

"Fuck," I mutter and let my foot off the gas, gearing down as I slow the car and pull over to the side of the road.

The police car stops behind me. I watch in the rearview mirror as the driver's side door opens and the officer steps out.

I let out a frustrated breath and roll down the window.

"License and registration," the officer says in a stern voice.

I hand him my license and the rental agreement.

"Do you know how fast you were going?" he asks, flipping over the rental agreement.

"Not really," I say flatly, looking at him through my black Persol sunglasses.

"What are you in town for besides speeding?"

I chuckle sarcastically, looking straight ahead. "Come on, I wasn't going that fast. I grew up here. I'm...visiting."

"This isn't a racetrack."

Looking over, I see him reading the rental agreement and checking my ID. I hate cops. All racers hate cops.

"We don't often get celebrities running through here. How long are you in town for?"

However long I want. Last time I checked, there wasn't a time limit. It is a free country.

I zero in on his name tag. "I'm not sure, Officer Mays."

Everyone in this town knows who I am. It's all over social media that Ford Keller grew up in Airy, North Carolina.

"Hang tight," he says, walking back to his cruiser.

This cop is a dick. I don't know what crawled up his ass or what donut he didn't get to eat this morning. Not that he looks like he eats donuts.

He looks in his late twenties. One of his toned and sunbronzed forearms has a sleeve tattoo of skulls and other random shit. With a clean-shaven face, gelled dark hair, and eyes hidden behind mirrored glasses, he looks like he belongs in a "Say No To Drugs" ad.

He walks back. "You were going ninety-five in a forty-five. I could arrest you. This isn't Le Mans, F1, or whatever you race, kid."

Kid?

"So I'm guessing you don't want my autograph?"

"Sure I do. You can sign your ticket."

"Can I go now?" I say caustically.

He hands me my license, rental agreement, and speeding ticket. "You can go. Be sure to slow down... have a nice rest of your day."

I rev the engine to annoy him. His jaw grows tight. I rev it again like a visceral snarl. "You too, officer."

I wait until he gets in his car and drives off to get back on the road.

Dick.

I drive steadily into town, turn left at the light, then right on Wilson Street. I've been thinking about coming home for the past six months. I'm tired of random hotel rooms and living out of a designer suitcase while flying to different countries. Eating gourmet meals that taste like shit. Drinking until I didn't know what day it was. Sleeping with different women who didn't fill the void. The only thing that kept me going was winning, but when the race was over, I was right back where I started. Unstable.

Rolling down the street, I notice the town looks the same. The same stores line Main Street with fresh paint. The antique turret clock tower that sits in the center of city hall at the end of the street, the black streetlights that line the sidewalks, and the grocery mart that closes at six every weeknight.

I drive to the next block and see the sign Sugar Coated Sweets Bakery. There is an old van parked out front with the bakery's logo. I wonder if she is in there now. I check the time and see that I'm early.

I don't know what I'm going to say to her. Will she remember me? And if she does, will she tell me to go fuck myself? I've thought about her a lot over the years. I could never get her out of my mind if I tried. The way she looked at me the last time I saw her. The way she smelled when she got in my car soaking wet that day after school. She smelled of rain and sugar. I imagined tasting it on her skin. I've had a lot of women since then, but I don't remember any of their scents except hers. I also remember the regret I felt when I dropped her off without asking her out. For not telling her how beautiful she was when they would call her ugly or how delicious her cookies were.

I've ordered a batch every week for the past four years online. I also made sure everyone knew that her grandmother's bakery was the best since she doesn't have a social media account.

I park near the high-end boutique stores to avoid drawing any attention to myself as I'm sitting there idling in the expensive rental car.

It's almost five o'clock. The jewelry store is about to close. I don't want an audience when I finally get to see her.

When it's five minutes until pickup time, I run across the crosswalk. I hesitate, but if I'm going to see her, it's now or never.

When I'm almost to the door, an elderly woman walks out with a big box cake in her hand. I catch the door above her head to let her pass.

She turns her weathered face to look at me. "Oh...thank you, young man," she says with a slight quiver to her voice.

I give her a polite smile. "You're welcome."

The smell of sugar, cake batter, cinnamon, vanilla, and even a hint of chocolate from baked goods lends a sugary note that hits me, followed by the bell as the door closes.

From behind the counter, not looking this way, Dulce's busy setting a platter of muffins onto the display. I remain motionless for a moment, taken aback.

She's beautiful without trying— her long, straight dark brown hair is tied back in a ponytail, a few strands framing her face. Her lips are plump but not too big. Pretty brown eyes that slant a bit at the ends. Skin clear and smooth. She is wearing a pink dress with folded sleeves on her slim arms. Her waist is still small like I remember. I swear I could wrap my hands around it.

I walk casually to the counter.

"We're almost closed for the day," she says. "We're all sold out except for muffins."

"I'm actually here to pick up an order I placed."

She looks up with a polite, blank expression.

She grabs a tablet. "Name?"

My eyes run over her slowly. Unapologetically. The tension rides thick as I take in every inch of her, trying to see a flicker of recognition in her gaze, but there's nothing.

She doesn't recognize me.

DULCE

I ignore the way my stomach flips at the sight of him as I stare at the iPad, playing it off like I don't know him. Like his name wasn't on the cover of *Sports Illustrated*, in commercials, and on every sports racing channel in the world. Seeing his face is unavoidable just doing everyday things like watching TV, using social media, or even glancing at the magazines in the checkout lane at the supermarket.

"Ford Keller," he says, with a fire in his blue gaze.

My fingers tingle as I scroll to his order like I didn't know it was the batch of chocolate chip raisin cookies I made cooling on the rack behind me.

"It'll be just a minute."

I turn around and put together a box and tissue paper, placing the cookies carefully in neat rows, trying to calm my shaking hands. Letting out a small breath, I calm my racing heart, ignoring the memories of that night when I was ready to share a part of me with him.

"Dulce?" he says softly. My name rolls off his lips like a caress, like he knows me intimately.

My throat feels like I swallowed a large pill.

I close the box, seal it with tape, and turn around. "Is there anything else I can get you?"

"Dulce?" he repeats gently.

My fingers tremble as I avoid his gaze. I tear the yellow copy of the invoice and place it on top of the box.

"Dul—"

"You can place orders online." I interrupt. "We ship internationally to you."

"Why are you pretending you don't remember me?"

The memory claws its way back, intense and sharp. Sweat prickles at the back of my neck.

The trickle and heat of blood feels thick, trickling down my thighs. The sensation lingers like a black stain.

"Why wouldn't I? Is there something memorable I missed?" I reply.

Of course I'm pretending because I could never forget him. But I'm not giving him any part of myself, not even recognition. Never again.

He pauses, looks at the coffee machine, and then scans the menu above with a furrowed brow. "Are you open for breakfast?"

"That's what it says," I say monotonously. My face remains expressionless.

He digs in his pocket and places a wad of cash in the tip jar. "What time?"

"Eight to eleven."

"Every day?"

"Monday through Saturday. We're closed on Sundays."

"I want to place an order for the same cookies every week. Is there a way it can be a recurring order?"

"Of course." I unlock the iPad to set a calendar reminder and pull up the menu. Knowing he will be around makes my heart race. "How many?"

"Fifty to start."

I swallow.

"Are you going to leave a card on file?"

"Yes, but I want you to personally deliver them."

"That's not..."

"Or I can pick them up every Monday at a specific time."

I don't want him in my space where I don't have control over how long I have to be around him. If I deliver them, I can drop them off and leave.

"Delivery is fine," I reply flatly, keeping my gaze unfocused like it doesn't bother me that he is here again, turning my life upside down.

"Great, can I have a number to call you directly?" he asks hopefully.

"Unfortunately, I don't give out my personal number to customers," I reply bluntly, the words falling flat between us. "You can call the bakery, and if I'm not in, you can leave a message." I grab the wad of cash out of the tip jar and slide it back to him on the counter. "We don't take tips in the store when we are closed."

His mouth pulls into a frown and glances at the money like it's diseased, and I'm sure he knows I'm lying.

I don't want his charity. All this time, he ordered the same cookies I gave him that day when he dropped me off. It was under a company name that I thought was a couple of towns over. A courier would pick them up every week. Same day. Same amount. He's been out of the country this whole time, so who did he send those cookies to?

He sighs, grabs the money, and shoves it into his pocket. "Do you have the information from the credit card used for this order?"

"I do," I mutter, barely looking up. The words slip out almost inaudible, as if he is robbing me of things to say.

He smiles like he won a rare collectible in a contest. "Good. Use that."

"Where do you want them delivered?" I ask, trying to hide the curiosity in my tone as I tap the screen to enter the address. The need to know where he is staying burns like hot coals in my stomach.

He smiles, writes on a blank order form, and says, "Here is the number and address."

I input the number under a new customer profile with his name. "Alright, you're all set."

He grabs the box, and I follow him to the door. After flipping the sign to Closed, I open the door. His blue eyes linger on my face. He bends close, his woody bergamot cologne caressing my senses, and says softly, "See you soon, Dulce."

I close the door and watch him walk across the street. His scent still in the air.

I back away from the door. A shuddering sob escapes my chest. Tears prick my eyes. Memories flash unbidden like a sudden vivid snapshot. The bathtub filled with blood all around me. Screaming.

My fingers press into my temples. My head pounds, robbing me of breath. I look down my legs and close my eyes. The room spins. I take gulps of air from the sudden surge of uncontrollable panic.

"It's a panic attack, Dulce," I mutter. "Breathe…" I let out a puff of air through my mouth and nose. "Breathe."

I wipe my eyes with the back of my hand and jolt when I hear a knock on the door.

I look through the storefront window and sigh in relief, opening the door when I see it's Officer Mays. "Hey."

"Are you ready?" he asks softly with a boyish smile.

I take a steady breath. "Yes. Um…let me get my bag and tablet." I walk behind the counter to grab my bag, phone, iPad, and charger.

"Are you okay, Dulce?" he asks in quiet concern, careful not to push too hard.

I look up at his handsome face, trying to calm my racing heart and sweaty palms. "Yeah. I guess I'm a little tired."

"Is this about earlier? About…"

I shake my head. "No, I'm fine, Off—"

"It's Danny," he interrupts with a nervous smile.

"Sorry, I'm not—"

"There is nothing to be sorry about." He grins. "I think we are past calling me Officer Mays."

He's right. We are past that. Since I started working at the bakery full time, he stops by every day at closing time to ensure I'm okay.

He checks his watch. "I know you agreed to Friday night." He clears his throat. "I thought maybe we could get a burger or something?"

"I don't—"

"You still have time before Mary is due to leave," he says with a hopeful expression.

"I'm sorry, Danny," I say softly, letting him down gently. "I need to get home."

He nods, looking at his shoes. "I understand."

But he wouldn't. No one would. Every minute I spend away from my grandmother is a minute I'll miss when she's gone. She's the only person I have left. It's why I'm still here in this shitty town, where I only have my grandmother and the bakery. Because everything else has been taken away from me.

I pull into the shitty hotel in town and park in the deserted parking lot. It is the most inconspicuous hotel I could find without going to Mooresville. I refused to go to my parents. They aren't happy that I left, and I don't have time.

As the doors slide open, the cold air and the scents of disinfectant and cheap air freshener assault me as I enter the lobby. A far cry from the luxury I'm used to.

The girl behind the desk calls out, "Welcome to the Ramada," as I approach the front desk. "Checking in?"

"Yes."

"Name?"

I pull my hat low. "It's under Derek Smith for Ford Keller."

I had my manager make a reservation in his name to buy me time until I arrived. I didn't plan where I would stay permanently once I got here. If it didn't work out, I could always go back. I could always prepare for the next race.

She looks up. "Yes, I have one room with one king bed for Mr. Keller. I need to see your ID."

I nod, hoping she doesn't recognize me when I hand it to her. She takes a minute to look at the license, making sure it matches the name.

She hands me my license and a key card with a flirty smile.

"Do you need anything else? Take-out menus?" She peers over the counter. "I see you made it in time to Sugar Coated Sweets."

"They're the best in all of North Carolina," I praise.

"It is. It's a shame, though, about that poor girl's grandma," she says sullenly. "Cancer. She's still alive, but her granddaughter takes care of her, you know. Runs the bakery. Pays for her treatment. Any hope of that girl getting out of here was robbed."

"Did she marry?" I find myself asking.

She shakes her head. "No. Not that I know of. She keeps to herself mostly." Then says like she is lost in thought, "People wonder, though."

"About?" I ask curiously, making me sweat when it's anything that has to do with Dulce.

"Why she looks so sad all the time."

"Knowing you're going to lose someone to cancer does that."

"Yeah, I get that, but why wouldn't you want to be surrounded by people."

Because you were treated like shit most of your life because of the way you looked.

"Maybe she doesn't trust people."

She snorts, making her look even more ugly. "I can't blame her. I don't trust my husband isn't fucking the gas station clerk. He always needs to top off his car full of gas or get a snack from the gas station. When I ask to go, he picks a fight. I went there, you know, to see for myself. I bought something and paid with my card. When I asked her for a pen to sign the receipt, she handed me the one from his job."

She picks at the pimple on the corner of her lip she tried to cover up with cheap concealer only to make it look like a wart, and she wonders why.

"You have a nice night."

"If you need anything, call me," she says and then giggles.

What the fuck did I get myself into?

My room is on the third floor, which is also the top floor. I walk down the hallway with the multicolored stained carpet and wallpaper peeling on the sides. The smell of dirty feet and carpet cleaner gets worse the farther I go. I'm not surprised by the room when I open the door. The bed doesn't have a comforter, and the box air conditioner turns on with rattle, blowing air that smells like stale cigarettes and mold even though there is a No Smoking sign that they clearly don't enforce.

I glance at the bed, knowing the last thing I'm going to get is some sleep. I kept thinking about what the front desk clerk said about Dulce. How she is still taking care of her grandmother.

I open the cookie box and take a bite, closing my eyes at how good they taste just like the first time.

Digging my wallet out of my pants pocket, I open it and unfold the little paper she gave me four years ago.

The one with her phone number still on it.

MY PHONE RINGS FOR THE SIXTH TIME. I REACH OVER blindly to grab it and decline the call. It's 7 a.m. My tongue is stuck to the roof of my mouth.

My phone rings again, and an unknown number flashes on the screen. I answer, thinking it might be one of the guys on my team. I want nothing more than to tell him to fuck off for waking me up this early, reminding me how much my back hurts sleeping on this horrible mattress.

"Hello," I bark.

"Is that a way to greet your favorite ex?"

Squinting, I try to focus on the screen. I recognize that annoying voice trying too hard to be sultry, landing between forced and irritating. "Summer."

"It's been a while."

"How the fuck did you get this number?"

"Still mad at me?"

"It's seven in the morning, Summer."

"Trent gave me your number. Don't be mad at him. You know he can't say no when I ask him nicely."

"Bet you asked him nicely." She laughs.

"Wanna catch up? Have coffee? I live in Mooresville now, but you like driving, so..."

"Even if you lived next door, that's still a no."

"I miss you," she says softly. "I mean, I'll always miss you."

"As you can see from the tabloids, I haven't missed you."

She sighs. "Why are you so bitter?"

Hmm...let's see, after I broke up with you, *you* lied to me that you were on the pill. Told me you were pregnant in hopes it would stop me from leaving. When that didn't work, you told my parents I knocked you up so I would be forced to marry you, then had an abortion, six weeks later, got drunk, and fucked Trent before prom night to make me jealous so I would hate my friend.

"I'm not."

"Then why are you so grumpy? Is there anything I can do?"

"Yeah, fuck off."

I hang up. I'd rather get drunk and titty fuck the front desk clerk downstairs than see Summer. Knowing her, she probably posted on social media that Ford Keller is back in Airy.

I get up and head to the bathroom. Ignoring the mildew under the toilet, I take a piss and step into the yellow-stained shower that was white once upon of time. I stand under the hot spray, letting it ease the knots in my aching muscles.

After I shower, I give up trying to dry myself, chafing my skin with a towel. I dry my wet feet on the shitty carpet and sit on the bed. I check the time on my phone. I'm meeting Trent around noon. The bakery opens at eight o'clock. I definitely have time to go see Dulce and have her serve me breakfast.

FORD

Pulling into the space in front of the bakery, I look at myself in the rearview mirror. I took extra time picking out what to wear—loose dark wash jeans, fitted white designer T-shirt loose at the waist, white designer sneakers, and a pair of black-and-gold aviators.

I wait ten minutes after she walks in and flips the sign to Open before hopping out of the car.

I feel like I'm getting ready for my first date. My palms are sweaty, my stomach churns, and it isn't because I'm hungry. I'm nervous for the first time since she got in my car four years ago. It was the only way I could talk to her with no one around, and she wouldn't tell me to go fuck myself.

In part, it was my fault. I should have done something sooner before Summer and her friends made her a target. By the time Dulce Webster had my attention, it was too late. I had Summer's attention and fell in line with the rest of my friends.

I kept telling myself it was for the best. That high school isn't forever. I thought back then that if I showed Dulce any attention, I'd make it worse for her, but now I'm not so sure.

When I walk into the bakery, the smell of freshly baked pastries and coffee greets me. The large display in front of the counter is decorated in different shades of pinks, listing colorful cakes in assorted flavors, some with sprinkles and different colored frosting. It smells sweet, like her skin.

The door opens, and two ladies walk in, chatting. I walk up to the counter toward the coffee machine, ready to order breakfast, but the moment my eyes land on the young woman behind the counter, my anticipation is replaced by a nagging disappointment.

"Welcome to Sugar Coated Sweets. What can I get you?" Katie says in her best voice.

"Dulce."

Her eyebrows rise, unsure how to respond. Then her eyes gleam. "I'm sorry, but I don't speak Spanish."

I remove my sunglasses. "I came to see Dulce," I clarify even though I can tell from the sassy once-over she gives me that she knows exactly what I meant.

"How can I help you?" she asks defensively.

"You can help me by getting Dulce, please."

"I mean, I can go ask her if she wants to see you. What's your name?"

I quirk a brow.

Right." She rolls her eyes. "One second. I'll be right back."

I give her my best fake smile. "Sure."

She lets out an exasperated sigh, turns around, pushes the back door, and calls out, "Dulce!"

The whirring noise stops. "Yeah?"

My heart beats frantically in my chest, hearing her voice.

"Someone is here to see you."

"Tell him his coffee is ready, and can you give him what I made this morning?"

Him?

"Sweetie, it's not him. It's…" She looks at me. "Can you come out here? He's making me hot."

My grin widens. Hopefully, Dulce appreciates her sense of humor.

There is a loud bang like something hit metal, then Dulce walks out, making my heart ache after beating so fast.

"Good morning, Dulce," I say softly.

Her mouth pulls into a frown, and her eyes cut to Katie and then to me. "What do you need?" she says curtly.

If you only knew, sweetheart.

"I wanted—"

The bell from the door cuts me off. She glances behind me, and her frown turns into a grin. "Oh, hi."

"Good morning, beautiful."

I turn around and come face-to-face with the dickhead cop who pulled me over. He just called her beautiful. What the fuck?

Looking back at Dulce, I see her wiping her hands on the pretty pink apron with Sugar Coated Sweets engraved on it around her waist with a blank expression.

"Excuse me," she tells me dismissively, and then she flashes the dickhead a full smile. "How are you, Danny? I'll be just a minute."

She goes to the coffee machine without asking what he wants, so clearly, she knows. She grabs his fresh brew and prepares it with a familiarity that grates on my skin.

She is even more beautiful in the morning. Her face is free of makeup, but I spot a hint of lip gloss on her pouty lips. I can't help noticing her form-fitting uniform and hate the fact that the dickhead cop has her attention.

The dickhead steps in front of me, blocking her from my view. He gives me a hard look. His eyes drop to the full sleeve of tattoos on both of my arms, comparing mine to his. Nothing can compare to the intricate detail of the track and the supercar from my first race, the skulls, and the shading from a celebrity tattoo artist. Then he zeros in on my Richard Mille timepiece on my wrist before reaching my eyes with a look of disdain.

I return his look, having zero fucks to give that he's a cop. I'll still kick his ass if he gives me even half a reason to.

"Here you go," Dulce says in a soft voice, placing his coffee and food on the counter. A bagel with raisins, strawberry cream cheese, and a cream-filled pastry. I threw in some fresh macarons, too. If you don't eat them while you're out serving and protecting us today, put them in the fridge when you get home to keep them fresh."

"Thank you," he says. "You didn't have to go to all that trouble, but I appreciate it."

I'm sure you do, asshole. Now pay and get the fuck out. But I'm stunned when I don't see her pull out her iPad or him moving his hand toward his wallet. Fucking freeloader.

Digging my hand in my pocket, I pull out about five hundred bucks and move around him to slide it into the tip jar. "My donation to support those who 'serve and protect.' In case they can't afford to feed themselves."

"Damn," Katie mutters. "It pays to race cars, huh?"

"Only if you win," I reply with a flirtatious grin, "which I do."

The two ladies in the back are drinking their morning coffee. One of them makes a tiny squeal and says to the other one, "I told you it was Ford Keller."

I smile at them.

The blonde to the right says, "My friend thinks you're hot." Her friend elbows her in the ribs. "I'm sure you get that a lot, though."

"I never get tired of it," I say with a charming smile.

I turn my attention back to Danny the Dickhead as he grabs his food and coffee off the counter and tell him, "Enjoy your free breakfast."

Danny flushes red, his throat turns purple, and he looks like he wants to say something but is biting his tongue. I'm sure he's worried about saying something that will ruin his chances with Dulce.

His jaw tics as I stare him down. "Is that your Porsche outside?" He nods to the window. "It's double parked."

We both know it's my car, and it isn't double parked. He wants to do this outside. Alright, I'll bite.

I turn to Dulce, who's watching. "I'll be right back, Dulce." I drop my gaze to her lips. "Don't go anywhere." I open the door and give the Dickhead a fake smile. "After you, Officer."

He walks out and stops in front of his cruiser, holding his stuff. "What the fuck do you think you're doing?"

"Getting breakfast," I reply with a shrug.

"You know exactly what the fuck I'm talking about."

I smile. "No, not really. Just getting breakfast. I hear Dulce's food is the best."

I see the way his eyes flicker when I mention her name. He's knee-deep crazy about her. I just hope the closest he's come to her is thinking about her while he jerks off.

"What are you doing here?"

"I'm from here. Unlike you."

"Yeah, well, news flash. This is my town now, not yours. You might have some people here falling at your feet because you're a celebrity, but I'm warning you. That woman in there? You leave her the fuck alone."

"Is that a threat...Officer?" I say coldly.

He gives me a chilling smile. "You think I can't make your time here difficult." He opens his driver's side door. "You have a lead foot, Mr. Keller. Be careful where you step. I've heard about how you and your friends treated her in high school. You made her life miserable for four years. Actually, eight years, but at least for the past four of them, I've been there for her while you were off doing nothing good for anyone except yourself. You don't give a shit what happens to her."

I don't answer and watch him leave. I let him think whatever he wants before going back inside.

Dulce Webster is mine.

"You know Ford Keller, and you didn't tell me?" Katie asks as soon as Danny and Ford go outside.

"I don't know him," I deny, pretty sure she can hear the lie in my voice. "We went to the same high school."

She looks doubtful. Then her eyes widen in horror as I pull the wad of money from the tip jar. "You're not giving that back. It's not like he has trouble keeping the lights on."

I drop it back in the jar grudgingly.

She cleans out the coffee machine. "He is so hot," she says with a dreamy look in her eyes. "Don't you think he's hot?"

I check the orders for the day on the tablet, and my tone is informal. "I have eyes."

"The way he looked at you... Jesus..."

I almost drop the tablet. "What are you talking about?" I ask, confused.

She grins and lowers her voice so the two ladies don't overhear. "Ford Keller wants you."

I shake my head. "No, he doesn't."

I'm the last thing he wants. Right?

"He isn't the only one. Officer Mays wants to marry you, I think. He definitely wants to fuck you."

"Katie," I scold, but my cheeks flush, looking over at the two ladies still seated at the small table. I'm glad they're engrossed in their phones, probably posting that they spotted celebrity race car driver Ford Keller.

"That is the last thing that crossed my mind."

She grins. "Well, you should."

I look up like I didn't hear her. "Should what?"

This town is full of gossip about shit that's nobody's business. Katie thinks she is playing matchmaker, but she has no idea how evil the people here are. If they want to keep you quiet, they will. They're all liars, and you can't trust anyone.

I had my heart in my throat the whole time Danny and Ford were both here, having a silent stare off like two wild animals ready to fight.

One man wants me to be someone I can't, and the other is the reason I can't be that person.

I couldn't help the feeling of fear and anxiety churning in my stomach. I didn't plan on giving Danny all that food. It was supposed to be a homemade bagel and a coffee.

Four years ago, I fell for their little game and paid for it in blood. Does he know what his friends did to me? He had to be a part of it somehow, right? How else did they get my number?

The truth is, I want to put it past me, but as much as I try, I can never seem to stop hating him.

Ford shows up in my dreams, nightmares, and now my bakery. Since he left, I try to avoid seeing or hearing about him as much as possible. I ignored him on the news. Changed the channel when any of his races would pop up. I tried to tell myself he was just another celebrity on social media and TV. A person you know based on what they did in front of the world.

I don't know why he's come back, but I'm pretty damn sure it's not to apologize to me or try to make amends.

"He's been around," Katie says, scrolling through her phone. "Models, socialites, fans. Different women. Different countries."

"Good to know. I'll make sure I don't touch him with my hands."

"Why not?" she asks with a smile, her voice lifting at the edges, but her eyes tell me she is curious to know why.

My head snaps up, and I meet eyes the color of blue glass not realizing Ford walked inside. Ignoring the way my insides flip every time he looks at me.

"I wouldn't want to catch anything," I say, playing it cool.

Ford smiles, causing my heart to race. "I'm clean."

"If you say so. What would you like to order? I'm running behind," I say impatiently.

"Are you working on something new?"

"No," I say a little too quickly.

I always am, but I'm not doing this with him right now. It's been so long since I've been near him, and I don't know how I feel about it. I've played out scenarios in my mind if he ever came back, and this wasn't it. How is it possible that he looks better than yesterday? Muscle and tattoos, eyes bluer, and his cologne more exotic. My pulse quickens at the undeniable wave of attraction. But then, disgust follows, like a shadow creeping behind me.

I hoped he would have forgotten me or at least given me the courtesy to stay away. That he would've taken the hint yesterday and realized he wasn't welcome here. Maybe call and cancel his order. But he didn't. He made sure I was aware of him like he did in high school. He could be in any room, out of sight, and I could feel his stare mocking me.

"How about a bagel and those macarons?" he orders with a gleam in his eye.

"You know you could head over to Betty's diner," I say sharply. "She is still in business. Get a full breakfast."

Everyone here is still in business, and from what I've learned, if they look the other way and keep their mouth shut, it will stay that way.

He leans in, his eyes scanning my face. "I like your cookies," he says, lowering his voice. "I'm sure everything else you make is just as good. Maybe even better than anything I can find in this town."

"Macarons are originally from Italy. I'm sure they taste better over there."

He has raced for Lamborghini. That was the magazine I couldn't help seeing in the checkout line at the grocery store. The town of Airy's own celebrity hero.

He smiles. "I've had them, but your cookies are better. Pretty sure everything of yours is better. I want to taste it all."

He's clearly talking about more than my baked goods, but I'm not playing his stupid game.

"Alright, I have bagels, macarons, banana nut bread—"

He interrupts. "You know what? All of them."

My hand hovers over the screen of my tablet. That means I would have sold out, and it's only 8:45 a.m.

A few seconds stretch to almost a minute.

"Is that okay?" He says each word slowly.

I swallow.

"Of course."

"How about dinner?"

"We close at six."

When he doesn't reply, I look up, and his eyes are fixated on my mouth. I hate when he does that. He never used to do it, except that day alone in his car.

"I meant dinner with me. You and me Friday night?"

Katie starts having a coughing fit. I look over, and I can tell she is faking it, but I ask, "Are you okay, Katie?"

She pulls out a bottle of water from the fridge. "I'll be fine," she says, but she's still coughing, and her eyes are wide.

I turn to Ford. "I can't. I have plans."

He raises his brows skeptically. "How about Saturday?"

"Weekends aren't a good time."

He frowns, looking annoyed and suspicious. "Oh—"

"I don't want to go out with you."

I don't think anyone has ever rejected Ford Keller. In another universe, I would have said yes, flushed, and felt those little butter-flies I used to feel when I tried to get him to notice me in high school, but those butterflies turned to knives, cutting me on the inside so I could bleed out.

I should scream at him and tell him he is a monster, but I don't. I can't because I know there will be an underlying threat after it. Another lawyer will pay me a visit.

"Is there a—"

I cut him off. "Anything else I can get you? Coffee?"

"Coffee would be good."

"Good," I say, my stomach churning. "Katie can finish ringing you up. Have a great rest of your day, Mr. Keller."

I turn away and push through the door to the kitchen, letting it swing close.

I slide down onto the floor, placing my hands over my face, stifling a sob. I cry because the one boy I liked took everything from me, and now I'm not sure if he was part of it or not.

It's been four years, and he still makes me feel a strange mix of longing, fear, and hatred.

Four Years Ago
DULCE

I glance at my phone with a flutter in my chest like tiny wings beating simultaneously, still not believing the message I received from Ford asking me out to prom. The Friday, May 31st prom ticket I thought was useless is taped to the old dresser mirror in my bedroom.

I turn to the side in the floor-length mirror, giving myself a critical once-over in my mother's prom dress and pushing the fear from facing everyone at school.

The dress flares out, snug at the waist, and almost knee length. It feels smooth against my freshly shaved legs. The white cotton thong made me feel like I wasn't wearing any underwear. The dress was strapless. I couldn't afford to buy a strapless bra to push up my breasts, but I didn't need it. Half my breasts were uncovered, and it gave me a sense of confidence. A dreamy feeling filled with excitement ran through me that Ford would find me attractive.

"You look beautiful, Dulce."

I look at my grandmother's reflection in the mirror and feel a pang inside my chest. She looks tired. The sky is overcast, and the lights in my bedroom make her look pale like white salamander.

When I was in ninth grade, she was diagnosed with cancer in her lymph nodes. She underwent treatment and went into remission. Now, it is back with a vengeance, wanting to finish the job. Cancer is a bitch. It's evil. It makes you watch your loved ones die slowly. Treatment gives you hope, but it doesn't make it easy.

"Thank you, Grandma."

"Who's the lucky boy?"

I smile. "Ford Keller."

"Ford Keller," she repeats but doesn't seem surprised for whatever reason. She knows who he is. I mean, who doesn't? His parents are rich.

I look at myself once again in the mirror, smoothing my dress. I almost declined his invitation when I received the text at 3:30 after school from an unknown number. I didn't plan on going. I had already told Mary to leave for the day. At first, I wasn't sure if the invitation was real. When I asked who it was, Ford's name popped up. My heart beat wildly. Blue eyes swam behind my eyes as my fingers typed the only reply that would make all my dreams come true. *Yes.*

"Are you sure you will be okay until I come back?"

She waves her hand from her wheelchair. "I'll be fine," she says.

She needs the wheelchair because the cancer has metastasized to the bone, and she can't walk. I bathed her when I got home because she hates when Mary does it, and then I made her dinner —mashed potatoes and meatloaf.

"Are you sure? It was last minute. I could send him a text and tell him I can't go. I know I told you I wasn't going."

"Dulce Webster," she says with a horrified look. "You will not stand up that boy. He asked, and you accepted. I know you're nervous, sweetheart. It's what happens when the guy you have a crush on asks you out."

I whirl around. "Grandma..."

She sucks her teeth. "You can't lie to me, Dulce. I see the look in your eye every time someone mentions Ford Keller." She pushes the button on her refurbished motorized wheelchair, which I found on eBay for half the price, and goes to her room. "Can't blame you, honey. He's a looker. I heard he is moving to Europe to race cars. This is your chance, so don't waste it on an old bird like me. I want to see you happy before I..."

My chest squeezes as she stops herself from finishing the sentence. I know what she was about to say, of course. I know what's coming, even if we never say it out loud.

She's dying, and there isn't shit I can do about it. Except watch her slowly and painfully wither away.

Nothing, but watch her die slowly.

"I don't want to leave you, Grandma," I tell her with tears stinging my eyes, knowing I'm not just talking about being apart from her tonight.

"I'll be here when you get back," she assures me. "This is the first time I've seen you smile in a long time. This is your night. Prom is one of the most memorable nights in a girl's life. If your parents could..." She seems to struggle to catch her breath like she always does when she talks about them.

I don't want to see my grandmother unhappy, so I smile and tell her, "Alright, Grandma. Let's get you to bed. Ford will be here soon."

"What time did he say he would pick you up?"

"Seven thirty."

I don't want him to see how run down the inside of our house looks. We need new floors and fresh paint. The kitchen is outdated because we updated the bakery to keep business going. All the money we make goes to the mortgage and keeping the lights on. We never have to worry about food because we work *with* food, but there isn't room for anything else.

I follow her to her room, my late mother's silver heels making the loose floorboards groan. She pauses near the stairs. "Hold on," she says and reaches for her phone in her pocket. "Stand over by the staircase," she says and then coughs.

"Grandma..."

"I need a picture of you in the same spot your mother stood when it was her prom. Make sure you take pictures with Ford."

I blink back tears, realizing how much this means to her. I stand at the foot of the stairs, smoothing my loose hair and smiling as she snaps the picture.

"Gorgeous," she says with glassy eyes. "You look so much like your momma."

I smile. "Thank you, Grandma."

I follow her to her room near the living room and wait until she turns the chair so that it is easier for me to assist her to bed. I carry her bridal style, balancing steadily in my heels and feeling how frail her body is in my arms as I place her gently on her hospital bed.

"I could have walked, Dulce. I don't want to wrinkle your dress."

"Oh, Grandma. I don't care if you did."

She gives me a once-over after I make sure she is comfortable and secure in her bed. "Good." My grandmother's Rosewood Grandfather clock chimes. "It's already seven thirty. It's not wrinkled, and you don't have a hair out of place."

For a fleeting moment, dread sinks in when I glance at my phone. There's no text from Ford. Has he stood me up?

I try not to, but I can't help wondering if I've fallen for another prank. Picturing myself waiting for him all night while he's at prom, laughing with his friends

Maybe agreeing to go was a bad idea. If I'd said no, I wouldn't have to worry about being made fun of. I wouldn't have to face them.

School will be over in two weeks. My attendance is perfect, and my grades are good enough that I can miss the rest of the year and still graduate. I wasn't planning on going to graduation, anyway, since my grandmother can't go and I have no other family to watch me take the stage.

My phone pings.

> Ford: I'm outside.

I get up out of the chair in nervous excitement, realizing my grandmother is already fast asleep. I place a soft kiss on her cheek and make sure she is hooked up to her monitor.

> Dulce: I'll be right out. Wait for me where you dropped me off.

I shut the front door, making sure it's locked. The sun has already disappeared in the horizon. Gripping my clutch, I walk up the square trail of steps leading to the main road, careful not to get my heels stuck between the cracks. A large black SUV gleamed under the single streetlight.

I bite my lip and squeeze the clutch in my hands. A sense of dread comes over me, causing nausea to snake up my throat. I only prayed for one night. One special night.

The back door to the SUV opens. Everything happens so fast. The door slams shut. The locks click, and the SUV bolts forward.

My eyes go wide, dread making my skin crawl. "You look pretty tonight," Trent drawls from the front passenger seat with a dark smile. No.no.no. Please, God.

My chest feels tight, and my vision blurs.

I turn my head, and the seat next to me is empty. Chris watches me from the rearview mirror. They're both dressed for prom, but it's just the three of us in the SUV.

"Where's Ford?" I croak.

They both laugh.

"Where's Ford?" Chris mocks.

"Did you actually think Ford would ask an ugly cunt like you to prom?" Trent says with a gleam in his eyes.

"Where are you taking me?" I ask.

"Somewhere special," Chris says, "where desperate cunts like you go when no one wants them."

"Please, take me back home," I beg, panic seizing my chest.

"I'm afraid it's too early. What would Granny think?"

I try to open the door, but it's locked. I pull the lock, but it quickly slides back in place.

"Tsk, tsk. Not yet, baby," Trent says with a sinister grin. "We haven't reached the best part."

I unlock my phone, but Trent snatches it from my hand.

"Give me my phone," I demand in a hard tone.

"I'm afraid that is not going to happen," Chris says flatly.

I jolt when Trent's finger rubs down my arm. I pull away from his touch, making me want to throw up. "Fuck off, Trent."

"You know what, Chris? I kinda think she looks pretty tonight." Trent leers at my chest. Nausea crawls up my throat. "I didn't know she had a rack like that."

I sink in my seat and move closer to the door trying to the handle. "Let me out, Chris!"

Fear swirls in my gut. They wouldn't?

"All the pretty sweet skin," Trent continues like he didn't hear me. "I bet your cunt is just as sweet."

I wipe my eyes. Fear squeezing my chest. "Stop it, Trent. You're better than this. Both of you. Don't..."

The car stops to a screeching halt, causing me to fly forward and hit the back passenger seat. It gives me whiplash, and I feel my neck snap.

"What the fuck, Chris!" Trent yells, rubbing the back of his neck.

"We're here," he says calmly and gets out.

I look out my window and see nothing but darkness and trees

on both sides of the road. We're in the middle of nowhere. There are no houses. No signs of life.

"Where are we?" I ask in a shaky voice.

My door opens. "Where the fun begins," Chris says and grabs me by the arm, dragging me out of the car. "You said you wanted out."

"What are you going to do?" I say between sobs.

"Whatever the fuck we want," Trent says, breathing heavily.

"What—"

Chris shuts the door. "Let's go. We got her out here. Fun is over."

"You're leaving me here?"

Trent throws my phone on the ground, stepping on it with his dress shoes for good measure and causing it to shatter. Then he says, "Yeah."

I wipe my face. "Why? I never—" I sniff. "Did anything to you."

"Someone had to be the end-of-the-year prank this year, and none of the girls like you," Trent says.

Chris opens the driver's side door and calls out, "Let's go. We're going to be late."

Chris's hard stare aims directly at me, and I wonder how I got it all wrong. He was supposed to be the nice one. Sometimes in study hall he would smile at me, at least when his friends weren't around. But apparently, he's no different from them.

Trent turns to open the door.

"Please, don't do this, Trent," I beg, my legs shaking. "Why are you doing this?"

He pauses for a second, then says, "They hate you because you're good. You don't make mistakes, and you're beautiful without trying." He gets in, slams the door, and the SUV takes off.

I watch the taillights until they are tiny specks disappearing into the darkness. I'm surrounded by tall, foreboding trees on the dimly lit road. A shiver creeps down my spine with each rustle of leaves. The faint moonlight dances and twists as it barely breaks through the dense canopy of clouds.

As spring makes way into summer, the air is thick. The heat presses like it's weighing down everything.

When I pull up the freshly paved drive, the Porsche's exhaust growls as I pull to a stop. The garage looked brand-new compared to the historic town. Trent's garage is upscale. It is a big white building converted into a warehouse with a vintage neon sign reading AMERICAN MUSCLE under it. Trent, Chris, and I would hit the track on the backroad and race to see whose car was the fastest. I was into imports, and Chris and Trent were into American muscle. Chris is more modern, and Trent loves the classics. Barracudas, '69 Chevys, and his prized possession—an SS Camaro.

A couple of guys give me stupefied looks like I'm a little lost or stupid for bringing a German car into an American shop.

As I get out, though, the guys' mouths drop open. They clearly recognize me.

"I'm looking for Trent."

A blond kid with overalls and grease under his fingernails stares at me like I'm an enigma. "I didn't think they were telling the truth in this town. You're really from here."

"I sure am. Is Trent here?" I ask.

The kid with the dark hair, mechanic's shirt, and jeans that haven't been washed since he bought them pops up and says,

"Sure, I'll get him." He walks inside through the main entrance and shouts, "Yo, Trent! You have a visitor."

"If it isn't a girl with big tits and a nice ass, tell them to fuck off," he shouts back.

Trent was always a sarcastic son of a bitch.

"This is better," the kid shouts. "I bet he can beat you in a race."

"Alright, alright. I'm coming."

Trent walks out, squinting against the blazing sun. "Son of a bitch. You made it."

"I promised I would."

The last thing I said to Trent before leaving that night was that I would return, and we would open a garage together despite what our parents thought. We didn't want to be part of the country club or be a CEO at one of their companies, trapped in a high-rise in the city fucking the secretary during lunch like our fathers did. We had dreams. Goals. His was a garage and, hopefully, pit crew at NASCAR. Mine was to drive professionally, and Chris's was to go to college and figure shit out.

Trent has scruff on his face like he hasn't shaved in days. "You look like you popped out of the set of a commercial," he says with a smile.

"Is that your way of telling me I look good?"

"Shit, better than I do." He looks down at his mechanic's shirt and low-ripped jeans with grease smeared near the pockets. He has tattoos on his forearms and neck—I bet his parents loved that one.

He motions me to follow him.

"I bet you're driving the ladies crazy," he says with a chuckle.

I walk in and wait a bit for my eyes to adjust to the fluorescent lights gleaming on the garage floor. The garage is immaculate, filled with the nostalgic smell of rubber, oil, and gasoline. He has eight lifts in the center. All classic muscle cars with gleaming paint jobs like works of art. The back walls are fitted with tool cabinets and vintage road signs. Rolling toolboxes are neatly placed on the other two walls. I'm sure they have every tool needed to build a car.

"Hey, some girls dig the mechanic look," he says, then looks over his shoulder as I follow him to his office. "I bet you've had more pussy than an all-you-can-eat buffet."

He isn't wrong. The first two years were wild. I bought more boxes of condoms than I did toothpaste.

"Trust me, it gets old after a while. Different cities—"

He interrupts. "A variety of pussy."

"They get attached," I reply, the words coming out on a dull monotone.

He walks into a modern office with the latest Apple studio desktop and takes a seat in his racing desk chair. I take a seat on the shiny red vinyl couch, letting the air-conditioning vent cool my heated skin.

"They all get attached. Famous or not," he says, leaning back in his chair.

"Sounds like you speak from experience."

"You should talk."

He means Summer. I didn't care if he slept with her. Despite what she thought, it's not like she was my real girlfriend, and Trent knew I didn't love her. He knew why I was with her. Chris, too, but I stopped talking to Chris when I told him I wanted to leave. He hated it. He was a good friend in the beginning. He was adopted when he was thirteen. It was always Trent and me at first, but then Chris showed up, and we hit it off until I left.

"What's up with Chris? What's he up to?" I ask, my voice carrying a light probing quality.

Trent looks up from his phone. I can tell it's not good. "He left for college and was kicked out three months in."

"How come?" I probe.

He shakes his head. "Don't know. He wouldn't talk about it, and his parents wouldn't say. You know how reputation is around here."

"Where is he?"

"He bought a house with the rest of his college fund when he moved back. His parents flipped the fuck out. They wanted him to take over the real estate company in town, but he told them to go fuck themselves. He isn't the Chris you know when you left, Ford. He's changed. Spends his time having wild parties. Races on the backroads with the high school seniors and whoever wants to race. Fucks around. Smokes weed. Drinks. It's like he's running a frat house."

"What's his deal with you?" I ask, wondering why he went off the rails all of a sudden. Trent stayed and is doing what he planned to do after high school. Why did Chris change? Chris was the nicest one out of all of us. The most liked and easy to talk to.

Trent looks away, but I know there is more he won't tell me. "I don't know. We don't talk anymore."

I look around his office. I notice he doesn't have any pictures —just him and his classic cars. "Are you seeing anyone? Are you married? Do you have a girlfriend?" I ask, wanting to know more.

"Nah. A couple of girls come and go, but nothing serious. I don't have time since I opened. Mine is the only one in town now. Old Theodore closed his shop before we graduated. He was too old to work on cars anymore."

I smile. "So you saw an opportunity and took it."

"Damn right, I did. My parents hate me right now, but I don't care."

I see the way he taps nervously on the desk. He looks at me and then looks away.

"I was planning to open the first exotic sports garage in Airy," I confess.

His eyes light up. "What about driving?"

I shrug. "I need a break. I'll go back to it. I have contracts and sponsors, but I'm tired of living out of a suitcase."

He nods, scratching the scruff on his chin, and asks, "What do you need?"

"Nothing right now," I tell him, looking around. "I came to

see what you have been up to. I need to buy land to start everything up.”

“Do your parents know you’re back?”

“They should. It’s already all over social media.”

He chuckles and asks like he doesn’t already know. “Where did you head to first?”

“Sugar Coated Sweets,” I confess.

He clears his throat, but his eyes are unfocused and distant. “You saw her?”

My eyes cut to his. “I did.”

“Told you to fuck off?”

I nod slowly but don’t like the way the hair on the back of my neck stands.

“Pretty much.”

He lets out a shaky chuckle. “Let that go, man.”

I sit up and lean my forearms on my thighs. “I can’t,” I admit truthfully.

He snorts. “You can have any woman on the planet. You’re Ford fucking Keller, and you’re telling me you still want the poor bullied girl from high school?”

“You know why, and I’ve never stopped wanting her.”

“Is that why you gave her a ride that day on her birthday?”

My stomach plummets. “What?”

He furrows his brow and tilts his head. “You didn’t know? That was why Vicki was talking shit about her parents dying when she was ten. They were killed in a car accident on her tenth birthday. You know how people talk gossip in this town. I thought you were giving her a pity ride home because she was walking in the rain on her birthday. I told you I was sorry for going along with them. You know why the girls hated her.”

It was her birthday?

Trent always went along with it because he was always a hardass. The one who would bully the dorks at school. He always got in trouble with his slick mouth. Girls loved him. He was funny, and at times, you'd think he gave a shit, but his empathy is as deep as a puddle.

"Has anyone bothered her since then?"

"You're going to kick their ass or hire someone to do it?"

I scoff. "Answer the fucking question asshole."

He rubs his eyes with the pads of his thumbs. "Not that I know of. I'm not into cakes and pastries. I'm more of a beer and burger type of guy."

"Is she seeing anyone?"

He takes a deep breath and sighs. "How the fuck should I know? It's not like I talk to her like we are good friends. Do you think she would want to talk to me after high school? If I ordered a cake from her, she would probably poison it, but I did hear a cop likes her."

That has my attention. "What about him?"

"He's a dick," he replies, looking at me straight in the eye. "He gives Chris a hard time for racing on the backroads even though it's on private land."

I frown. "Who owns it?"

"Chris. He bought that, too. Pissed the fucking cop off when he did."

"He gives you shit?"

He snorts. "All the time."

"Why?"

He shrugs and looks away. "I don't know, but I heard he loves going to the bakery." I scowl. He laughs. "I went to the super-market where old lady Persie still works. Overheard her complaining that the Dickhead cop turned her down after she tried to set him up with her daughter. Said he would be fifty by the time Dulce Webster gives him the time of day."

"What do you think?"

"Me?"

"Yeah?"

He has been here the whole time since I have been gone. He hears shit, obviously.

"You want to know what I think?" he says when I look at him straight in the eyes. "If Dulce Webster would give me the time of day, I would show you our wedding pictures, and you would meet my kid while the other one was on the way."

"Touch her—"

"And you'll kill me. I understood the day you socked me in the eye for checking out her ass."

He could have any girl. Any of my friends growing up could, but not her. Trent did me a favor by sleeping with Summer. Summer thought I punched Trent because of her, but all the guys knew the truth. The way I looked at Dulce when she wasn't looking. It was gut-wrenching every time I had to ignore her. I protected her from what they would do if they knew I wanted her. But something in his eyes doesn't sit well with me. He's holding back for whatever reason.

"How's therapy?"

I narrow my eyes. "Good. Why?"

He shrugs. "Just asking. Now that you're back and all."

"You know what? I need an empty warehouse," I tell him, changing the subject. "My cars are being delivered next week."

He tosses me the keys. "It's yours for as long as you want it." He pulls out a carefully rolled blunt. "Where are you staying?"

"Ramada."

"Far cry from the Ritz."

"I didn't want to be spotted."

He chuffs a laugh. "You rode in a Porsche dressed like...that."

He isn't wrong. I wanted to impress her, but not with the car, of course. That's business. Dulce doesn't give a shit about that. I wanted to see if she would look at me like she used to in class, but she wouldn't.

"It's business."

"Sponsor?"

"Yep."

He lights up the end of the blunt. The cherry end glows like a red eye in the dark sky and he says before he takes a drag, "Shit, must be nice. Why don't you stay with me until you figure out if you're staying or want to be my silent partner."

"Where are you staying?"

"Here," he says and blows smoke toward the ceiling. The smell of marijuana floats in a cloud of smoke. "I have a loft on the second floor."

"That works."

He grins, holding out the blunt. "It'll be like old times."

"I'm good. I'll be back." I motion for him to follow me outside. Sliding my glasses on, I open the door to the Porsche, reach in, and hand him half of the macarons I bought from Dulce.

"Are those macarons from—"

"Yeah, give them to your staff. I'm sure the guys will appreciate it. Also, order breakfast from the bakery every morning and send one of the guys to pick it up. Make sure you order cakes, pastries, and whatever else she sells from her and not the supermarket. They get plenty of business from everyone else."

"Playing the hero again," he mocks.

"Someone ought to be," I shoot back.

His eyes narrow slightly. His shoulders tense. He takes a drag and blows smoke before he looks away. It's the second time he's looked at me that way when I mention her.

"You should forget her. She would never go for it, and it's not a good idea."

My guard goes up. It's the second time someone has warned me away from her. "Why is that?"

"Too much damage. Keep in mind you stood by and did nothing," he says, reminding me like rubbing salt in a wound. "No one did. And your therapist said so. It's why you left, no?"

I don't give a fuck what the therapist thinks or what anyone thinks. That's the problem.

And I'm not leaving until I find out what he means because something doesn't add up.

As I walk in the front door, Mary is already getting her things together. "I'm home," I call out.

"Hi, sweetheart." Mary greets me with a smile.

"How is she?" I ask with a worried expression, my stomach in knots.

"Hanging in there," she says with a polite smile.

These past few months, my grandmother has been getting worse. I know it's only a matter of time. She has lasted way longer than expected since the doctor put her on hospice the last time he saw her. He gave her six months, and that was four months ago.

"Is she awake?" I ask hopefully. She is usually asleep after her dose of pain meds when I make it home late. I had to stay later than usual to place an order for more supplies since Ford bought me out.

"Yeah, I think she's waiting for her bath."

Grandma met Mary at the doctor's office when she went in for a routine checkup. On the twenty-ninth of June, the day of my parents' wedding anniversary, the doctor diagnosed her with cancer. In my sophomore year of high school, she started chemo, and things began to go downhill fast.

"Alright, I'll get to it," I tell her, placing my bag on the chair right outside her room. "Could you lock up for me?"

"Sure thing, love," she says, walking toward the front door. "If you need me—"

"You're a phone call away," I finish for her.

She puts on her sweater and grabs her keys. "Dulce?"

"Yes?" I ask, masking the emotions clogging my throat whenever I walk home. I know it's only a matter of time before she'll be gone.

"Are you...okay?" she asks with a worried expression.

"I'm fine," I lie.

"Don't forget to get a checkup at the doctor, you hear?"

I swallow thickly. "I know. I mean, I will."

"Good." She smiles. "I'll be here in the morning."

"Oh...um, Mary?"

She pauses before she closes the front door. "Yes, love?"

"Could you stay with her a little later Friday night?"

"Is everything okay?"

I lick my lips nervously. I've never asked her to stay later, especially on a Friday night. I owe it to her to tell her why. She was there for me when—

"I promised Dan—Officer Mays—I would go out to dinner with him on Friday."

Her brows gently rise. "Oh..." Her eyes twinkle. "Is it a date?"

A flush creeps up my neck. "I think so."

"You finally accepted."

I accepted before Ford showed up when I was making the batch of cookies.

"I did."

It's no surprise. Everyone knows Danny, and all the ladies are drawn to him. Some call the police station to report things, hoping he shows up to the call. There is no doubt that he is handsome. The kind of man who makes you feel safe.

"I think he would be good for you, Dulce. He seems to like you. You've known each other for some time."

I give her a wry smile. "I know. I felt bad all the times he asked me, but I didn't want to leave Grandma alone." It wasn't the only reason. The truth is, I'm unsure about Danny. He has been there since it happened, and there is no question he is attractive, but I'm afraid to trust anyone. You don't know how people are underneath; it's only what they end up doing when you least expect it.

"You don't worry about that. I'll keep an eye on her while you're gone. You deserve a night out. He's been patient with you. There is no doubt about that. You shouldn't feel guilty about leaving her to have a few hours to yourself."

He hasn't seen you running naked with blood and dirt dripping down your body in the middle of the night, screaming at the top of your lungs.

"I know. Thank you, Mary."

"My pleasure."

When she closes the door, I walk into my grandmother's room. I made sure it was repainted, and the floors were redone. I also bought her a new bed with an adjustable frame. It's the nicest and most updated room in the house because I want her to feel comfortable.

"You're here," she says with a pained smile. Her hands are folded over her stomach.

"I am. How are you feeling?"

I look at her weathered hands. Her blue veins are like road maps under her thin skin. There are dark circles under her eyes. She tries to smile, but I know she's in a great deal of pain. She tries to skip her morphine dose every evening to see me come in from work. If she takes it, it knocks her out, and it's like I missed a day speaking with her. I'm glad she took it prom night.

She doesn't know what happened. In her mind, I went to prom with Ford Keller and had the most magical night.

"Like I'm ready to go out dancing," she says with a glint in her eyes.

"You want to borrow my heels?" I tease.

"You got those black ones I like?"

"Better, I got the kind with the red soles."

She laughs, her light brown eyes shimmering with love. Then

she grimaces from the pain, causing the light in her eyes to dim. Her life is like a light going out slowly.

I don't have any heels, but it's a little game we play. I help her get ready like I'm helping her prepare for a night on the town.

"So who is it this time?" I ask.

"Tonight, I'm going out with Jim Coates," she says with conviction.

"The owner of the supermarket?" I ask in disbelief. "The old man with the thick gold chain like he got it off the set of an Italian mob flick?"

"He didn't always look old, Dulce. He was handsome. You should have seen him in his prime. He was smooth and a gentleman with the ladies. He could charm the skirt of any girl back in the day. "

"Old Jim?" I make a face. "He's a grouch. Every time I see him, he looks like he got a flat tire coming into work."

She smiles, but I see something in her eyes—like she's keeping a big secret. "Wait...how do you know so much about Jim Coates?"

"He kissed me junior prom," she admits. I can see it in her eyes that she's telling the truth.

"Where was Grandpa?" I ask, confused.

My grandparents grew up in this town. My mother married her high school sweetheart.

"He went with a girl named Dolores."

"But I thought—"

"I met your father in high school, but I wasn't his girlfriend until the second month of our senior year."

"How come?" I ask curiously, tugging the blanket off her.

"He was screwing the girl who hated me," she says with a bite in her tone.

"So you went with Jim Coates to junior prom."

"Damn right, I did. It's why he gives you a discount." She sighs. "If you ever wondered why the old man was nice to you. Now you know why."

I grab her nightgown and toiletries. Pull her wheelchair. I catch her gazing out the window like she's reliving a memory. Now I know why the old man gives me a discount. He always said it was because our businesses were in the same strip mall and wanted to help out the locals.

"So how come you didn't end up with Jim?"

"I turned him down."

"Why?"

"Because I was in love with your grandfather," she confesses.

"Did you and Jim…" I trail off when she looks up. I can see it in her eyes. She would never have slept with Jim if she had been in love with Noah Webster.

"What's this I hear about a date Friday night?" she asks, changing the subject.

My cheeks heat. My ears burn, and my lips break into a shy smile as I push the wheelchair against the bed. "I'm going out to dinner with Officer Mays."

I carefully transfer her to the wheelchair. Our eyes meet. My heart sinks when she sees the truth written on my face. "You don't look excited."

"I am," I lie like a piece of cake you're forced to try yet don't want to hurt the person's feelings by telling them that it's horrible.

"I know when you're excited. I saw it that night." I glance at the picture she has of me in my mother's prom dress on her night-stand. I quickly blink back the moisture from my eyes. How happy I was in the photo only to have it crushed by the horror as soon as I stepped out of the house. "He isn't Ford Keller."

"No, Grandma. He isn't." I don't want him to be.

"I heard he's back in town," she says like she was in the bakery with me when he showed up.

"Gossip travels through trees around here."

"It sure does," she says as I push the wheelchair to the bath-room, wiping the tears that manage to escape behind her back. I hate that I keep secrets from her. The weight of them left an indelible stain on my soul next to the scars. "Has he been by to see you at the bakery?"

"He has..." I turn the water on, drowning the thoughts of Ford. The thoughts of that night.

"And?"

I place the shower chair in the center of the shower and let the water warm the seat. "He ordered."

"You turned him down," she says quietly, removing her clothes and placing them on the chair.

"It was one night, and nothing happened. He is not for me, Grandma."

"You're right. Mary heard someone at the clinic say he knocked up the mayor's daughter."

I drop the body wash.

"I heard she lost it. Everyone said he never liked her. He broke up with her before, though. Who knows," she says with a little shrug. "She was a snobby thing. Poor girl."

My hands tremble. "What else did Mary say?" I hope it's not about that night I asked her not to say anything or the day I had to go to the ER. Please, God. Please...

"Nothing much. She did tell me to keep reminding you to go to the doctor for a checkup. Once a year, Dulce."

"Yes, Grandma."

"I remember when I had a period cramp that bad. It looked like pig's blood spilled all over the toilet. It went away after I had your mother." She looks up. "Did you know that?"

I shake my head and give her a weak smile. "No."

It wasn't period cramps, but I can't tell her. I could never...tell her the truth.

P ulling up to the starting line, I roll my window down and look at Trent in the GTO next to me.

Trent smirks. "Are you ready, bitch?"

He revs the exhaust of his nine hundred horsepower '69 GTO, drowning out my response. The smell of gasoline from the smoke floats like a cloud of dust in the light breeze. I look down the two-lane backroad we used to race as kids. There is no one out here, just us. After my cars were delivered, Trent was itching to race like a kid wanting his piece of cake.

I gave him a choice between the three cars I had shipped here from where they were parked at my house in Vegas, a mansion I bought just to have a place to hang out between races. "You think that clunker is going to beat me?" he taunts.

"Stop being a pussy and find out."

I can hear the challenge in his voice, but he hasn't heard me rev my car. I put the Lamborghini in neutral and press the gas. The deep, powerful sound drowns out the noise, causing the birds to fly away from the tree line. The roads mimic a medium-sized track hidden between massive trees. There is only one way in and one way out to these roads.

I look over at him and see the unease flicker across his features. He knows he doesn't stand a chance. Not even with nine hundred horses.

"Let's go," I yell.

He revs the GTO. It trembles like a beast waiting to feast on the open road. His back tires squeal when they kiss the pavement to get traction.

I set the launch control by pressing down to click into Corsa mode. I press the ESC off. A siren wails, and I lean my head back on the seat.

"Fuck." I look through my rearview mirror, recognizing the police cruiser, and sure enough, it's Officer Mays.

I shut the car off and glance at Trent. A sadistic smirk plays on his lips, and he says, "I swear this guy loves cock."

Officer Dickhead walks between the cars, looking at me and then at Trent. "Looks like you boys were going to break the law again," Dickhead says with a smirk, the glare from the setting sun causing me to squint.

"You know stalking is illegal," I tell him.

"I'm on duty," he points out, straightening his shoulders with an air of authority.

I play dumb, looking around. "I don't see how we are breaking the law."

He points down the track. "You were about to race."

"No, we weren't," Trent says after he shuts off his car.

Dickhead stares straight ahead like he is trying to read a sign. "You know, Keller, I'm surprised you hang out with the commoners."

"Hey," Trent sneers, his body halfway out, peering over the roof of his car, "who the fuck are you calling a commoner, pig? Why don't you get your broke ass to the station and get off my dick."

"Not my style, Trent," he replies. "I don't answer to trust fund pricks like you."

"Jealous?" Trent says with a menacing smile.

"My personal business is not your concern, Keller," Officer Dickhead says.

"Ah, I don't buy that. A good-looking guy like you?" My

hand, itching to punch him in the face. "I'm sure you're answering calls all over town." I get out, shut the door, and lean on my car, looking for a crack in his demeanor. I don't buy the good cop bullshit.

"Wouldn't you like to know?" he sneers.

"Don't worry. Sooner or later, everything comes to light," I say darkly.

"Don't I know it? Isn't that right, Trent?" he says, looking directly at me and making my blood boil.

"What's that?" Trent says, acting like he didn't hear.

Dickhead walks idly toward the back of my car, staring at the mufflers, and says, "Doesn't everything come to light in this town?"

Trent drums his fingers over the roof of his car with a challenge in his gaze aimed right at Dickhead. "You want to hear a story, Mays?"

"Go ahead," Dickhead says.

"When I was a kid, my father told me I could be anything I wanted. I said I wanted to be a cop or a fireman. This was before I was into cars. I wanted to help people. They kept putting posters up at school, telling people to give back to the community. How important it was not to break the law. One day, I told my father I wanted to be a cop when I grew up. He laughed at me. I asked him what was so funny. He said he would rather me be a thief than a police officer. I was initially confused and asked him why. He said there was no point in being a police officer when I had money."

"I'm missing the point," Mays says.

"There is no difference. A thief. A cop. It's all the same. They both fuck people for money."

"Are you trying to tell me something, Trent?"

He's trying to say his silence can be bought... or it has been bought.

"Not at all. Are you trying to bust me for something, Officer? Are you trying to fuck me for money?" Trent says scornfully.

Dickhead gives me a bewildered little smile. "That depends. I could give you boys a citation for an improper start. See how you get off on that and have these cars impounded for being illegally modified."

I suck my teeth. "That's all you got? Seems to me this is about something else."

I'm not sure what his deal is with Trent. It could be that Trent is an asshole with money who gets away with shit because of who his father is, but with me, it's personal. This is about Dulce. What gets me is how he knew how I felt about her. He was hired about the same time I left town, and the first time I saw him was when he pulled me over as soon as I passed the welcome sign. Something doesn't add up. It looks like he was waiting for me to come back. Like he was expecting me.

"What do you think, Keller?" Dickhead asks like he cares what I think.

I cross my arms. "I'm with Trent on this one. I think you fuck people for money."

"No, I think you're worried I'm going to get in the way of whatever the fuck brought you back or, better yet, who."

My leg shakes, trying to calm the urge to beat the shit out of him.

"There is no law against that," I point out.

"No, there isn't, but I don't trust you, Keller. I can honestly admit that I don't like you."

I chuckle sarcastically. "You could have fooled me."

"I can see right through your pretty boy smile. You think you're hot shit. All of you. That friend of yours—Chris, is it? He's a real piece of work," Dickhead says, placing his glasses on top of his head.

"I wouldn't know about that," I tell him. "I just came back into town."

He looks at Trent. "What's your business here?"

Trent glances at me.

"Cars," I lie.

"I think you're lying, Keller."

"That's a strong statement, Mays," Trent says. "That type of statement can get you in trouble. A cop targeting a celebrity. You know that won't fly in this town."

"Last I heard, he isn't the mayor's favorite." I can see the gleam in his eye when he continues, "Both of you, but especially you, Keller..." He pauses. "Weren't you fucking his daughter?"

"I would be careful what you say next," Trent says, shutting the driver's side door.

"Or what? Are you threatening a police officer?" he warns, placing his hand on his gun.

Trent walks around, leans on the back of his car, and crosses his arms. "No, but our families will. When they hear you're spreading things about people way above your pay grade. You can give us all the tickets you want. They will just get thrown out of court."

"Because you have money?" Dickhead sneers, the corner of his mouth pulling up in a disdainful smirk.

"That's right. Keep that in mind when you take out your notepad. Now go do some police work and leave the rich folks to play with their toys."

"Alright," Dickhead says a little too quickly. He starts to leave and comes back. "You know, you should really check on your friend Chris. He really looks like he's going off the deep end."

"He's a big boy," Trent says, making me frown.

I haven't gone to visit Chris yet. My cars were supposed to be delivered on Monday but arrived today before the weekend. Why would Mays say that? Why would he bring up Chris? Something is not adding up.

"I think he should slow down." Dickhead glances at me in warning. "He parties too much. Noise complaints. Rowdy behavior."

"Ah, come on," Trent says with a smile like they're old friends. "You act like you are so much older than us. Like you didn't have fun. What are you, twenty-six?"

"Twenty-eight," he replies.

"You're not that old," I point out.

"Old enough," Dickhead counters.

"Trying to settle down?" Trent asks, his grin widening like he gives a shit.

Mays smiles disarmingly and looks at me. "That's the plan."

Trent gives a short, derisive laugh. "Last I heard, you were dating that girl—" He snaps his fingers like he can't remember her name, then raises his dark eyes to Mays. "Oh, yeah. Roxie. That was her name."

I watch the color drain from Mays's face. I guess someone needed their cock polished while he was being there for Dulce.

"See, Officer, I guess we all have secrets," I say with a menacing smile.

Dickhead plays it off and checks his watch like he's late for an appointment. "I gotta go," he says.

"Hot date?" Trent says sharply.

Mays opens the door to his cruiser, looks at me directly, and says a little too easily, "It's Friday night. You guys, be careful and stay out of trouble." The way he looks at me before he gets in his cruiser causes something to sicken my gut and puts a sour taste in the back of my throat.

"Why do you think he backed off and left suddenly?" I ask Trent, watching the cloud of dust from the police car's back tires as he drives off.

"I don't know."

"I don't trust that son of a bitch."

Trent laughs. "That's because you know he wants to fuck Dulce. He's all over your ass because you're a threat."

"She turned me down," I admit.

"You asked her out?"

"Yep."

He burst out laughing.

"Dulce Webster turned down the great Ford Keller. This..."

He holds his fingers toward a mock gesture like he is taking a picture. "Is a picture worth having. It should go down in history."

"Fuck you," I spit.

He drops his hands. "What are you going to do? Go to Mick's bar and drown your sorrows in some pussy?"

"No, asshole. I'm going to keep asking until she gives me a chance."

I catch a glimpse of something in his eyes. Something that almost seems like...fear? What does he have to be scared of?

He looks away, but I catch the same look before he slides into his car and fires it up.

After he drives off, I sit in mine, idling. The race is forgotten. Something happened after I left. Something I missed.

I should've never let her leave my car without telling her. I could have told her how I felt and what my plans were. She wouldn't have left because of her grandmother, but we could have had something. I could have had something to live for, waiting at the finish line. If I could go back and change that moment, I would.

I called the number she gave me that day, but it was disconnected, or maybe she changed it. Either way, I wasn't supposed to call. That was the point of me leaving.

I press the call button on the steering wheel. "Call Derek," I say to the Bluetooth.

The phone rings for a few seconds. "What's up? Everything good with the delivery?"

"Yeah, yeah. I'm not calling about that. I need a favor."

"Shoot."

"Do you still have that contact at Tiffany and Co?" I ask.

"Yeah?"

"I need you to get me something and deliver it to this address."

"You're not going soft on me, are you?"

"I sent you the picture of what I need."

"Fine, when do you need it by?"
"As soon as possible."

DULCE

"**D**o you think it's too much, Grandma?"

She looks up from the trashy romance novel she's reading and gives me a once-over with a critical eye. I'm nervous. I've never been on a date before, but she doesn't know that. I'm wearing a yellow bohemian summer dress that stops mid-thigh. It was hers when she was in high school. I bought the espadrille platform wedges with a raffia braid wrapped ankle ties on clearance at Mrs. Wilk's boutique shop at the end of the strip mall.

"You look gorgeous," she says. "Mary, come in here."

"I'm coming," Mary calls out from the kitchen.

Grandma coughs, and my heart breaks from the guilt of leaving her to go out. She takes a deep breath, catching her breath. Mary walks in, adjusting the oxygen and checking her O2 level. When she is done, my grandmother continues, "Take a look at Dulce."

"Mary comes into the room from the kitchen. Her eyes light up when she looks at me. "Oh my. You'll give that young man a heart attack when he looks at you."

"Are you sure I look okay?" I ask worriedly.

I've seen the other women my age around town. They dress differently. More chic and some more provocative. They get their hair done at the salon. I wish I could apply more makeup, but I'm on a budget. The best I could do is a tweezer for my brows and lip gloss from the health and beauty aisle at the pharmacy while waiting for Grandma's medication.

"You look beautiful, Dulce." Mary smiles warmly. "Turn around in a circle so I can get a good look at you." I turn around like a little girl in a princess costume like I used to do for my mom when I was little. My long dark brown hair whips around my shoulders.

"Did you wear it?" Mary says naughtily with a knowing smile. I flush. "Yes."

"What is she talking about?" Grandma asks, looking between us.

Mary walks over and fluffs her pillows so Grandma is more comfortable. "I got her a thong so she wouldn't have panty lines in that dress."

"It feels like you're wearing nothing, Grandma. You should try it," I say playfully.

"Good. Mary will get me one next time I go dancing," she teases.

"A red one," I say.

"Black," Grandma says, "so it will show when I wear a short white skirt."

"Grandma, you're worse than Mary."

The doorbell rings, and my stomach drops. "He's here."

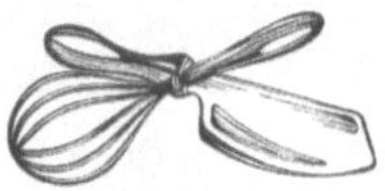

DANNY TAKES ME TO MICK'S, A BAR AND RESTAURANT tucked away on the corner of Main Street. It's inviting, with warm-amber lighting casting a soothing glow over the pavement below, and it is the nicest dining establishment in town.

The air was heavy with the subtle scent of hops, grilled steak and the richness of freshly polished wood within. Made of dark wood, the bar's surface was smooth and weathered from years of laughing and friendly elbows. Behind the bar, the shelves were adorned with rows of meticulously organized bottles, each catching the light and demonstrating the precision of choosing them.

DANNY GIVES ME A TENTATIVE SMILE WITH A HOPEFUL glimmer in his eyes as we wait to be shown to our table. He has been a gentleman since he picked me up. I was a little embarrassed at the state of the house, but he didn't seem to notice all the things that needed to be fixed.

"You look beautiful, Dulce," he says softly as the hostess approaches. My cheeks feel hot, and I hope I don't look as red as a tomato.

"Right this way," the hostess says.

Danny leads, following her to our table. I fidget with the hem of my dress. My eyes dart around the room, searching for a familiar face and hoping I don't run into Ford.

The music is loud, but I can still hear the boisterous laughter and pool play from the bar area in the back of the restaurant.

We are seated at a table with a view of the bar section nestled near a window. I sit across from Danny. My hands are sweaty in my lap. I'm not used to eating in a restaurant. I don't know what to order and don't want to make it obvious that this is my first date. The last time I went out to a formal restaurant was when I was nine. There was a kid's menu with only four choices, and my mom ordered for me.

I look down at the menu, the letters swimming before my eyes from the many selections. I flip the menu over, and the drink menu is worse. Different wines, spritzers, beer, and soft drinks.

"Are you okay?" Danny asks, his voice barely a whisper. His eyes soft as he watches me.

I've never been to a restaurant as an adult, but I can't say that. I can't tell him I've never been on a date or had my first kiss. It's embarrassing. It will bring up the past, and that is the last thing I want to do right now.

"Yes," I say, a bit uneasily.

I've been so nervous since he showed up. I felt like such an idiot when I almost slipped getting in his truck. I wasn't aware the steps opened automatically. He must think I'm stupid for giving him one-word answers. It feels like I have mothballs in my mouth.

I look up for a minute and see the effort he put into his appearance. He looks different outside of his uniform. He smells nice and wears blue jeans and a light blue short-sleeved shirt neatly pressed open at the throat. His skin is smooth and bronzed from the sun. His hair looks the same, combed over to the left side. My eyes fall on his arm, where all the tattoos disappear under his sleeve.

The server approaches our table with practiced ease. Something dark flickers in her gaze when she spots Danny. A worried look crosses Danny's features.

"Welcome to Mick's. My name is Roxie," she says with a saccharine smile. "How are you two enjoying your evening so far?" It must be nice when someone calls and shows up."

My appetite plummets at the familiar way she looks at him. I wasn't aware he was seeing someone. Underneath her brittle smile, she is pretty. With curly brown hair with highlights you could only get at a salon, expertly applied makeup, and a full figure, she's making me feel imperfect, a feeling I'm well acquainted with.

"Don't do this, Roxie," he says in a low tone.

"I don't know what you're talking about," she says with a forced smile, her jealousy seeping through the veil of professionalism. Her eyes land on me, and I want the chair to swallow me under the dirty looks she gives me. "What can I get you to drink?"

"I'll have water," I rush out. "How do you guys know each other?"

She glances at Danny and back. "We went out on a few dates. *Overnight* dates. Did he not tell you about me?"

I give Danny a questioning look.

"Roxie," he warns in a hard tone.

She ignores him. "We were supposed to go out two weeks ago, but he didn't show up and wouldn't take my calls." My eyes drop to the menu, the beat of my heart hammering like a drum.

I guess he can see the look in my eyes because his eyes soften a bit. I'm not sure if it's pity like I've seen so many times.

"If you'll excuse me," I mutter, grabbing my purse and standing, looking for the women's restroom.

"Dulce," Danny calls out. "Please...let me explain."

There is nothing he can say. Deep down, I knew this was a mistake. He kept asking me out every month for the first two years since prom night when he found me and every week for the last two.

I finally spot the bathroom sign. I push the door, quickly find the last stall, and lock myself inside.

When the bathroom door opens, I hear footsteps, but then there's only silence. I wait a few seconds, but there is no sound of another stall, the sink being used, or anyone leaving.

I try to see through the small space between the stalls for someone, but it's empty. I swallow nervously and slide the latch.

I walk out, and my breath catches in my throat. The room shrinks around me. My heart pounds, and everything fades as I stare at Ford Keller.

"What are you doing here?" I ask tensely.

His gaze travels slowly, like he's seeing me for the first time. "It looks like you need a ride home?"

"How did you know I was here?" My thoughts are scattered like a pinball machine. He gives me a devilish smile that makes my stomach flip.

"I was at the bar, and this beautiful woman walked into the restaurant," he teases. "Everyone turned around and couldn't help noticing that she was with the wrong guy. So they sent me."

He's joking, trying to make me feel better.

"People at the bar sent Ford Keller after the poor humiliated girl on a date?" I reply playfully.

"Is that why you turned me down?" he asks, crossing his arms with a playful smile.

I look away, not meeting his gaze.

He steps forward. "Why don't we fix that?" he offers.

"I would like to go home," I say truthfully.

"I can do that."

"I don't trust you," I admit. "I don't trust anyone right now."

"Hmm...Tell you what. Call your grandmother and tell her you'll be home. Send your location to her or whomever is with her right now so they know where you are."

I don't have a ride home, and it's at least five miles away. Walking is not an option. Uber doesn't work in this small town, and the cab drivers are out for the night.

I pull my iPhone from my small crossbody and send Mary my location from the Maps app. After two seconds, a text comes through with a thumbs-up. That was one thing Danny had taught me since that night.

"Okay."

He smiles, and his blue eyes flicker with a promise. "Alright, let's go."

He turns around, and the bathroom door swings open. Three women stumble inside, smelling like cigarettes and beer. Their eyes widen in recognition when they see Ford, and then their gazes slide to me.

"Oh my God."

"Is that—"

"Good evening, ladies." He takes my hand and moves, leading me out of the bathroom and pushing open the door to the rear exit.

The cool breeze brushes my skin with the smell of seared steaks from the kitchen vents, making my stomach growl.

"Hungry?" he asks with a smile.

My stomach takes the opportunity to let out a low growl.

"Starving."

"My car is right this way. I had to park on the side to avoid people noticing me. I already had many posing to take pictures in front of it at the gas station."

He stops in front of a newer model Lamborghini like the one he was driving that day he gave me a ride home in the rain. Except this car is lipstick cherry red with black seats.

He rushes to the passenger door like he's stealing a car. It swings up like I remembered.

"Be careful. This one is a little lower than the last one you were in."

"Okay," I say and try to get in, holding the back of my dress without flashing him my ass.

When I'm inside, he leans to buckle me in. His cologne causes the bad memories to fade and leave the ones I felt that day in the rain. A burst of butterflies flutters in my stomach. His hand inches from my thigh. He turns his head, our eyes meet, our lips a breath away, and then, it happens. He kisses me. Slow at first, like he's memorizing the texture of my lips.

He groans low in his throat. I breathe him in, memorizing the scent of his breath mixed with something fruity and mint. But I'm frozen, not knowing what to do with my tongue or hands.

His eyes never leave mine when he drags his tongue over the seam of my lips like he is sampling how I taste in slow, deliberate strokes. There is no hate or fear, just...want. A dark want that was always left unfinished. A love story with missing pages that needed to be written.

I wanted to burn all the bad pages that ruined it. The ones that haunted me with thoughts of what they did. Because they took something from me. Something that belonged to him, and he didn't even know it.

His kiss burns. His tongue marks my soul. The first that would never be forgotten.

The way his hand hovers over my thigh, needing to be

entrapped in his hands, to look at me the way he is looking at me now. Unbidden.

"You taste so sweet," he whispers against my lips. "I've wanted to kiss you for a long time."

My heart melts.

It caves.

He sets it on fire.

All I ever wanted was a kiss from the boy who stole my heart and shattered it under the blue firestorm of his gaze.

Even if he could never be mine, I was his ashes. Ruined for anyone else. Too far gone in the web of lies and secrets this town created.

I accepted the truth that night.

We weren't meant to be together.

In the same way, I couldn't bring my parents back from death. I couldn't save my grandmother from dying. But I had one kiss, and it was all I ever wanted.

Four Years Ago

DULCE

A twig snaps, sending a jolt of terror through my body. My heart thuds in my chest, echoing in my ear. I look at the ground where Trent shattered my phone, and it's unrecognizable. The screen shattered into a tiny mess of glass. I pick up the phone, but the pieces break apart.

All I can think of is walking in the same direction we came from until I can call for help or until someone comes.

I hear another twig snap. There is a distant hoot of an owl followed by a breeze. Trees sway. The wind slips through the leaves.

After walking for a while, the sense of someone watching me

is overwhelming. I take my shoes off. My feet are aching from the straps digging into the knuckles of my feet.

My breaths come in shallow, rapid gasps. The smell of dirt and moss heavy in the air. My hands sweat. My tongue sticks to the roof of my mouth. I try to think how long we were in the car from my house until they left me here, but I come up empty. I ignore the sting from tiny rocks under the pads of my feet. The unfamiliar sounds of thrashing branches, casting shadows across the road.

Then I hear breathing sounds followed by padding of feet coming behind me. Like an animal. A coyote or bear. Whatever it is, it's coming. I glance behind me, but I don't see anything. The sound grows louder. Whatever is behind me is picking up speed.

I start to run, not sure where to go, but I push my legs. My bare feet pound on the pavement. The wind is whipping my hair. The skirt of my dress is flying behind me. The air bites my lungs, tears sting my eyes and blur my vision, and my legs are cramping, but I push harder. All I could think about was my grandmother. I have to get to her. I can't leave her to die alone.

I stop abruptly at the fork in the road. My breaths are frantic, and I'm not sure where to run, but the movement of something between the brush causes a scream to erupt from my throat.

I drop my shoes and small clutch on the ground. I look ahead. The grass on both sides is tall. The moon disappears behind the clouds, and it's pitch black. I can hardly see my hand in front of me, but I start running again.

I look over my shoulder, and my gut clenches in fear. My hands shake. A dark figure stands in the middle of the road. The hairs on the back of my neck stand up. I blink, and then, it's gone.

I turn and run toward the brush of grass and slip down a ravine. Hard pricks from the rough ground scratch the skin on my thighs. My dress rips like a zipper opening. My arms flail when I can't feel the ground and keep falling. I cry out when needles from the bark of a tree cut my hands and feet when I finally land with a thud. The sting makes my eyes water.

I can't see anything.

Something scrapes my skin. "Please..." I whimper in the dark. "Why, Ford?"

Why did you do this to me?

My heart knocks against my ribs as I gulp air, struggling to steady my breathing. The jagged texture of something scrapes against my skin. Finally, I find even ground, pushing my way through the damp leaves.

The muscles in my legs tremble. My ears are on high alert.

Something stomps wildly behind me through the under-brush, followed by screams like a bird being mutilated. My blood turns cold, and suddenly, I feel something heavy on my head, and then pain, so much pain. Then darkness.

She freezes. I pull away, scolding myself for moving too fast. My heart beats in my throat. The only thing clouding that thought is my obsession. Her.

I briefly close my eyes and pull away. Her lips are swollen. The taste of her sweet breath on my lips. My hard cock dying to be inside her and making her mine is at war with the blank look in her eyes.

She was into it, and then something happened. She wants to push me away, but at first, a part of her wanted to pull me close for some more.

I hesitate to want to give in to the side we both want, but I don't want her to think I'm using her. For her to think it was a mistake.

I want nothing more than to finally have her. To give in and let her see how she really makes me feel.

When I pull away, I rub the pad of my thumb over her bottom lip. "Hey?"

She blinks a couple of times.

"You went off somewhere?"

"I'm sorry," she says, looking away.

"You look beautiful, Dulce, and I'm not sorry for kissing you," I tell her and shut the door.

As I pull up, my car roars under the moonlit sky, drawing attention from people coming out of the restaurant.

Mays, leaning on his truck, is absorbed in his phone.

He looks up, and I roll down my window, offering a smile. "Next time you ask a girl out, make sure you've ended things with the one you're with first. You should know better. News travels fast in this town."

His gaze slides to the passenger seat. A crease forms on his forehead, a bead of sweat dripping down his temple. "Dulce, get out of the car," he demands. The words rush out, tumbling over the next, causing my fist to clench on the steering wheel as he continues, "Dulce, listen to me. You can't trust him. I'm sorry. I'll take you home. Please—"

"Stop," she thunders.

His throat moves as he swallows, and hurt glimmers in his eyes. "Could you...call me when you get home?"

She looks away, dismissing him, but I don't understand what the fuck is this guy's problem.

He glares at me. "You do anything to her, and I swear—"

"Don't threaten me," I warn. "She obviously doesn't want to talk."

I drive off, leaving him watching me as I pull onto the road. I lick my lips, full of the scent of her sweet breath and the taste of sugar from her lips entangled with mine.

"Thank you," she says apologetically, biting the corner of her lip.

"For what?" I ask, trying to keep from reaching for her hand.

"For coming to get me. For giving me a ride. I honestly didn't know how I was going to make it home."

"Were you going to stay in the bathroom stall all night?" I ask playfully.

"Maybe."

I glance at her briefly, loving the way she looks tonight, but I don't want to make her uncomfortable by staring. "Are you okay?"

"I am now," she says quietly, and all I want is to keep driving and not come back. I want to keep her forever, but I can't. Not yet.

Instead, I ask, "How long do you have until you're expected back home?"

I don't know what her situation is at home, how bad her grandmother is, or how long she has left.

"Umm. "

"You know what? Call home and ask who is hungry."

She glances at me. "Why?"

"Because we're bringing dinner."

"You don't have to do that, Ford."

I smile, putting her at ease. "It's no trouble."

I STEP INTO THE DOORWAY, BALANCING TWO BAGS OF take-out barbecue pulled pork and mac-n-cheese and following Dulce into her house. The house smells like a hospital. Sterile and antiseptic mixed with rich wood that has seen better days. The house is clean but needs a facelift.

My eyes soften as she walks cautiously into what I assume is her grandmother's room. It's the only room so far that is completely remodeled.

"Is she awake?" Dulce whispers to a woman named Mary sitting in a chair by her grandmother's side.

Dulce said she is a nurse that works at the local doctor's clinic and takes care of her grandmother while Dulce works.

"I'm awake," her grandmother says with a quavering quality to her voice. "You think I don't have gas in the tank, but I do, and I hear you whispering away like you're hiding something. Tell me, how was it? Did Danny behave himself?"

Danny was a shady bitch who got caught.

I step forward, the bags drawing her grandmother's attention.

I'm met with the same brown eyes that have haunted me since the first day I fell into them.

"Grandma," Dulce says.

"You're not Danny," her grandmother says, trying to sit up. Mary gets up to assist her.

"No, ma'am, I'm not," I say quietly.

"You're Dulce's Ford."

"Why yes, ma'am, I am," I say, liking the way it sounds.

I step farther into the room, but she freezes me on the spot with a stare. Then looks at Dulce. "What happened to Danny?"

Dulce smiles, but it doesn't reach her eyes. "It didn't work out."

"Oh...small town?"

"Yes, it is. Word travels fast," Dulce says.

"You should know, Ford," her grandmother says.

I'm not sure if she is talking about the past with Summer or my racing, so I reply, "I do. It goes with the territory."

"Not my granddaughter's—"

"I wouldn't dream of it," I interrupt.

"Good. When I decide I'm good and ready to kick the bucket, Dulce will go to college. It's not too late. I told her she should have gone after she graduated, but she didn't want to leave me."

"Let me take those, Mr. Keller," Mary says, taking the bags.

"Please call me Ford," I reply, helping her with the bags and following her out to the hallway with Dulce behind me.

Like the driveway, the rest of the house is twenty years overdue for repairs. The kitchen is the same, with dated wood paneling and chipped Formica cabinets. Yellow ring marks on the counters from too much use. The appliances also need an update, but I admire Dulce's strength in taking care of her grandmother's business and the house while taking care of her grandmother.

"Alright," Mary says and glances at Dulce. "Will you come and help me get these served?"

"Sure," Dulce says reluctantly, opening the cabinet and grabbing the plates.

The kitchen is small, so I walk back to her grandmother's room, wanting to get to know her.

As I walk in, her grandmother pins me with a look, scrutinizing me and giving me a chill down my spine.

When she looks at me, it's like she is seeing inside my soul—something my own mother couldn't do.

"What's your business with my Dulce? Are you passing through, or are you planning to stay?"

"I'm not sure. It depends."

"On?" she asks with a challenge in her gaze.

My eyes zero in on a picture of Dulce on her nightstand; it doesn't look like it was taken long ago, but it's not recent, either. She is still gorgeous, but in this picture, she looks breathtaking. I've never seen her smile with such a light in her eyes. She looks so happy.

I point at the picture. "Can I?"

"Oh yes. Of course. I'm sure you remember that night."

I pick up the photo and look at Dulce's beautiful smile. Her dress. Vintage but gorgeous on her perfect figure. My eyes cut to the old woman, looking quizzically for a moment.

"I was upset that she didn't bring me pictures of you both."

"Pictures?" I ask, confused.

"The prom? She was so happy when you invited her at the last minute."

A sick feeling crawls up the back of my throat.

"You sent her a message, and she wouldn't stop looking at it the entire time she was getting ready."

My stomach self detonates. The walls feel like they are closing in. What is she talking about?

"I want to thank you for putting that smile on her face," she says with a soft expression, remembering the way she looked that day.

Something is not adding up. I don't remember seeing her in that dress before.

Dulce and Mary walk into the room with a plate in each hand. I place the photo back, wanting to keep it but knowing I can't.

"What's going on, Grandma?" Dulce says, but I see when she notices the picture I just put back. Her eyes widen in fear. Her face looks pale.

She lied to her grandmother, and I'm guessing who she went with when I see the trembling of her expression. I can tell she made it all up to please her grandmother about going with someone to prom. I should be annoyed, but I'm not.

"I was thanking Ford for taking you to prom," her grandmother says, looking between us.

The plate slips from Dulce's hand and crashes on the floor.

"Mary—" Her grandmother trails off, her voice weak.

"Dulce?" I rush to her side, but her face is white. She is trying to take large gulps of air like she's suffocating. Something is wrong.

"It's a panic attack," Mary says, putting the food down and rushing to her side. "She gets them sometimes."

Before Mary can reach her, I pick her up bridal style on instinct to soothe her. "Shh..." I rock her in my arms, placing a strand of her hair behind her ear. Her eyes are snapped shut. I can feel her heart racing like a racehorse. "It's okay," I say, trying to soothe her in hushed tones. "I've got you...breathe." Her chest rises when she takes a deep breath and then lets it out. "That's it, Dulce. You got this, baby." Her eyes open, looking around in a daze, and I smile. "I've got you."

"Come, lay her down in her room," Mary says, guiding me out of the room.

I lay her on her bed on the small mattress with pink sheets. I slide in next to her, holding her. I want to know why she has panic attacks.

"I'm sorry," Dulce mutters.

"There is nothing to be sorry about. Relax and breathe."

Mary checks her to make sure she's okay. Then she excuses herself to tend to Mrs. Webster.

I remember seeing someone on the track at a race have a panic attack. The most important thing is to take them to a quiet place and calm them.

"Uh, Ford," Mary calls.

I look up, then at my chest to see Dulce sleeping, her breaths even. "Yeah?"

"Could you walk me out? Mrs. Webster is already asleep, and I need someone to lock the door behind me," she says, but when I place Dulce gently on the bed and walk out of her bedroom, I see something in Mary's eyes. She wants to tell me something. "There's something you need to know."

FORD

No one was happy when I left town. I never thought they would go after her or stoop so low. I get that those girls in school hated her, so I was careful not to sneak glances when I was around them. I ignored Dulce as much as I could. I hated to laugh at some of their jokes, so it seemed believable, but fuck if it didn't eat me up inside. It fucking wrecked me that I couldn't do anything about it. I had my parents' money, not mine.

I drive for what seems like hours, the sun heating the road as I push the Aventador to its limit down the backroad where Mary said it happened.

I look left and right like it will give me a clue of who is responsible, but in my eyes, they all are.

I place the car in park, open the door, and scream like a wild animal until my throat is raw, hearing the whoosh of birds flying from the trees in panic. My chest heaves as my lungs burn with rage.

I get back in the car, and there is only one place I can go right now. I check the time on the dash; she should be open at eight o'clock. It's the last place I thought I would visit since I came back. I have a doctor I see on a regular basis in Italy, but he doesn't know this part of my past. The part I keep hidden from the world.

I reach the small house turned into an office building three blocks from my old high school. There is a white Toyota Camry parked in the doctor's space.

I walk inside and write my name down on the walk-in sheet and have a seat until the receptionist slides the glass window open and calls me inside.

The door slides open after ten minutes, and a soft, professional voice calls out my name. "Mr. Keller."

I stand and meet green eyes I haven't seen in a while, belonging to Mrs. Forester. "Hello, Ford. It's been a while."

"It has. How's Bob?" I ask pleasantly.

The skin on the corner of her eyes crinkles when she smiles. "Still a pain in the ass," she says, wasting no time in opening the office door.

She knows I'm here because it's an emergency. Just like old times. "She will see you now."

"Thank you, Mrs. Forester," I say before walking inside the familiar office.

The same old plant and blue couch are against the far wall, but different board games are on the coffee table. The same painting of four irregular black-and-white shapes hangs right above it.

The brown wood desk belonging to Dr. Alice Bregman is on the opposite side of the room. She sits behind her desk, her black hair in an elegant chignon with the same white pearls at her throat. She wears a collared white blouse with blue slacks and a professional smile she reserves for all her patients.

"Long time no see, Ford. I was hoping this was a friendly visit, but I see that it's for an appointment."

I take a seat on the right side of the blue couch and stretch out my legs like old times. "It is."

She takes out my chart, which is about an inch thick. It was where she wrote all her notes from every session we had throughout my high school years. "I see you're back in town. How is everything?"

"I am," I say, looking directly at her.

"Is this about her?" she asks, writing something down.

"Yes."

"Same feelings," she asks, "like before?"

I snort. "They never went away, Dr. Bregman. I did. Like you recommended."

She nods like she understands, but she doesn't. She hasn't been obsessed with one girl for years.

"And now that you're back, these feelings for Dulce are magnified."

I scratch my neck. "You could say that, but I'm not here to cope without her. I'm here to ask you how I can safely channel my thoughts and feelings while I pursue her?"

She places an elbow on her desk and rests her chin on the palm of her hands, listening intently. "And do you think that is a good idea? How does she feel about you?"

"I think it's a great idea. I always have, despite what my parents think. At this point, I don't care what anyone thinks; I just care about what Dulce thinks and how it will affect her. I think she is attracted to me, but she doesn't trust me."

"Then earn her trust. Form a healthy relationship and work on that. Don't let obsession bend your positive thoughts. Attraction is healthy. So is sex but not when it's abused. Anything in excess is not healthy, Ford. It is why I was on board when you told me your plans to pursue your dreams of racing. Why I agreed that the best thing to do about your obsession with Dulce was to find yourself. Build a healthy relationship with yourself. See the world. Meet new people."

"I did," I quip.

"And?"

"She is still the one thing missing, Dr. Bregman. I crave her. I want her, and I'm not going to stop until I have Dulce Webster."

DULCE

On Monday, I place the cakes in the display case and turn the temperature to the right setting to stay fresh.

"So Danny turned out to be an overlapper," Katie says, packing today's deliveries.

"An overlapper?"

"Yeah, it's when a person starts a relationship while still in another one, knowing that the current one will not work out. They suddenly break up with the person when they feel secure in the new one."

"I've never heard of that?"

I don't have experience in any kind of relationship because I've never had a boyfriend, but that sounds like a lame thing to say to someone like Katie. She's spunky and full of spirit. She's had three boyfriends and has more experience than I do when it comes to guys.

"Yeah, it's like an emotional airbag. Some are even habitual or serial overlappers."

"Sounds like they're serial killers."

She snorts. "Yeah, of people's feelings. They try to convince themselves that they're not cheating when, in fact, emotionally, they are because they are trying to forge a connection with the next person."

"I think it's cheating. How can you string someone along like that, giving them hope when you know you're not interested in them anymore."

"Ford Keller raced to your rescue, huh?"

"He was there at the right time."

"Do you think it was a coincidence or the luck of the draw?" she asks curiously.

I never thought about it. I was so wrapped up the entire weekend when he stayed until the sun came up to make sure I was okay. I cleaned and spent time with my grandma for the rest of the weekend. I was thinking about what it meant that he stayed and how I responded to being in his arms. I felt safe. None of it made any sense. I should've been afraid, but maybe my subconscious was trying to tell me something.

"I'm not sure. Ford was—"

"Perfect?"

I sigh. "He isn't perfect, but guys like Ford usually seem like they are, and women want to believe it."

"How many hearts do you think he's broken?"

"I'm sure plenty. He's famous, rich, and good-looking, but I won't be one of them."

"Why not?" she asks, placing the orders gently on the counter.

I grab my back from underneath the counter by the register. "It would never work. He's him, and I'm...me."

And I'm not sure if he had anything to do with what happened.

Even if he didn't, a guy like Ford doesn't end up with a girl like me. I'm stuck in this town like most of the people here.

She snorts, giving me a doubtful look. "I think you're selling yourself short."

"You haven't lived in this town long enough."

"You're probably right, but I'm here working with this town's best baker. Here are the invoices, keys, and the address for Ford's delivery." My stomach does a little flip thinking about seeing him again for some reason, and I slide my hands down the front of my uniform.

Katie gives me a knowing smile. "You look great."

I check the time, knowing Danny will walk in any second for his coffee, and I don't want to see him. I grab the invoices, keys, and three boxes while Katie grabs the other three, and we head out to the white van.

After securing the orders in the back, I open the driver's side door, ignoring its weird sound, followed by the loud slam when I close it. The van is old. Some would say it was considered a piece of shit clunker.

The starter whines and then pops after a series of spluttering backfires, but it finally catches. A cloud of smoke spills from the back. It's a hot day. The heat and the smell of burning oil and gas float across the parking area. I place the van in reverse, and it jerks. It's worse than last week, but I don't have money for repairs, and the last place I want to go was to a mechanic who would break my heart with the estimate to fix it.

After the first delivery, I start the van, surprised they don't call the cops for a noise complaint as I drive down the road. I set my phone's GPS between the cracked gray vinyl on the dash and follow the directions.

My heart starts beating wildly in my chest when I notice I'm on the road heading to the middle of nowhere, following a ribbon of asphalt. Flashes of me in the dark, running naked toward red and blue lights, breaks through the memories I tried to suppress.

I blink, and the sunlight glistens with heat. The air conditioner doesn't cool as much but blows air over the blanket of sweat on my skin. I check the dash, and the car starts making a funny noise. I press the gas, and it doesn't pick up speed, making my heart curl in my throat. I glance at the GPS, and it says I still have fifteen minutes until I arrive at my destination. I let the van crawl, but it's slowing down by the second. I press the gas, but nothing. It doesn't pick up speed. I tap the brake and change gears with the shifter by the steering wheel, and that's when the car slows. I changed it back, and I'm screwed.

"No, no. Not again. What is it with this place?"

The engine of the van stalls, and it rolls until it comes to a stop.

It's the same road, but this time, it's daytime without a cloud in the sky.

The sun peeks through the tall trees, casting shadows over the road. I've never had a delivery this far.

I grab my phone and exit the map, looking for the nearest tow truck. I'm glad I have enough battery and signal.

Someone picks up. "Dean Towing," the man says through the phone.

"Hi, my name is Dulce Webster—"

I get out of the van when it gets too hot, fanning myself. The man on the phone named Dean said it would take about thirty minutes for him to show up. I'm glad I was smart enough to place the cookies and cake in a cooler. I don't want to open it and check because it could allow heat to filter in. I walk around to the other side, closer to the grass on the shoulder, and look into the trees. I see something brown through the streams of light. I step closer to get a good look and notice a small house—more like a cabin.

It wouldn't be surprising that plenty of people live in cabins in North and South Carolina. Looking down the road, I see if I can find the place where Danny found me, but I can't. It could have been farther up, but I know it's this road because I can feel it like evil fingers tickling my skin, reminding me that I was here stranded and attacked four years ago.

Four Years Ago

DULCE

There were times when I wished I died with my parents. If it weren't for my grandmother reminding me of all the beautiful things in this world, I would have done something to be with them. I never told a soul because there wasn't anyone I could tell.

Perhaps it was her subconscious telling her she needed me. To take care of things when her cancer came back, and it wasn't fair if I was gone too. But who would be with me when it was my time to go? I knew the answer before even thinking about it. No one because everyone hated my existence.

I thought of death many times since then. How would it happen? How would it feel? Where would I go? Would I float in the air or go out like the tide? Would it hurt? I knew the answer when I felt death was looming. I wanted to live, and I wanted the pain to stop.

My eyes open, and I take a large gulp of air. My lungs burn, making a strange sound like a broken bellows, each breath a short, wheezing burst. The pain between my thighs swallows me whole, like from rubbing alcohol in an open wound. I don't remember a pain like this. This pain is anguish.

I sit up, and my head feels heavy like a brick. My clothes are completely gone, and I try to remember what happened when a trickle of something wet drips on the side of my face. My hair sticks to my neck. I wait for my eyes to focus in the dark. I place the palm of my hand on the ground, feeling the wet dirt and leaves on my fingers. The moonlight breaks through the trees, and I look down and see dirt, leaves, and...blood smeared over my skin. How I got here. Memories come flashing. Something crusty between my thighs. With trembling fingers, I touch the inner part of my thigh, hoping it's from dirt. Except it isn't dirt, it's blood.

No. Please God, no.

I try to stand, but my wobbly legs feel like hundreds of needles are stabbing them. With a cry, I fall back down. I look up at where the moon kisses the trees while I try to breathe through the pain. When it subsides for a few seconds, I turn my head and follow the trees to the embankment and catch a glimpse of the road.

A twig snaps, and there's a subtle rustling of leaves some-where nearby.

Panic seizes my chest. Fear causes me to crawl up the embank-ment with a strangled cry, ignoring the burning pain with an elec-tric jolt as my heart hammers like a drum. I make it up to the road.

Using a tree trunk to pull myself up, I begin staggering down the asphalt.

Two headlights head toward me like yellow eyes on a black canvas, blinding me. Then the familiar red and blue lights flash like a beacon. A sob rips from my throat. My knees almost buckle when I flail my arms.

I let out a hoarse scream. "Please! Help!"

The car stops.

The headlights blind me. I let out a guttural cry when the familiar blue and red lights shut off. "Oh...please! *God*."

I hear a car door open. "Ma'am?"

I shudder at the sound of the man's voice. I cross my arms, my hands shaking as I tuck them between my legs, trying to cover my naked body. "Please," I gasp.

"You're saying you were supposed to be at prom with Ford Keller?" Detective Fisher says.

I stare at the white wall in the hospital, refusing to look at Detective Fisher directly standing across from me in his wrinkled black suit jacket and yellow collar on his white dress shirt from wearing too much cologne. He looks like he hasn't slept in days.

I nod. "Yes," I say hoarsely.

"But that he didn't pick you up."

I grip the blanket under my chin. "That's right."

"Who did?"

My lip quivers. "C-Chris Ellis and Trent Walker. T-they left me."

They started an IV and drew my blood, but I refused everything else. I want to go home. I cannot afford another hospital bill. The cost of the ambulance that brought me here is probably already in the thousands.

The door opens. A nurse and the police officer who found me walk in, but I've been sitting on the bed in this cold hospital room for hours, wearing a gown and wrapped in a blanket.

"Detective Fisher, are you done here?" the young police officer asks with eyes the color of his black police shoes. His hair is expertly combed to the side without a hair out of place. "The doctor is asking for you."

Detective Fisher straightens. "I'll be right out." He turns back to me. "Miss Webster, this is preliminary. I know right now isn't a good time, but I need you to try to remember how you were attacked."

"Detective, she was assaulted, and she's in shock. The questioning can wait," the officer declares with a frown.

Detective Fisher's eyes cut to the police officer. "I'm aware, Officer Mays," he says in an annoyed tone. "According to the statement from Mr. Ellis and Mr. Walker, they were at the Airy High School prom with their dates around the time the attack happened. We have no suspects. Even if she agreed to take the rape kit, we cannot test it if we don't have a suspect in the state of North Carolina until the law passes, and she doesn't recall if she was assaulted or what exactly happened."

"She's scared," the nurse asserts, angrily raising her voice.

They both pause and cut her a glance.

The nurse looks at me with a soft expression before glancing at them. "Can you give her a minute?"

My hands shake. The dirt stuck under my fingernails stains the white blanket. "They left me..."

The nurse places the tray in front of me, causing me to pause, and then she glares at the detective.

"I don't disagree," Detective Fisher says, "Maybe I can get statements from the boys. I'm sure they already have their lawyers on their way. If you could answer one last question before I go, Dulce."

"I'll try," I say darkly, having a good idea what he is going to ask.

"Were you sexually assaulted by Chris or Trent?"

I turn away. My mind tries to search for anything. A clue, a memory—anything. But there's nothing. It's dark. *It burns. The blood. You know what will happen, Dulce. They will make you pay. It's now or never.* I shut my eyes. The little voice in my head won't stop. Damned if I do, damned if I don't. No name. No witness. No description. Nothing. Maybe I just made it all up? Or maybe it's a nightmare, and I'll wake up in the morning and realize it didn't happen.

"Miss Webster," Fisher calls out.

"I don't...NO..."

Be careful what you say, Dulce. It will be used against you. Trust no one.

"Even if they didn't assault her, they abducted her, broke her phone, and left her in the middle of nowhere—"

"I understand, Mays. I was trying to get them on a personal property charge, but the phone is less than two hundred dollars. I checked," Fisher says. He isn't wrong, but it was the way they left. Why they left me. What they said to me... "I'm trying to find out what happened as much as you are. All we have is a high school prank gone wrong and a broken cell phone. Keeping her in the car against her will is a crime, but she told them she wanted out of the car when she realized she got in the wrong car. They did pull over and let her out but broke her cell phone. Unless we have evidence of anything else, there is nothing we can do." He looks at me. "Is there anything else you can remember? Something, an animal, or someone."

"I don't know. I was hit on the head and blacked out." I tuck my chin in as two tears run as my chest tightens, hating that I have to say it. "I woke up like this. My clothes missing and..."

"Dulce, I'm so sorry. I know it's hard. But an examination would help us find out what happened to you and who did it."

I shake my head. "No, please. I need to go home. My grandmother..."

"We already notified her nurse; Mary is with her now. Your grandmother is fine and asleep," Officer Mays says softly.

"Thank you," I say softly.

"If you're done, you can leave," the nurse says firmly.

Detective Fisher nods, hands me a card, and says, "If you remember anything, you call me right away."

I nod. "Thank you."

"I'll be right outside when you're ready to be discharged to give you a ride home, Miss Webster," Officer Mays says with a nod and follows the detective out the door.

"My name is Sharon. I'm the registered nurse assigned to you. I'm not sure if the charge nurse told you, but I need you to take these," the nurse says, holding out a cup with water and another clear cup with pills. "The antibiotics are just in case and help fight any infection. You'll be sent home with a prescription to continue taking them when you're discharged. It's important that you finish the course of antibiotics. Your lab results so far are negative. We have to wait for the rest of the results."

Nodding, I take the cup of water and pills and swallow them in one go. I wince when they slide down my throat. It feels like a sharp nail scratching me on the inside. "When can I go home?"

Your discharge papers should be ready for you to sign," she says and gives me a concerned look. "If you don't want the examination and the rape kit, will you please see your primary doctor? It is important. I'm sure he or she can do one there."

The last thing I want is to be touched or prodded. "What you just gave me..."

"It's an antibiotic to cover the basics. If anything doesn't look, smell, or feel normal, you come back right away."

I lower my head. "If I get a fever..."

"Right. I'm sure the charge nurse and the doctor went over it with you when you came in, but I'm making sure you understand. The number for the hotline is in the pamphlet. It's free. If you need to talk to someone. This is important. I overheard what the officer said, and I know you're scared, confused, shocked. It is why..."

"You urged me to go to my primary and have the examination there."

She has no idea how I feel. She is just doing her job. Empathy is what they are taught to feel. Not sympathy. She will go home tonight and talk about me to her boyfriend or husband. Feel pity.

I'm stupid for refusing an exam and that she would've made better choices if she were me. But she's not me, and she can't know how she'd feel if something like this happened to her.

"It's important to go as soon as possible. It will help the police catch whoever did this."

"The way this town is, people will know…"

"Maybe, but the police will catch whoever did it since you can't remember."

"They don't have a suspect. The law to test hasn't passed in the state. They will leave it on a shelf somewhere, or someone will make sure it stays that way," I blurt.

It's all over the news the law they are trying to pass to test the rape kits that have no suspects or enough people to test. There are hundreds of them. Hundreds of cases. It's best I keep quiet for now. Maybe I will remember if I go home. If I open my mouth and say the wrong thing, my grandmother will find out. My life will get worse. Everyone at school will blame me. Chris, Trent, and Ford. Their families run this town. They all have money. It will be me against them because they are the ones who left me there for it to happen. Their parents will come after me with everything they have. I'm eighteen.

A shiver runs through me. "I don't…"

"You're still in shock. Are you sure you're okay to go home?" Sharon asks with concern etched in her features.

I have to. Mary needs to get home to her family, and my grandmother can't wake up alone or, worse, find out what happened. This will crush her.

"Yes. I want to go home."

Present

There was no reason for me to look up different types of wild animals in the area to report like the detective asked because a coyote or a bear didn't attack me, but a man—an animal of a man who made sure to keep what he did a secret.

I went one step further, trying to get a close look at the small house to see if someone lived there because, to this day, I don't remember. But my body remembers. It remembers what my eyes can't see, what my mind can't figure out as panic grabbed me. I vividly recall my breath becoming stuck in my throat and refusing to escape. As if engulfed in a black hole, the world around me shrank until I could make out nothing but the pain. With a trembling palm, I reached out for anything solid, but all I could feel was empty space and the crushing realization that I was completely alone.

The sound of a loud, powerful engine cracks through my focus. As I turn back around, I see a flatbed tow truck drive around my van, parking in front of it.

I hear a door slam, followed by the rattle of a chain hitting metal. His stomach hangs like a teardrop over dirty jeans caked in grease. His white beard is long like Santa Claus decided he wanted to tow cars in his spare time before Christmas.

He grabs a pair of gloves and slides them on. "Dulce Webster? You called a tow?"

I sigh in relief. "Yes, my van made a funny noise and then died."

He nods, looking at the white van with rust caked in the corners. "Okay. Where do you want me to take it?"

I lift my hand to shade my eyes from the sun. "I need to make a delivery."

"I can take you up to a garage so you can see it before it gets fixed."

"Is it too far out? I was heading down this road."

He gives me an appreciative glance that makes me lose my appetite.

He secures the cooler in the back of his tow truck and the van on top of the flatbed. I get in the truck and pull down the hem of my dress.

Dean clears his throat. "What are you doing delivering cakes this far out from town?"

"We all need to make a living, Dean. I'm sure you understand. It's like asking you what a guy like you is doing towing cars this far out."

His watery eyes tinged with red around the white find mine. "There is only one difference, Miss Webster. No one would take a second look at a greasy old fat fuck like me."

He said it, not me, but I get his point.

The truck's engine rumbles low as it lunges forward, sounding like a purring cat, mixing with the air whirring from the air conditioner.

At least it was cold, but the cabin smelled like aged gas and stale cigarettes. The kind of smell you would have to shower to get out of your hair.

He nudges toward the side of the road, the tree line whizzing by. "I saw you peering through the trees when I pulled up. It's hard to see it, but that's old man Moody's cabin."

"Does he still live there?" I ask curiously.

"Don't know," he says with a shrug. "He's an old bastard. It's why they call him old man Moody. Probably why he lives out here in the woods."

"Why do you think he lives out here?"

"I think... maybe because he doesn't like people, or maybe people don't like him. He's old, pushing seventy, but he's a dirty old man."

My stomach clenches. "What do you mean?"

"Likes 'em young."

Bile rises in the back of my throat.

"How do you know that?" I'm trying to steady my breath and swallow down the nausea without him noticing. The bottled-up stench in here isn't helping.

"You know how word gets around in this town. I've heard stories. Like how he got handsy with a cashier at the grocery store. She was wearing a dress like you are, bent down to pick something up, and he just shoved his fingers up inside her."

I cup my hand over my mouth, my fingers trembling. "Seriously?"

He laughs. "That's what they say."

I frown. "They didn't arrest him?"

He shakes his head in disbelief. "He played the blind old man excuse. Conveniently provided a medical diagnosis that he was completely blind in one eye, and since he was old and the girl eighteen, they do what they always do in this town."

"They brush it off, look the other way, like it's some wild secret."

"That's right. No harm, no foul."

My throat is full of acid, but I manage to ask, "Is he still alive?"

"I haven't seen 'im. Not for a while. I thought maybe the son of a bitch died. Ain't no one going to miss the sick bastard. I didn't buy that blind excuse. I don't think no one did, but the girl moved to another state, and old man Moody returned to his cabin with his peaches." He laughs on the last part, finding it funny while I was falling apart inside.

We pass roadkill, and it's a dog with his guts spilled out over the road. Probably didn't see a car coming in the middle of the night.

"Poor thing," I mutter.

"You'll see that a lot in my line of work. There is always a poor animal bleeding out his asshole and a crowd of flies around his eyes on the road."

"That's disgusting."

"Ah, you'll get used to it. I've seen worse. Dead bodies from car accidents."

I look away, thinking about my parents and how they both died in a car accident on the way back home from getting me a surprise birthday present a few towns over.

He pulls out onto a main road, which is freshly paved. "Here we are."

I look at the big white building, freshly painted sitting in the middle of nowhere, oddly placed. I read the sign, and a wave of dread washes over me. This is the last place I want to go, but my phone chimes and says, "You have reached your destination."

I frown and look at the order form. This is the same place I was headed, and it's the last place I would think Ford would be staying when he asked me to personally deliver his order.

"This is Trent's garage."

"That's what it says," he says sarcastically. "It's the only mechanic shop still open in town. The last one closed. The owner called it quits and retired. If you want your van fixed without paying hundreds to another shop outside of town, I'll gladly do the tow. Call me, and I'll give you an estimate per mile. If not, Trent is the only one that can help you." He gives me a wink. "He's not a bad-looking guy. I'm sure he'll give you a good price."

A darkness creeps in from the edges of my memory and threatens to swallow me whole, fragmented, disjointed—a series of flashes and sensations that refuse to fade. But the fear, profound and unfathomable terror is still as real as it was at that moment, always lurks just beneath the surface, ready to drag me back into that place.

I swallow, trying to calm the lump in my throat.

"You never went to school with him."

"Oh, so you know 'em."

"Something like that."

He pulls to a stop and gets out, giving me a full view of his plumber's crack as he slides off the seat.

Walking up to the overhead door, I catch a glance from a few guys working on a Mustang out front.

"Is Trent here?" I ask, my voice cracking on the last part.

"Let me do it." Two guys are arguing. "I want to do it."

"Whatever, man," the other kid whines.

"Yo Trent, we got a customer!" a blond guy says, giving me his lame attempt at a sexy smile.

I roll my eyes and wait, listening to the flatbed system from the tow truck as it tilts.

I hear the deep growl from an engine. Then it roars so loud that I squint and cover my ears.

"Woohoo!" someone cheers. "That sounds awesome!"

"Yo, Trent!" the blond guy fires off.

"I'm coming," he yells, his voice cracking in frustration from somewhere in the back, and then I see him. My nightmare in the flesh.

"I have a delivery, and..." I look over my shoulder at Dean unloading my van, dragging the chain away from the tires and back. "I need an estimate to fix my van. I broke down on my way over."

He casts a hesitant glance at the van and then at me. "You need me to fix your van?"

I fold my arms protectively over my chest with the order form from the cookies still clutched in my hand, not caring that I'm crumpling it. I do," I reply and look away, not wanting him to see the tears I'm holding back. "I don't know what is wrong with it. It was backfiring earlier, and then it died on the way over here."

"Alright," he says softly. A far cry from the way he looked and treated me back in high school. I haven't seen him since it happened. I hoped I never would.

"Here you go, Missy. That will be three fifty," Dean says with a clipboard in his hand. "I need you to sign here. After you pay, I can hand you the keys."

"Let me get my cooler and bag out of your truck."

I turn around and run into a hard chest. I look up, and eyes the color of blue flames hold me. "Good morning, Dulce," Ford says softly.

"Good morning," I murmur, hating that he's here with Trent and hating Trent more. "I brought your order."

I walk around him, but he holds me gently by the arm. He leans close and kisses my cheek softly, washing away the hate and replacing it with a fire. "Are you okay?" he whispers and looks warily at Dean and Trent. "Did Dean do anything, say anything?"

I shake my head.

"Good. Let me help you."

He follows me to the tow truck, helps me with the cooler, and then carries it inside the garage.

I open my pocketbook and grab the money. "You have a great day, Dulce," Dean says, passing me and getting inside his truck. I frown, watching him back out after he blasts his horn. He didn't take my money. I glance at Ford, and he gives me a wink before glancing behind me, narrowing his eyes.

I turn around, and Trent remains standing in the same spot, watching me with a worried look. What is he afraid of? Or who? Is it me? Why would he, of all people—

Then it hits me. Ford is back in town. And Ford doesn't know what Trent and Chris did to me. Maybe he doesn't know they ruined my life.

Four Years Ago

DULCE

After feigning a headache from a long night, Mary was sick with worry when she found out what happened but promised me she would not tell my grandmother. She would be devastated. She told Grandma this morning that I was tired from prom.

There's a knock on the front door. I squeeze my eyes shut, hoping whoever it is will go away, but then another knock is followed by the doorbell. I drag myself out of bed before my grandmother wakes up. I look at myself in the hallway mirror and cover the gash near my hairline. There are dark circles under my red eyes from crying. Red splotches on my cheeks. My lips look like I had lip fillers. I look horrible. I look hung over, and I'm too young to drink.

I look through the peephole. A man in a black suit holds a briefcase. The top of his head is bald, and the gray hair is short on the sides.

Maybe it's a different detective.

The man smiles. "Good morning."

"Can I help you?" I ask cautiously.

"I'm Attorney Richards, and I'm representing Chris Ellis. Can I have a few minutes of your time?"

"I don't think—"

"Just a few minutes. Chris and his family want to ensure you're okay. It's unfortunate what happened. I assure you my visit is in your best interest." His eyes are cold like a shark.

"Miss Webster?" His voice is low and commanding.

I nod. I don't want to, but I feel like I need to know why he's really here. I step forward and shut the door behind me.

"What is this about?" I ask in a hard tone, crossing my arms to keep my hands from shaking. From the look in his gaze, I can tell this isn't a friendly visit.

"Look, I know high school can be tough, and it sounds like you've been through a lot. My client said you were the target of a harmless prank gone wrong."

I scoff and let out a humorless laugh even though I'm screaming inside. Harmless prank? Is he kidding?

"I understand you are in a tough spot right now with your grandmother's illness and running the bakery," he continues without waiting for me to answer, his mouth lifting in a sickly smile that doesn't reach his eyes. "If you want to keep it open, I suggest you move on from this." He lowers his voice. "Everyone knows your situation. It would be a shame if your grandmother had to close her bakery after being in business for so many years," he says, leaving a rigid taste in my mouth. "My client's family understands lineage, and they have the power and means to end things the way they see fit or make it better by making sure rent at the bakery is affordable. Maybe helping you out for six months after graduation. I'm also very good friends with Trent Walker's family ..." He pauses. "They also hope you can accept as a way to resolve things."

They think they can pay me off? Bastards.

"And what if that's not good enough for me? What they did was a crime."

"I recommend not going that route. Your story has holes, starting with Ford asking you to prom, seeing that he left the country yesterday at five o'clock. Chris and Trent have alibis, and you have no proof of who did any of it. Not to mention, you don't have anyone to support your side of the story, and this town doesn't tolerate liars." I want to slap his threatening smile off his face. "You and your grandmother risk losing everything."

My grandmother would be heartbroken, and we would be penniless if we had to close the bakery. The bakery is what pays for her medications that are not covered to keep her comfortable. State long-term care gives her eight hours Monday through Friday to pay Mary for personal care and homemaker for four hours each. Anything over that needs to come out of pocket, or I have to do it myself. Chris and Trent's family have the power to destroy me. They have the power to pay people off to look the other way.

"I understand," I say through clenched teeth, hating him— all of them.

"My clients are willing to replace your cell phone and any medical bills you received in urgent care if you keep things to yourself. If you need to see a doctor, one will be provided for you at no cost." He smiles like a car salesman. "I hope you feel better, Miss Webster, and good luck. My secretary will be in touch." The bloodsucking lawyer turns around and walks down the broken steps. I want nothing more than for him to trip and fall on his smug face and then scream at the top of my lungs.

Dulce looks terrified as I guide her into Trent's office. The cookies smell delicious, and I feel bad for making her come out this way, but I had no idea her van was in such bad shape. There was a moment when I thought it was better to pick up the order myself every week in a desperate attempt to see her, but I've had a change of plans, and now I need her here.

I guide her into Trent's office, ignoring the weird way he has been acting since she arrived. I need a minute alone with her to make sure she's okay. The last thing I want is for her to have a panic attack like the one she had on Friday night, and if she does, she comes first. Fuck everyone else.

"Do you have any orders left for the day?"

She shakes her head, clutching her bag like a life jacket.

Trent walks in and sits behind his desk, fumbling with his computer, probably pulling up the year and make of her van. I want to tell him not to bother fixing it. What she needs is a new one. The van she has is an old rust bucket, but I don't want to make her feel bad and would never point it out.

I'm sure she bought it with her own hard-earned money. I understand the pride one feels despite coming from a family that has everything. I know the feeling when someone flexes their wealth. Everything I have, I've earned. No one can take it away or tell me it was handed to me. I'm sure she feels the same way.

"I found the year, make, and model. I'll have my mechanic take a look at it," Trent says awkwardly, avoiding eye contact with Dulce.

"When was the last time you guys saw each other?" I ask, leaning against the wall, able to see the expressions on both their faces.

Trent's fingers pause over the keyboard. "School," Trent says.

Dulce is silent, staring at the wall like in a trance.

He's lying, so I say, "Hmm..."

"What did you expect? We weren't exactly friends with her."

"How was prom?" I ask sharply, looking directly at Trent.

From the corner of my eye, I see Dulce's legs shaking. Her hands tremble between her clenched thighs, and it looks like she's digging her nails into her palms. Trent leans back in his chair, not meeting my eyes, glancing nervously back and forth between Dulce and me.

"Don't fucking look at her," I warn firmly, my tone hard and unyielding.

Dulce looks up with terror in her eyes. I don't want to scare her, but I'm pissed off. I'm willing to commit murder. Trent sees the threatening look in my gaze. The way a person does when they want to make something or someone disappear.

"I went," he says.

"And Dulce? Did she go?"

He shakes his head slowly.

I push off the wall. "How come? I heard she went with me?" I stand next to him on his desk, looking at the computer screen where it says no charge on Dulce's invoice. "What's wrong, Trent?" I say angrily. "You're usually so vocal."

His Adam's apple moves up and down. My blood boils. "Answer me!" I scream, causing Dulce to jump in her seat.

I point at her but stare at Trent. "I'm not mad at you, Dulce. I would never hurt you, but this piece of shit in front of me..."

"She was the end-of-the-year prank," he says quietly.

My body trembles like rocks bouncing off the earth. My teeth grind so hard they are going to snap off. "Why?"

"It's what everyone wanted after you left."

Chris and Trent were the only ones who knew I felt this way, so why?

"Tell me!" I snap my fist, landing on the desk, causing him to jump.

Dulce continues to shake, but she's listening. She deserves to know.

"When you left your phone with us after we dropped you off at the airport," Trent finally says to me, his voice tight, his reluctance obvious. "Everyone had these crazy ideas for prom. The end-of-the-year prank was the biggest one. Summer, Vicki, Heather, Gwen, and all the guys. Practically, the entire class. Dulce's name came up, and all bets were off. Summer was pissed off that you left. I mean, we all were." He pauses, giving me a pleading look, willing me to understand, but I don't. Not when it comes to Dulce. He knows better.

"Using you made it sound more convincing. It was the only way we could make it look real. No one else at school that wasn't us knew you left the night before prom. That day you dropped her off was a perfect way to convince her. We were going to make it look like you stood her up. You were the most popular guy at school, so we were positive she wouldn't back out."

"How?"

"Chris and I picked her up in a blacked-out SUV, and we drove out to the backroad, ten minutes from my garage. And we..."

"You what?" I ask angrily.

"We left her stranded in the middle of the dark road." He hesitates to wipe the sweat forming on his brow, staring at the back wall like he's trying to erase a bad memory but can't. "I smashed her phone so she couldn't call anyone."

I stare at him menacingly.

"I'm sorry, Ford," he pleads, but it's falling on deaf ears. "So...

fucking sorry. Dulce...I didn't know you were going to be attacked..." I see tears run down his cheeks,

"Then what happened?" I ask, wanting to see how much more he knows.

"He found me helpless, running naked in the middle of the road," she continues, looking accusingly at Trent. "I begged you. I begged you both not to leave me there." Her voice breaks into a sob on the last part.

I quickly walk around the desk, pull her in my arms, and she cries in my chest. I want to take it all away, and I wish she could trust me enough to believe me, but all I can do right now is stare at Trent with a wintry smile. "Now what?"

Pulling up to Dulce's house, I notice the same mailbox leaning to the side like a pole after a hurricane. The vinyl stickers remain faded, but the numbers on her street have nearly peeled off.

When I think back on her car situation, I press the brake to stop the car and turn to face her before she gets out. "I can rent you a car," I offer.

"That's not necessary," she rushes out.

"Why not?"

She needs a car. She has a business to run and needs to get to and from work, plus I'm sure she has deliveries. It's the least I can offer right now.

She turns to face me in her seat, her voice shaking slightly. "Why are you doing this?"

"What?" I frown. I'm not sure if she's asking why I'm offering to rent her a car or why I keep showing up.

She stretches her hands out wide. "This?" she says sharply. Her face is splotchy from crying, but it doesn't diminish her gorgeous appearance. I instinctively want to protect her, which brings out my possessive edge to ensure she has no reason to cry.

I play dumb. "Are you upset at me for taking you home?"

"I could have called a cab."

"It's late and expensive," I reason.

"I'm not your responsibility, Ford. I appreciate you helping me the other night, but..."

"I am responsible, though."

She shakes her head. "You weren't even in the country when it happened. It was my own fault. I was stupid and naïve..." She closes her eyes, struggling to say things she doesn't want to.

It's not like I expect her to open up to me and tell me her innermost secrets, but I have to help her with anything she needs.

After a few seconds, she opens her eyes and stares out the window, and it feels like the first time I took her home four years ago. It felt good when I did it, the same way it does now.

The tension lingers in the air.

In her mind, she believes that I'm just like everyone else in this town. I may not know her very well, but considering everything she's been through, it's clear that Dulce is strong. Resilient. Honest. She is determined and kind, putting all her dreams on hold. A human being who doesn't deserve what life has thrown at her.

"Stupid to think what?" I ask after a while when it's evident she's not going to say any more without being pushed a little. I don't want to say goodbye yet. Not without finding out what is going through her mind right now.

She sighs in defeat and opens the door. "Nothing. I-I...thanks for the ride, Ford."

I reach out just as she is about to get out but hesitate and grip the steering wheel, not wanting her to be afraid of me. "Dulce, wait. Wait, please."

She pauses and looks over her shoulder with an unreadable expression, giving me hope.

I'm sorry, Dulce, for everything," I say honestly. "I know you might not believe me right now, but... I want to help you."

Her chin jerks up a little with a determined expression. It triggers my instinct not to let her go, but I want her trust more than anything.

"No one can help me, Ford, and you're the last person I expect anything from." She gets out and shuts the door.

I watch as she walks on the little path of broken pavers toward her house, skipping every few steps to avoid the potholes. It takes everything in me to keep from going after her. My fixation with her erased everything else going on in my life, leaving nothing but her.

Trent's confession probably brought back memories she's been trying to forget for the past four years. But I think it's important for her to share what happened to her with someone. I can be that person. I know I can, but I don't think she's ready to believe when I tell her she's not stupid and it wasn't her fault.

Guilt runs through me like venom. Back in high school, I did nothing. I was a coward. I stood by and watched her endure the bullying. I believed I protected her by ignoring the bullying, hoping it would eventually stop.

But I wouldn't have stood by and allowed what happened to her on prom night. Would she believe me if I told her that, though?

If we're assigning blame, Trent and Chris are at the top of the list. But someone else was involved, too. Someone who did something way worse.

For four years, no one has helped her get justice. The money and power of Chris's and Trent's well-connected families have made sure of that.

Dulce Webster may not be important to anyone in this town besides her dying grandmother, but she is to me.

I place the car in first, peeling out as the back tires kiss the pavement. The adrenaline rush as the car hits one hundred and ten does nothing to calm the storm brewing in my veins.

By the time I make it back to Trent's garage, the sun is setting with purple and orange streaks in the sky. The red neon sign outside the building shines brighter as the sun disappears. The two young guys constantly bickering outside seem to have left for the day. When I park, the only car in front is Trent's GTO.

I walk in and hear Trent muttering a curse, followed by metal hitting aluminum with a clang. He must have sensed my approach because he looks around the raised hood of Dulce's van, caked in dirt and grease.

"I said not to fix it," I tell him tightly.

"Well, I never listened to my parents, so I'm not going to start with you," he says, turning around to grab a tool.

"I'm buying her a new one," I state.

He snorts. "Yeah, like she would take it coming from you. Why would she want anything from us, anyway? To be honest, you can't blame her."

"Not from you." I pause, hating him for what he did. The broken look in her eyes at his confession is killing me inside, making my anger boil and causing my fist to clench and the tic in my jaw to run rampant. "She could have died!" I yell.

I wanted to confront him as soon as I found out, but I had to wait because I want to kill him.

"Don't you think I know that?" he roars, glaring at me with bloodshot eyes. "Do you think I go to sleep at night knowing what I did to her?" He lets out a strangled cry of frustration, but I don't feel sorry for him. Not him or Chris. Not even me. We all destroyed Dulce in some way.

"I broke her fucking phone, man." He shuts his eyes. "She couldn't call for help. I..."

Something snaps inside me. I continue raining blows on his face, and he takes it. I'm losing control, but he deserves it. They all do. I'm surprised he doesn't fight back. Trent is not one to back down from a fight, even if he deserves it.

His back is against the front of Dulce's van, trying to keep from falling. "Don't stop," he manages to say through a bubble of bloody spit. Some land on my chin, but I don't wipe it off.

I land a few more punches. I split his brow. His lip. I'm out of breath. My arms feel like lead, so I drop them. My knuckles are split open. Sweat drips down my face, but I welcome the sting in my eyes. I watch his face swell in the scorching heat like a dead body would. His face is almost unrecognizable.

"Give me Chris's address," I demand between breaths. He attempts to spit on the concrete, but instead, a glob of blood-tinged saliva slides down his chin. Through the tiny slits in his swollen eyes, I can see that he understands.

I walk to the driver's side of the Porsche, and I'm surprised he can get inside the passenger seat after locking the side door. He presses an app on his phone. The garage door automatically closes.

I reach behind the seat. "Don't get dirt, grease, or blood on the car," I tell him, tossing the towel in his face. "It's a rental."

I program in the address Trent gives me to Chris's place.

"I'm sorry, man. I swear I didn't touch her. It wasn't me," he says as I speed down the road.

It doesn't take long before the GPS has me turning down a road with a large two-story house at the end. The grass looks three weeks overdue for a cut. The windows don't have blinds. It looks like a family moved in but didn't have money to cover the windows and decided to put sheets in different colors so no one could look inside.

I get out of the car, not bothering to wait for Trent. I don't care if he comes with me or not. As I walk up the steps to the front door, it sounds like a small party inside, with loud music blaring. In the dim glow from the outdoor light that's half full of dead bugs, I see a doorbell with a missing button. I bang on the wood door with scuffs and peeling paint.

I'm about to knock on the door again when the door opens a bit. A woman's head pokes out, looking like a bird. A bad dye job on the woman's burnt hair has resulted in mottling between dark brown and green.

Her eyes widen, her pupils dilate, and she blinks like a lizard a couple of times. It takes her a few seconds for her eyes to focus on me.

She gives me a once-over. "Who are you?" she asks.

"Where's Chris?"

She leans on the door and smiles. Her yellow teeth and the black tartar surrounding her gums make me want to throw up.

"Around, inside, outside," she says, and then lets out a drug-induced laugh, causing her to shift on her feet. The smell of stale smoke, beer, and rotten wood makes my throat thick with bile.

I swallow it down. "Get Chris," I grind out, barely restraining myself from charging the door and pushing the bitch out of my way.

"Chris!" she yells as loudly as her raspy smoker's voice can manage.

"Who is it?" he fires back, stumbling toward the door.

A hand with dirty fingernails grips the door above her head, and he comes into view. His armpit hairs are inches from her face, but she doesn't move. From the looks on both of them, I'm positive they haven't showered in days.

I have never seen Chris in this state. It almost makes me feel sorry for him. If it weren't for what he did to Dulce, I would try to figure out a way to help him.

When he recognizes me, his eyes widen, glassy and unfocused. "Look who decided to visit!" he says with a wide, crazed smile. "Ford Keller."

The woman's eyes go wide like she won a prize. "The racecar driver friend you told me about," she says, then cackles.

"The one and only," Chris says, moving to the side. "Come in." A shadow runs over the wall, and I know it's Trent standing behind me. "Holy shit, Trent. What the fuck happened to you?"

I don't turn around because I don't need to. After staring at Trent some more, Chris raises his brow at me. "You did that?"

I don't respond, and neither does Trent. After a few tense seconds, Chris nods.

"Because he owes you money, Ford."

I wish it was that easy.

"What do you think?" I ask, looking at him with a hard expression.

He shrugs his shoulders like a little kid. "I don't know," he says and then laughs. I watch as he scratches the meth sores on his arms, near the faded tattoos on scraped skin that looks like they were homemade from a tattoo kit you ordered online.

"Do they want to come inside?" the woman offers suggestively.

I would rather eat my own shit.

"That's okay. Maybe some other time," I reply, staring directly at Chris. "I just came to see how Chris was doing."

"He's doing fine, ain'tcha baby," she says, cupping his junk over his dirty blue jeans.

With a gleam in his eyes, he smiles. "Yep. I'm mighty fine, Ford." Chris nudges his head. "You and Trent should come hang out with us. I don't mind sharing."

"We're good," Trent says in a muffled voice.

When I get in my car and Trent shuts the door, Trent asks, "Now what?"

"I come back. Alone."

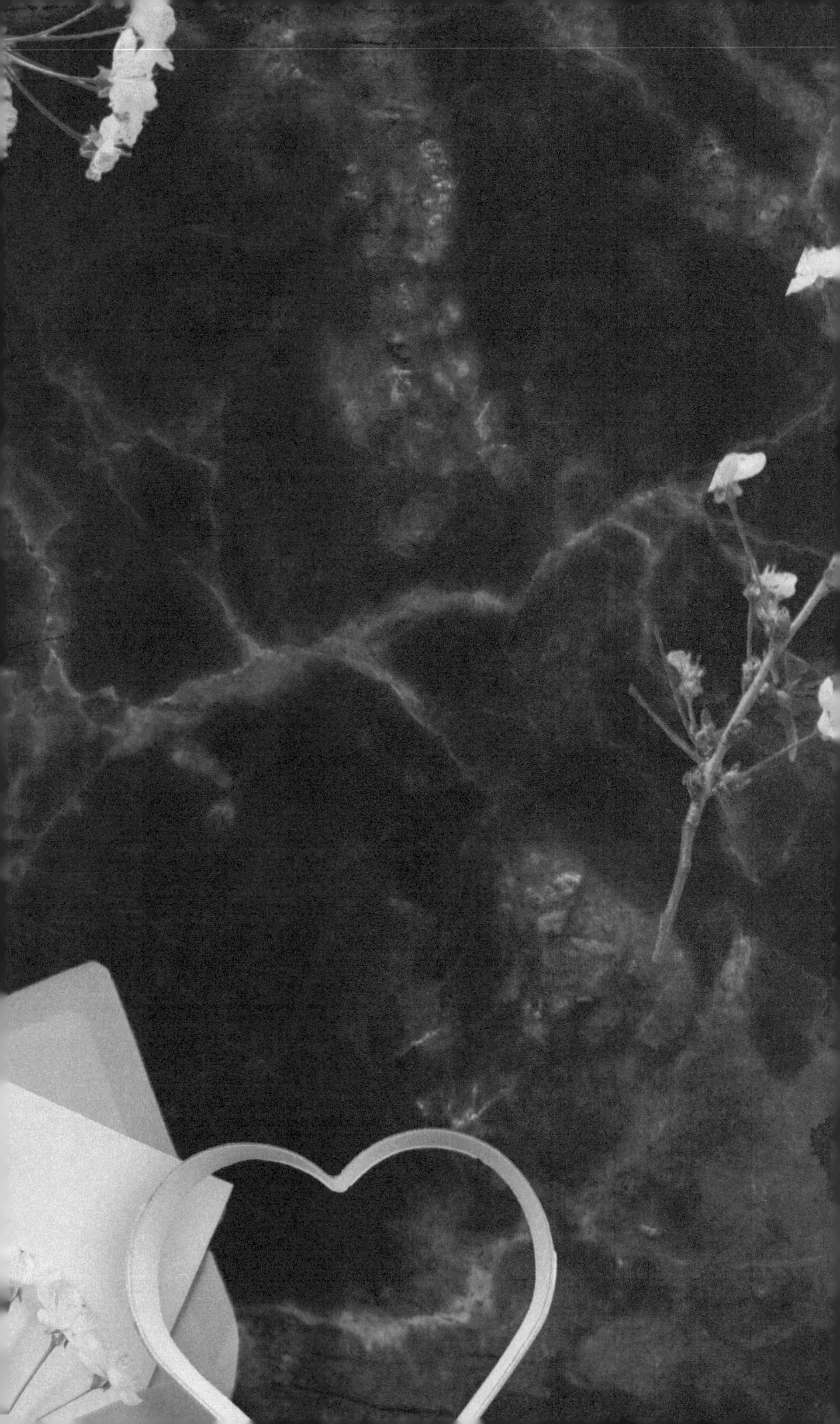

K atie's car pulls up in front of my house, near the mailbox, and she rolls down her window. "Your Uber is here."

"We don't have Uber," I remind her.

"That's because this fucking town sucks."

"You're catching on. This town does suck." I open the passenger door to her white Toyota Camry and get in, placing my bag between my feet. "Thank you for picking me up and taking me to work."

She waves her hand, places the car in drive, and makes a U-turn. "I don't mind. It's not like we aren't going to the same place, and you are a cool boss."

"I'm not that great."

"You're better than my last one working at the gas station back home."

"You're not a bad employee yourself."

"I'm your only employee."

"You have a point, but you could still be a bad one, and that's not the case."

"How come?" she asks curiously.

"You still have a job."

"What happened to the van?"

"I have no idea. It's at the mechanic shop. It was late and..." I don't want to tell her that Ford took me home.

I'll never hear the end of it. She thinks Ford and I are close because we went to high school together. Katie doesn't know I was the outcast.

"How did you get home?"

"Um... Ford gave me a ride."

"Ford Keller?"

I sigh. "That's the one."

"So you do know him."

"He was at the garage when the tow truck dropped me off."

"Oh?" she says. "How come?"

"The owner of the garage is one of his best friends."

"Ohh... What's his name?"

"Don't worry about it. He's an asshole. That's all you need to know."

She parks in the back of the bakery, and I quickly get out before she asks me why. The last thing I want to talk about is Trent and why I think he's a prick.

After Ford dropped me off last night, I couldn't sleep. I had nightmares about that night. I couldn't see. Panic gripped my throat, choking me of breath. I woke up gasping for air, reliving the pain I felt all over my body.

The last place I thought I would end up was at Trent's garage. Even if my van hadn't broken down, I would have ended up there to deliver the large order that came in yesterday evening through the online ordering system.

Chris and Trent haven't come by the bakery since that night, and I made sure not to go to Trent's for any car repairs. It's most likely why my van was in such terrible shape.

I unlock the back door and disarm the alarm, but something in the pit of my stomach tells me something isn't right and feels off. I turn on the lights. I take a quick look around the back hallway and then glance at the display, which is exactly as expected. Empty. Everything is neatly put away. The rich smell of vanilla and butterscotch is heavy in the air.

Katie walks in. I shut the door and flip the lock. When I walk to the kitchen, I see something on one of the prep counters. There is a weird sound. Whatever it is, it's moving like a worm.

"What is that?" Katie says when she walks into the kitchen, the door swinging back and forth.

"It's a rat," I tell her, stepping forward cautiously.

Katie grabs my arm, causing my stomach to drop. "Is that...?"

"Blood," I finish for her, taking two steps forward, and my heart slams into my ribs.

Next to the dying rat, big red letters in blood spell out SHHHH.

"What the hell?" Katie says,

"Don't touch anything, Katie," I rush out. I swallow thickly.

She nods nervously. "Who would do this?" she asks, pulling out her phone to take a picture while I stare at the dying rat covered in blood.

"I don't know," I say, my head falling into my hands.

But I do know. Whoever wants me to keep quiet. Is it Trent? Chris? Ford? It wouldn't make sense if it were Trent or Chris. It's been four years; why would they threaten me to be quiet now?

After ten minutes, Danny shows up, knocking on the front door. I had to close the shop for the day. It's not like I could serve customers with a dead rat on the prep counter.

"Are you alright?" he asks with a look of apprehension as he walks in.

I'm not surprised he came alone. I thought that usually when there was this sort of thing, cops would bring a partner or backup.

"Yes...and no."

"Let me take a look," Danny says, turning down the radio clipped to his uniform when the dispatcher addresses another call.

"Be our guest," Katie replies in a snarky voice.

She doesn't like Danny because of the date and how I ended up in the bathroom stall. However, I can also sense her fear in the way she bites her thumbnail. Hell, I'm scared.

Danny walks inside the kitchen to check it out while Katie and I stand right outside the door. I steady my breath, trying to calm the panic.

Someone broke into the bakery. There are only two exits, and none of them look like someone has broken inside. I armed the alarm, so it would've gone off. Katie was the last one to lock up. I have cameras by the register. There is no reason she would do something like this. I shift to the side and grab my phone, scanning the kitchen for anything amiss but finding nothing.

While I hear the kitchen door swing open, I check the footage on the app. "Do you have cameras in the kitchen area?" Danny asks.

"No, but I'm checking the camera by the register to see if anyone slipped behind the counter and entered the kitchen, but there is nothing. I was here yesterday until I had to make deliveries."

"Where's the van?" Danny asks curiously.

"It's in Trent's garage," I reply.

"Trent?" Danny says in a hard tone.

"His is the only car repair place in town, Danny."

"Trent placed an order from your bakery yesterday," Danny asks.

I don't want to tell him it was Ford.

"There is no way anyone went into the kitchen yesterday after you left, Dulce," Katie said, shaking her head. "I was working the register. We had about ten customers. I didn't go back to the kitchen after you left. I locked up at six o'clock and closed out the register. Then I armed the alarm and locked the door."

"I know," I tell her, waving my phone. "I saw."

I trust Katie. I wish I had told the guy who installed the cameras to install one in the kitchen, but it was extra, and I was on a budget. I needed the money for the van and the extra hours to pay Mary so I could work.

"He must have had something to do with it," Danny says.

"Who?" I ask confused.

"Trent," he says.

Katie looks back and forth between Danny and me with a confused expression. Katie doesn't know about my past or what happened. "Who is Trent, and why would he be involved in breaking in the prep table rat?" Katie asks.

I don't trust Trent, but he didn't place the order. It's possible that he knows who did it or who is behind the rat. Ford was asking him questions about that night, but I don't want to tell Danny about the argument they had or that Ford is prying into what happened.

"We can't rule anything out, but I'm not sure Trent is behind it," I reply, ignoring Katie's question.

"Why not?" Danny counters.

"Because Trent didn't place the order," I tell him. "Ford did."

Why would Trent or Chris be behind the rat? It wouldn't make sense. They wouldn't want to reveal the prank or bring up the fact that they abandoned me in the middle of the road, so why would they send me a message? Everyone from school knows about the prank on prom night. I still can't remember. I don't have a face. This last threat reinforces the fact that they want me to think it's Ford.

"Don't you find it strange that this is happening since he came back?" Danny says in an acerbic tone.

He means Ford.

I shake my head, not wanting to believe it, even though I can't think of an argument against it. I can't trust anyone in this town. The truth is, Ford kicked Trent's ass despite being friends, or maybe they aren't as close as I thought.

"I'll call the investigations unit to see if we can find any prints. Did you touch anything?" Danny asks, taking out his phone.

I shake my head. "Just the back door, the kitchen door, and the alarm."

"Good. Don't touch anything until they get here and do their thing." He gives me a soft expression. "I'll do anything in my power to catch whoever did this, Dulce."

Fear claws at my gut. I cross my arms over my waist. They never catch anyone, but I nod anyway. The dead rat is a message, and he knows it. I need to keep my mouth shut, or I'll end up dead like that rat on the table.

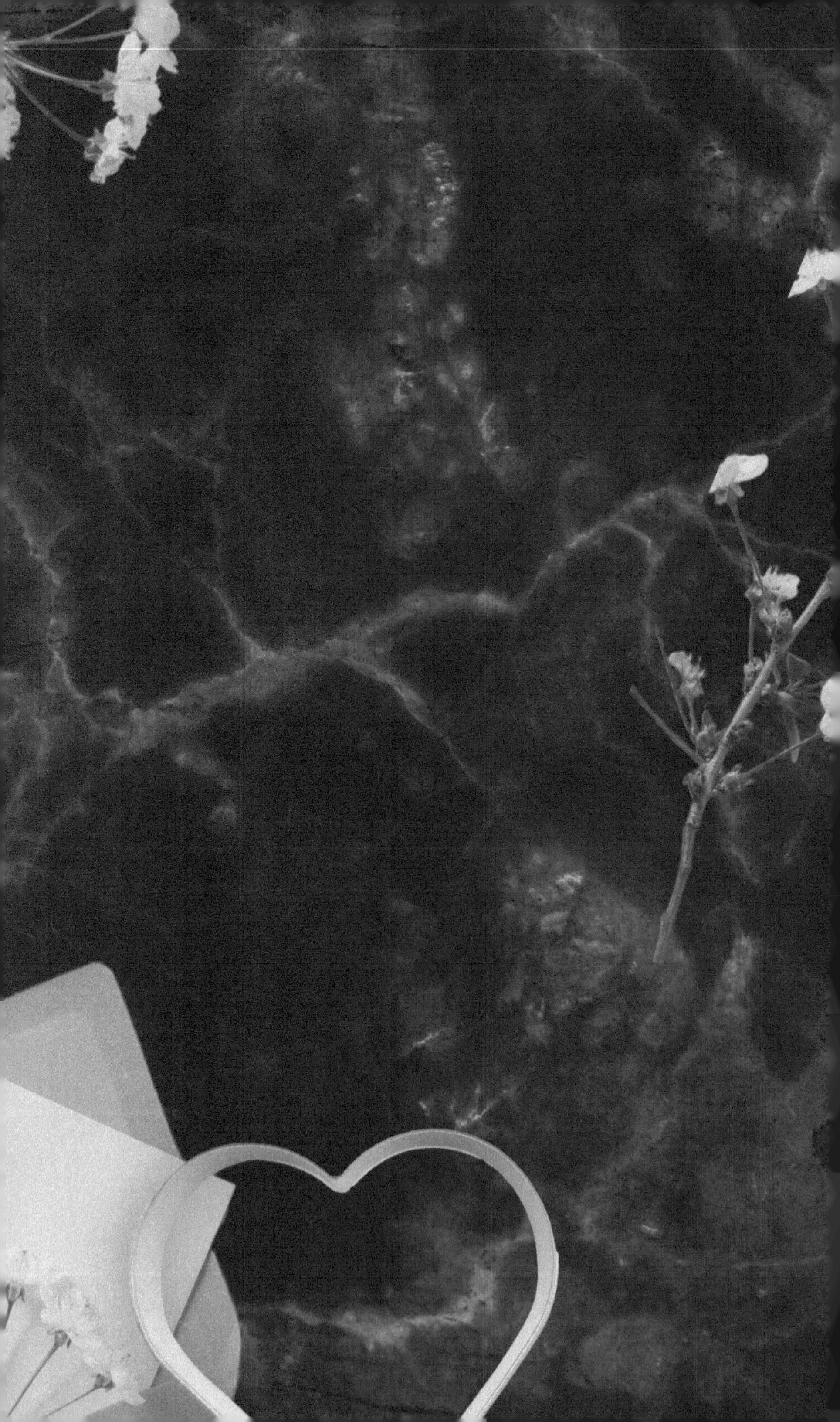

DULCE

After Danny calls the general investigations unit, Katie and I prepare our statements. It has been a madhouse so far. People are wondering what happened when they show up to find the bakery closed. Katie called the customers, canceled their orders, and issued refunds. I called Mary, and she told me my grandmother is okay and has already had lunch. I told her someone broke in but didn't take anything. I didn't tell her about the rat. I'm sure she'll find out soon enough. Nothing in this town is kept under wraps unless they want it to be.

Katie walks up while I stare at my phone. "The cleaning crew is here," she announces.

When there is a rat inside a food prep area, I have to call a company that cleans and sanitizes the entire bakery so OSHA and city regulations don't breathe down my neck when I resume operation. It's not like I would bake in there anyway or serve anyone. Rats are known to carry diseases. Whoever did it knew this would set me back and jeopardize my business.

"Perfect," I say, getting up. "The faster this gets done, the faster we can open back up."

"I'm sorry, Dulce. I know this is a setback you can't afford."

"You know what they say when it rains."

"It fucking pours," she finishes for me. She covers her mouth like a child who says a bad word in front of her parents. "Sorry."

I shake my head. "Under the circumstances, it's appropriate."

I watch as people file in wearing protective gear. "Could you take me to see about getting a new prep table?"

"Sure."

I'm not preparing anything on that table. When the cleaning crew finished, I instructed Katie to dispose of it.

I hear the bell at the door. I look up and see Ford. A calming sense spreads through me. My breath catches in my throat at how good he looks in a simple T-shirt and jeans. His arms bulge when he pushes his sunglasses on top of his head.

"Hey..."

"You heard?" I ask worriedly, causing sweat to slide down my spine. Making me aware of every movement I take.

"You know, people in this town talk about how when a store closes. It looks like you have an alien inside with all the people walking in and out wearing protective suits."

Karie scoffs. "Aliens?"

"It was a joke," he explains with a slight smile, causing my heart to skip a beat.

"Ha, ha," she says sarcastically.

He raises his brows and slides his hand into the front pocket of his jeans, looking around. "So...rats, huh?"

"Yep," I quip. "I'm about to head out, so..."

"Oh...um. You need a ride?"

"I think you've given me enough rides," I tell him, not sure if I should trust Ford to give me anything.

Katie snorts.

I glare at her.

"What?" She plays it off. "It sounded funny."

I sigh. "I need to get going," I tell him.

"I'll go with you. That's the reason I stopped by."

"Why?"

"About your van. I figured you wouldn't want Trent to stop by or call, so I thought I would."

"What's wrong with it, and how much will it cost me? I ask,

ignoring his comment, even though he's right that Trent is the last person I want to see. But right now, I'm only concerned with figuring out if I have enough on my credit card to pay for the repair.

"Um, to be honest," he says gently, licking his bottom lip, "it's best if you get a new one."

I laugh sarcastically. "Yeah, no. How much is it to get it to run and not leave me on the side of the road?"

"More than it's worth," he says convincingly.

"I can't…"

"I know," he says. "But I can fix that."

Katie looks back and forth between us with a grin on her face.

"I don't want you to fix anything."

"Fix what?" Danny says, walking from the back and standing behind Ford.

"We're talking about my van," I tell him.

Danny looks at Ford as if he wants to bag him along with the rat. "What about it, Ford?"

"I think Ford wants to buy Dulce a new van," Katie chimes in.

"She can use my truck," Danny offers like I'm not standing right here. Maybe he realizes he sounded rude because he gives me a quick, apologetic look. "You could use my truck, Dulce. It's no trouble. As long as you need it."

"I…"

"That's not going to work," Ford says.

"Why not?" Danny challenges.

"For how long?" Ford says. "In the end, she will still need a new van. Fixing the one she has isn't worth the trouble. It's not reliable anymore." He turns to me. "I can buy you a new one."

"I don't want to owe you money," I tell him firmly.

Ford shakes his head. "You won't owe me anything because it was a gift." I open my mouth to protest, and he cuts me off. "I can afford it, Dulce. Easily."

Danny scoffs. "You have balls, man. You think you can throw your money around, and that solves everything."

Katie ignores Danny and stands in front of me with raised brows and wide eyes. "We accept," she says. I turn to her and say, "Excuse me."

I shake my head, telling her she is out of her mind.

She nods slowly as if I'm stupid for not accepting his help, but Katie doesn't understand.

"Good," Ford says, satisfied. "The last thing she needs is to find herself stranded again. She has a business to run."

"What a hero," Danny says sarcastically.

"Can you two stop?" I interrupt, and Katie and Danny look at me like toddlers caught in a fight. With a sigh, I ask, "Why can't you get along?"

While I'm listening to them, anxiety causes my pulse to race. I hate to say it, but Ford is right. If I spend money to fix the stupid piece of shit van, there is a high probability of it leaving me stranded again. I shudder at the thought of finding myself on the side of the road.

"We can't get along," Danny says.

"Why not?" I ask.

"Because I'm trying to protect you. I'm..."

"He's trying to fuck you," Ford interjects. "Literally."

My eyes cut to Danny, and he glances at me with a warm expression. "It's obvious I like you, Dulce. Very much. I'm..."

"The last time I checked, you were still fucking the server at the restaurant. So that means, if I'm as good at math as I am at driving, you had an epiphany about a week ago when it came to Dulce."

"You son of a bitch," Danny growls, lunging at Ford.

I step between them, placing my hand on Danny's chest. "Danny, stop." I can feel Ford step close behind me.

"I should arrest you," Danny says angrily. The blatant hate for Ford in his eyes.

"For what?" Ford laughs sarcastically. "Go ahead, fuck with

me, and after I'm done with you, you'll be lucky if you have a job as a security officer at a grocery store," Ford warns.

I whirl around and catch Ford's blue gaze. "Please stop?"

His eyes hold me for a second. "Come with me. Let's go get what you need for the shop," he says. "Katie can stay. I promise to have you back before it's time to close."

I shake my head. "I…" The back of his fingers caress my cheek, causing the words to die in my throat and my stomach to flutter.

"Please, Dulce. Let me do this for you."

My eyes fall to his lips. The warmth of his skin on my cheek is easing my anxiety. There is no way Ford is responsible for the break-in or what happened at prom. I can feel it in my gut. He could have easily left the same way he did before prom, and no one would question him.

"Okay," I agree.

"You've got to be kidding me," Danny sneers as he walks around me, his gaze fixed on Ford. "You hurt her, and the only thing you'll be driving is a go-kart."

"Is that a threat, Officer Mays?" Ford says through clenched teeth.

"It's a fucking promise, asshole."

"Good," Ford says, glaring at Danny. "She needs someone to watch over her, not fuck her."

Danny bares his teeth. "Like that's not on your mind whenever you look at her."

Ignoring him, Ford simply walks around him and opens the front door, holding it for me to walk out first.

I guess we're going car shopping.

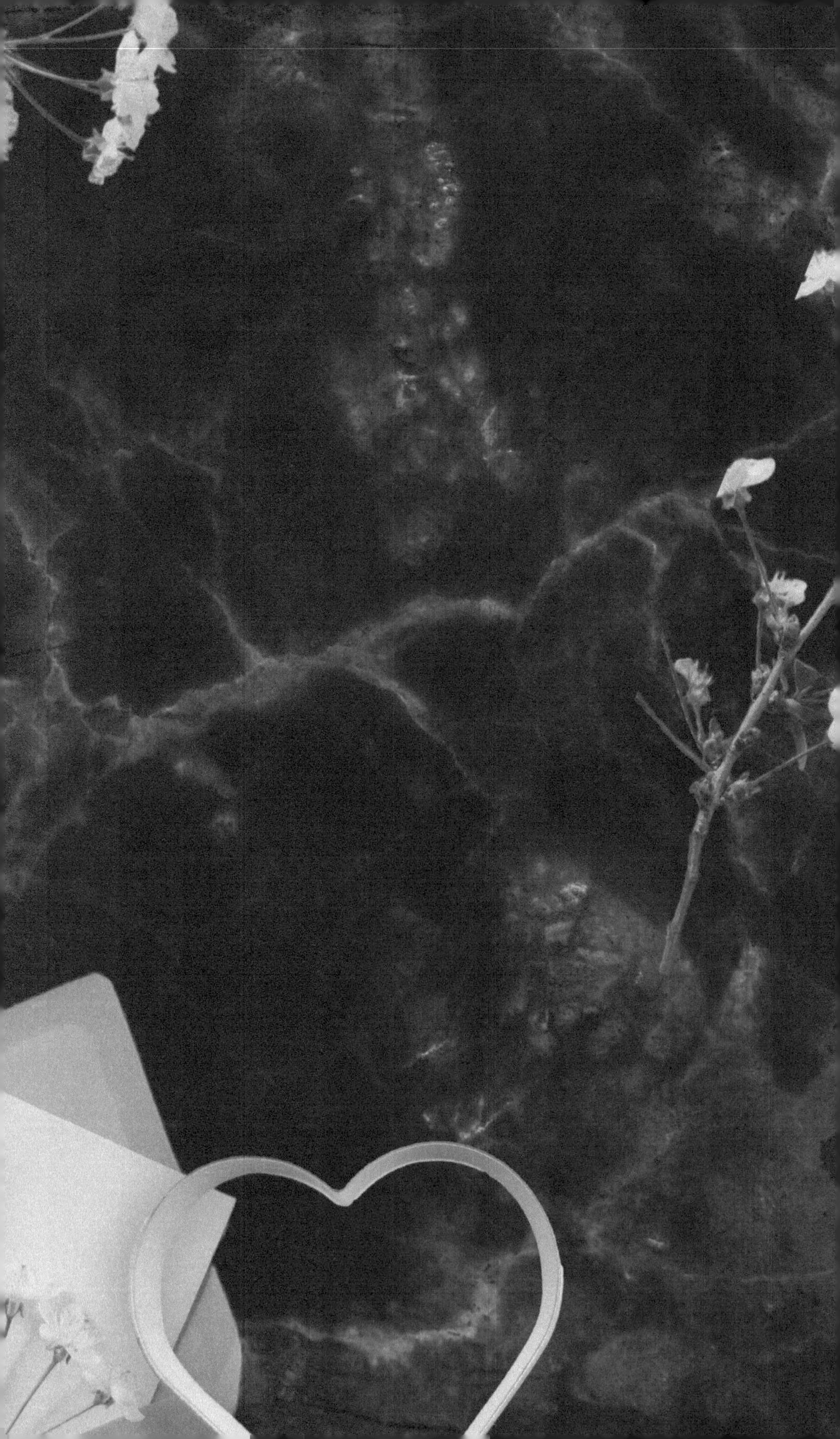

The car is silent as Ford drives out of town. The tension is thick, like breathing hot air under the sun. He hasn't looked at me since we left the bakery. I'm not sure what he was thinking or if what Danny said was true.

"Is it true?"

"Huh?"

"What Danny said back there."

"What? About my offer to buy you a van?"

"No," I say, moving the vent from the air conditioner so the cool air can hit my skin. "What's on your mind when you look at me?"

After a few seconds, I get tired of waiting for him to answer and look out the window. "Not the way he made it seem," he finally says.

"Oh," I say, giving him a smile of regret. "Of course not."

Maybe I shouldn't have asked, but I just want to know the truth. Why is he helping me?

Every few seconds, he casts a worried glance my way that I purposely ignore. The tension between us stretches, causing my hands to sweat. I check my phone and see a missed text from Katie.

Katie: What does it feel like to be in the same car as one of the most beautiful men on the planet?

Dulce: Hot, cold, and then hot again, but he isn't talking to me.

Katie: He's likely worried about saying the wrong thing. Danny was upset that you left **without him. You have competition, boss lady.**

Yeah right.

Dulce: Whatever, not interested.

Katie: You can't give up because one guy is a douche.

I snort, not realizing I had done it out loud.
"Is everything alright?" Ford asks.
A wave of heat travels up my neck. "Fine," I say, playing it off.

Dulce: I haven't met one that isn't.

Katie: Have faith. I think Ford Keller wants you.

Dulce: You're reading too much into it.

Katie: Yeah, right. Then why is he offering to buy you shit?

She doesn't understand that it's out of guilt.

Many nights, I sat in my room crying myself to sleep, trying to remember anything that night, but I only wake up from a nightmare, reliving it all over again. A faceless man haunts me.

Dulce: I'll tell you later.

Will I? I'm not sure if I should. I've never told anyone what really happened. Obviously, the doctor and nurses who treated me knew. Danny doesn't know what happened after that night. No one knows the consequences I had to suffer for my silence, and sometimes I think it was done on purpose to make sure I would never forget.

"Are you sure?" Ford asks.

I pocket my phone and reply, "I'm sure." He stops at a light, and I notice he drives us into the city. I clear my throat. "You know this is unnecessary, right?"

"I'm not following," he says, but we both know what I mean.

"You don't owe me anything, Ford," I say softly. "The past..."

"Dulce..."

"Don't you mean Betty Cocker?" I shoot back. "It's what you and your friends called me all the time, isn't it? Why stop now? It's like shit. It still stinks after you wipe it off."

I know it's stupid to bring that up and not accept his help if he is offering it, but I've managed to survive without it. I don't need his money to bail me out of my problems so he can sleep better at night. The other night, I realized the kiss was guilt-driven. Sometimes I think it must have been a cruel joke to make him feel good about himself because, deep down, they are all monsters.

"I've never called you that."

"But you never told them to stop," I retort.

What I remember from high school, he would stand next to his friends and watch them do nothing.

The crush I had for him was like a blanket covering the truth.

The light turns green, and a car honks when he takes a second too long to move forward.

"You're right. I didn't. I feel—"

"Guilty." I interrupt. "Is that why I'm here in your fancy car? Is it so you can throw money at my problems and feel vindicated? Free from guilt? Kiss the victimized high school girl to provide her with a sense of comfort and security."

A look of horror crosses his face. "No..."

"Then why am I here, Ford?"

He stops behind a parked car near a row of shops. He opens and closes his mouth, clearly not knowing what to say. I'm sure he never thought I would bring any of this up or call him out on his bullshit. But I'm not the shy, weak-bullied girl in high school anymore.

"I want to help you."

I open the door. "You want to help yourself," I shoot back, stepping out of the car.

"Dulce..."

I slam the door, not wanting to do this right now.

I spot a café next to a commercial kitchen store with small tables outside and a neon sign that says fresh coffee. When I walk inside, I stand in line, looking at the menu. It's already two in the afternoon, and I haven't eaten anything since the rat incident. When it's my turn, I order a simple coffee and bagel.

Ignoring the curious looks people give Ford, he walks in and scans the tables until he finds me taking a seat in the booth by the window.

I look at my phone, opening the last text Katie sent me so I can tell her to pick me up. I'll have her take me to Trent's garage and ask him how much it is to fix the van until I figure out what to do next.

The chair makes a rough sound when Ford pulls it out to sit across from me. "Why did you leave like that?"

"We have nothing to talk about. At least I don't."

"Why..." He stops mid-sentence. My eyes snap up. He can probably tell by the look on my face that it's a stupid thing to ask. "I don't feel guilty," he rushes out. "If you haven't noticed, I like you, Dulce."

One of the employees places my order on the table.

When they leave, and he glances at me, waiting for me to speak, I burst out laughing, almost spilling my coffee. He looks around, trying to find out what is so amusing, but I can't stop. Maybe it's because I've liked him since I was fifteen and saw him for the first time, and not once did he notice me in a room unless someone was poking fun at me.

When I manage to stop and catch my breath, I tell him, "I'm sorry, but I can't possibly believe anything you have to say."

"I know."

"Then why bother?"

He gives me a determined look. "Because I'm not going to stop until you believe me."

I lean forward. "Is that why you came back? Because you heard what your stupid friends did."

Something I can't define passes in his eyes when he says, "I didn't know what they did, I swear."

I know he didn't. His image is too important, but maybe that keeps him at Airy. People discovering that he isn't the decent guy everyone believes he is. I mean, you have to be some type of selfish asshole to be friends with people like Chris and Trent. I'm not sure if the rumors of him getting Summer knocked up are true, but I'm surprised none of those little details have popped out in the tabloids. Usually, the dirt from celebrity's pasts is aired at some point.

"You didn't answer my question," I press.

"I don't know why I came back." He looks at his phone when it rings. He stares at the screen, which keeps ringing with the name Derek flashing on the screen. It stops and then starts again.

I raise a brow. "Are you going to get that?"

He sighs and answers, putting the phone up to his ear. "What? I don't know." He pauses. "I know, but I'm not done here. Well, they can wait. I know I have to race, Derek. I told you I had to come back and figure things out...No..." He glances up at me and continues, "I haven't yet, but I will soon. No, I changed my mind. No racing shop."

So it's true. He had plans to open a race shop in Airy. I wonder what changed his mind. It means he didn't know what happened if he was considering it.

He hangs up, and I stare at him, trying to focus on my anger but come up empty. "Problems?"

"That was my manager. I planned to open a racing shop but changed my mind."

"Then why are you still here?" I push. "Don't you have to race cars in circles somewhere?"

He laughs. "You're funny."

"That's a first," I say, sipping my lukewarm coffee. "I've never heard that one before."

He grins. "You don't take compliments very well."

"I'm not used to them coming from someone like you."

"Someone like me?" he says unexpectedly. "That's a first."

"I'm sure you're accustomed to them, but not me."

"You should. Because it's true," he says honestly.

"I need to head back," I tell him, pushing my coffee away and picking up my phone.

"I had something planned," he says, confused. "I thought we were good."

"That's one thing we would never be. Good."

"It doesn't matter. I'm going to buy you what you need."

"Why?" I ask confused.

"Because in my eyes, we will always be good, Dulce. I just need to convince you."

This is a side of her that I have never seen before. But I like it. She has a fire in her eyes when she speaks to me as if I am gum beneath her shoe. It's refreshing.

She doesn't trust me, and I can't blame her. If I were in her shoes, I wouldn't either.

She asked me why I came back, and I hated lying, but I can't tell her why because it would make it worse.

"Why did you agree to come with me?" I ask. "You could have said no."

She shrugs and says, "I changed my mind."

"Changed your mind about what?" I don't get it. What's her problem? She needs help, and I can and want to give it to her.

"You."

"What about me?"

"I don't want your help, Ford."

"Why not?"

She raises a brow.

Okay, point taken. She has every right to tell me to go fuck myself.

"You don't want my money."

"No, I don't. To be honest, I think your being nice to me is a giant red flag. I don't need a savior.

"I can be."

She scoffs. "I don't believe in fairy tales, Ford. This isn't a fantasy. In my story, the knight doesn't exist. In my story, the damsel is fucked."

"Okay, how about a friend? Everyone needs one of those."

"I wanted friends. But your stupid friends and your high school sweetheart made sure I didn't have any."

She's right. I can't refute it. But I can change that.

"We aren't in high school anymore, Dulce. We're adults."

She clenches her teeth. "Yeah, but what your friends did..."

She gets up, making the small table rattle, almost knocking over her coffee cup. I get up, ready to go after her.

"Please, Dulce. Let me make things easier for you. I swear, this isn't about me. I want to help," I say honestly. "Let me prove it to you. I know you won't take my money, but there must be another way."

"There isn't," she says with determination in her eyes. "Can you please take me back? I can't be late getting home."

Her grandmother. Sometimes I forget that she has a sick family member to provide for.

"Alright. I'll take you back."

The ride back into town is tense. I'm careful not to say anything that could exacerbate her existing hatred for me. After the kiss and staying with her after her panic attack episode, I thought we were getting somewhere. Not that I want to take advantage of her or anything, but I like her. I have to prove it to her, and I have to figure out a way that she can pay for all the things she needs. There has to be a way for me to help her.

After I drop Dulce off, I stare at the wall with peeling wallpaper and yellow stains on the corners, thinking of different ways I can help her.

I give up and call Derek.

"Hear me out. I need your help."

His sigh sounds like a gust of wind. "What is it?"

"I need to help a friend promote her business here in town."

"What kind?"

"Bakery?"

He chuckles. "The cookies? You have got to be kidding me."

"I'm not," I say quietly.

After a few tense seconds that made me want to reach through my cell phone and strangle him, he finally relents. "Okay, so we're discussing publicity and promotion, correct?" Increase sales. People are ordering and buying... cookies," he says like he finds it lame to help me promote cookies. It's not the only thing she bakes and sells, but I bite my tongue.

"Yes."

"Ford, you have a phone and an extensive social media platform with millions of followers." He chuckles. "Post some fucking pictures of you and the owner eating fucking cookies. Take a couple more pictures and send them to me, and I'll take care of it."

"That's it?"

"Isn't that what you pay me for?"

"Yeah."

"Good. Send me the pictures and let me know when to send the bus with transport for your car. No more playing down memory lane if you're not going to do shit there. Sponsors are getting anxious. Remember, you have a race coming up."

A thought forms in my mind.

"Derek?"

"Yeah?"

"Do I have room for another sponsor?"

"Of course."

I stare at Dulce's number on the folded piece of paper and smile. "Good."

DULCE

The cleaning crew had finished by the time Ford drove me to the bakery. I was down a prep table and still needed to go by Trent's garage to see about the van, but it was late. Katie dropped me off at home in time to relieve Mary and prepare my grandmother's bath and dinner.

"There was a rat in the bakery," my grandmother says, surprise etched in her voice.

The bakery never had rats. We cleaned thoroughly every day and followed guidelines, but I couldn't tell her the rest or how we found the rat. There was no way I could tell her anything. She had enough to deal with.

Yes, but we've already addressed it. I have to replace one of the prep tables."

"I heard you left with Ford Keller?" she says with a knowing smile.

"News travels fast."

"I called the bakery, and Katie told me."

Dammit, Katie.

"It was nothing. It was to give me a ride out of town to look for a new prep table," I tell her.

"And?"

"And I didn't find one."

"You know your cheeks go pink when you lie, just like your mother."

I sigh. "Fine, I let him think that."

I can't lie to you about everything. Every time I lie, it consumes me deeply.

Every day, I can see it in her eyes. Her time is coming to an end. She's exhausted, and there is nothing anyone could do. She's stage 4 and on hospice. I'm surprised she can talk to me, given her constant pain.

Katie must have told her who else was there. Since the police were still investigating, I told Kaite not to tell anyone about the details of finding the rat.

"I wanted to make a point."

"To Danny?"

Busted.

"Yes," I admit.

"So you used Ford to get Danny off your back."

I close the drawer with her pj's in hand and look over my shoulder. "You figured me out, Grandma."

"It's clever, but I don't like the fact that you used Ford."

I almost snorted. If she only knew Ford was worse than Danny.

"Trust me, I'm forgotten as soon as they step out of the bakery."

It's not like I was hurting anyone's feelings. Danny is... involved with someone. Ford gets around. Literally.

"If you think so," she huffs.

After her bath and dinner, I sit with her, and she tells me stories about when she was young. She recounts my childhood activities with my parents. When she fell in love for the first time. She wanted me to always remember those moments. It made everything worth it. I could never get those stories when she was gone. Without her, I would have no one to share these stories with. There was no one to remind me that I had a family. I had people who loved me.

"You need to find someone to start a family with, Dulce," she says as I rub lotion on the wrinkly, pale skin on her feet. "Maybe not right now, but soon." While I sit in the recliner next to her bed, she looks over at me. "Find someone to start a family with. Create memories to add to the ones I've shared with you. It's what will give you peace and happiness."

"I haven't found the right person, Grandma."

I don't think I ever will, but I don't tell her that. I don't want her to worry more than she already does. I've accepted that there may not be anyone out there for me. At least, not until I can get out of this town.

It's not like I could hide it. At night, the nightmares will haunt me. A panic attack out of nowhere. Unexplained crying when I fall asleep. I can make excuses. Maybe I'll see a doctor when I leave here, but it's too late. The damage is done.

Sooner or later, whomever I'm with will know. There are only so many lies you can tell before they surface. Because they always do.

Keeping secrets is just a prison for the lies that can destroy you.

THE FOLLOWING DAY, KATIE COMES TO PICK ME UP TO take me to Trent's garage. I had to close the bakery for another day until I could get everything sorted out. Danny texted me to say he still has no news about the break-in. I'm not sure he ever will. This town only allows you to understand what they want you to know.

I make my way to Katie's car down the little path, careful not to twist my ankle. It's hot despite it being only eight o'clock in the morning. When I open the oven door after a cake finishes baking, I can sense the sun's heat radiating. A sheen of sweat coats the back of my neck by the time I make it to her car.

"It's hot as hell outside," I tell her when I get in the car.

"Tell me about it. Every time I breathe, it feels like cotton balls are in my throat.

"Thanks for picking me up."

"No biggie, we're closed today. We need to figure out what we are going to do about the van."

"Yeah, that is a wonderful place to start." The thought of going over to Trent's fills me with dread. "How's your grandmother?"

I smile weakly. "Um, she's still alive."

"I'm sorry, Dulce."

After ten minutes, she turns on a road that haunts me even in the light of day. I clear my throat, trying to remove the feeling of suffocating. Panic bleeds into my chest. It feels like all the air has been sucked out of my lungs.

"Dulce?"

I place my hand on the dash, not caring if my seat belt is cutting into the side of my neck. "Could you pull over for a second?"

She pulls over, and I hear her unclick the seat belt. "Dulce? What's wrong?"

I blink twice, trying to clear the spots clouding my vision. "I need a minute," I say between breaths.

"Are you having another panic attack? I don't mean to be nosy, but you should see someone."

"I can't."

"Of course you can," she says softly. "There are resources. Free hotlines."

I laugh, and it sounds crazy. If she only knew.

"What's so funny?"

"I'm not laughing at you, Katie. I can't do any of that."

"Why not?" she asks, confused.

I squeeze my eyes shut. "What I'm about to tell you cannot leave this car."

"Okay," she says nervously.

"It stays here."

"Okay," she repeats.

I tell her about high school. I tell her about Ford, Chris, and Trent. I don't tell her the rest or what exactly happened, but I tell her I was attacked without going into details because I'm not ready to visit the dark room in my mind; I've managed to keep it shut.

"Is that why you acted like you didn't remember Ford when he showed up?"

I nod. "Yeah."

She leans back in her seat. "Shit. Here, I was encouraging you and thought he was a racing god."

"It's not your fault, and what happened isn't his. Not really."

"But he could have acted differently toward you. I mean, before."

"He left the country before prom. It wasn't his fault, and I can't hate him for not wanting me, Katie. I can't blame me for being stupid enough to think he would look at me the way I wanted him to."

"Then why is he here sniffing around you?"

"I question myself every time I see him. Sometimes I think he is trying to absolve his friends or maybe his name. Reputation. Celebrities are worried about their past coming to light."

"Huh, Ford is really a bully. I could see it, but I never would have guessed based on the way he looks at you."

I shake my head. "No."

"Apparently, anything. So that is where Danny fits in all this, and he turned out to be..."

"A liar like the rest," I finish for her, looking down the road, trying to see if I can find the house I saw.

The trees shift in the light breeze. The sun shines through the trees, revealing a brown roof in the distance. The house is a small one, no larger than a cabin.

I open the door.

"Dulce, where are you going?"

"I need to see something," I say. Before I close the door, I look down at her. "I'll be right back."

My heart is racing, but I'm confident that either someone lives there, it is abandoned, or Dean from the tow truck was full of shit. Maybe the old man doesn't live there anymore. The story Dean fed me couldn't have been recent.

"Are you crazy?" Katie yells from behind me. Her car door opens and slams. "I'm not going to let you go alone!"

"I've been called plenty of things, but crazy was never one of them," I shoot back.

She catches up to me, out of breath, looking back every few seconds. "What are you doing out here?" She pauses when I don't answer. "Is this where it happened?"

"Yeah," I say, looking between the brush of trees, treading carefully.

"That's why you had the panic attack," she says, speaking more to herself than to me. "Is that…"

I look around. "Yeah. It's a cabin. I saw it when I broke down, and the tow truck picked me up."

I've been thinking about the cabin. If someone lived there, it could have been the person who attacked me. I didn't believe an elderly man could possess such strength, but someone did.

"Are you sure this is a good idea? Maybe we should call the cops."

I stop. "Katie?"

"Yeah?"

"I don't trust anyone in this town. You can leave me here. I don't want to put you in any danger. Go back to the car, and if you see that I'm in trouble, drive off and call the cops." I glance back at her car, parked on the side of the road. "Go," I say quietly.

"I can't," she says, shaking her head frantically.

"You can. I'll be fine," I assure her.

"No, you won't. What if there's a man who hurts you or a fucking psycho killer who cuts girls up for fun?

"I guess I'll find out, won't I?"

"Dulce. I don't think…"

"Go, Katie," I snap, and she jolts.

I regret talking to her like that when she has been the only person who has been nice to me, but this is something I have to do.

We walk between the trees, the sun causing me to squint until we see the small triangle shape of the rustic roof appear.

The door is tilted like it's been tampered with. It reminds me of those crack houses you see on TV in the city, where drug addicts hang out to shoot up drugs.

My eyes fixate on the fogged-up windows caked in yellow like they haven't been washed in years, but I can't see anyone. I get the courage to knock.

"Are you nuts?" Katie whispers.

I knock again. I wait a few minutes, ignoring the alarm bells ringing in my head, telling me to get the hell out of here.

There is a loud thump and then a curse.

"Shit. Oh my God. Someone actually fucking lives here. Dulce, let's get the hell out of here." Katie grabs my arm, trying to drag me away.

"No," I say with conviction, pulling my arm out of her grasp. "Go, Katie. There is still time. Get out of here."

"Hell, no. I'm not leaving you here."

I hate dragging her into this. I check to see how far we are from the road. If something happens, she'll have time to run to her car. I have to face this nightmare. I need to know. Whoever is behind that door could be my attacker. He could be the reason I can't sleep at night. The reason I want to fucking die. Maybe he could finish the job.

The door opens, and a man appears, looking like a corpse from *The Night of the Living Dead*. He has rheumy eyes, gnarly hands, and veins running down his alabaster skin like a road map to hell. It's the old man, Moody. Dean was telling the truth. The old man who likes young pussy.

"What the fuck do you want?" he asks, tucking his thumbs

into his suspenders to cover his stained white shirt, which does little to conceal his wrinkled skin and gray chest hair.

"Are you Mr. Moody?"

"Who the fuck wants to know?" he asks with a dirty gleam in his eyes.

"My name is Dulce Webster. Four years ago, someone attacked me in these woods."

His laughter makes the hairs on my arms stand up. "Let me guess. You think I had something to do with it? Does it look like I can run after a cunt like you?" He gives me a slow once-over, making my skin crawl. "In my prime, you wouldn't stand a chance, but I'm too old. My dick doesn't work, but if you would like to show an old man a good time, I won't hold it against you," he spits, and I want to throw up when I get a glimpse of his missing front teeth. "Your secret is safe with me, Dulce. I know who you are."

My throat seizes.

"You're disgusting," Katie says behind me.

Old man Moody leans his shoulder against the door. "I love a little girl-on-girl action. I kind of preferred it in my day. It's a shame he got you before I could."

What do you mean?" I ask, stepping back.

He chuckles. Darkness grows in his eyes like he knows more than he is letting on.

"What you said," I say, trying to keep my voice from shaking.

"What did I say?" he says with a malicious smile, showing me his rotted gums.

I swallow the ball in my throat. "You said he got to me first."

He chuckles and removes his suspenders.

"Dulce?" Katie calls in an uneasy tone, stepping back. "Let's get out of here."

"Who?" I press. "Who got to me first, Mr. Moody?"

His smile grows wider, like Art the Clown before a kill. The last suspender slides off a bony shoulder. "It couldn't have been me. He unbuttons his trousers, and they slide down his sickly skinny thighs. My stomach clenches.

"I think I'm going to throw up," Katie says through a cough.

He digs his hand inside his piss-stained underwear and pulls out his flaccid cock, surrounded by gray pubic hair, causing a ball of bile to burn the back of my throat.

I'm stunned.

Frozen.

"You see," he said, jiggling his small penis in his palm. "It's dead, Dulce."

"You're sick," I hiss.

He laughs.

Tears fill my eyes. He's disgusting. "I hope you rot out here."

He laughs louder.

I step back, pulling Katie with me. "I hope you rot in hell," I scream in frustration.

We run back to the car, and Katie fires it up, peeling out on the road toward Trent's garage. I wipe the tears of frustration from my face, trying to eradicate what I saw from my memory. The way he laughed. It's like he knew. But it wasn't him.

"I'm sorry," I finally say. I look down at my hands, which won't stop shaking. "It was stupid to go there. To involve you. I'm sorry."

"Don't..."

"If you want to quit the bakery, I understand."

I don't want her to quit, but who in their right mind would want to work for an unstable boss? I'm fucked up, and maybe I always will be fucked up. It was stupid of me to drag her into this. I know that, but I had to know.

"It wasn't him. It couldn't have been. Right?"

"Dulce?"

"Yeah," I reply, weakly looking at the clouds in the sky.

"I'm sorry."

"I understand."

"No, I mean, I'm sorry about what happened. I'm not going to quit on you unless you want to fire me."

"I could never fire you, Katie. You've been the nicest person to me besides my grandmother and Mary. I know I put you in danger, and for that, I'm sorry. That man..."

"Had a small, wrinkly dick."

I burst out laughing, causing snot to come out of my nose. "Oh God. I grab a napkin and wipe my face. "He did, didn't he?"

"Disgusting," she says with a laugh. "It looked like it was rotting with the rest of him."

I visibly shudder. "He didn't have teeth."

"I know, but he did know who you were. He knew you worked at the bakery. Have you ever seen him before?"

"Never. But in this town, nothing escapes people unless they want it to."

"I believe that. There's something off about the people here. It reminds me of those towns that look normal but have something evil hidden underneath."

"You should move while you can. This place isn't safe."

"How about I make a deal? I'll leave when you leave."

I smile. I've never had a friend before. One that would have my back like she did back there.

"Katie?"

She stops at a stop sign. "Yeah," she says, looking both ways.

Her face blurs. "Thank you."

She gives me a hug. One that I desperately need. "We all have dark and messy closets, Dulce. I know I have mine. I'll tell you sometime."

I nod, knowing that telling people about the past you're trying to run away from is hard. On the way to Trent's garage, all I could think about was how I'd had mine bottled up for four years, eating me from the inside like a disease. I just wish it would stop.

"Is this it?" Katie asks, looking at the modern garage in awe when she pulls up to Trent's garage.

"Yeah."

"This is the douchebag who broke your phone that night."

"Yep, the one and only." I get out and squint, dreading having to talk to Trent. "I have to warn you," I say, closing the door. "He's a dick."

She remarks, "I'm accustomed to guys who are dicks. You should meet my ex-boyfriend. He's a real piece of work."

"Is he the reason you're running?"

I don't want to pry, but I'm taking a wild guess.

"Why lie?" she says, walking in front of me.

When we walk inside, it's surprisingly cool, even with the overhead door open.

A man wearing a mechanic's shirt glances upward. I didn't see him the last time I was here. He was working on a car that resembled a supercar Ford would drive. A supercar that you find on the track. He drops a tool, wipes his hand on a towel, and walks up. "Can I help you?"

"Is Trent here?" I look around and spot my van in the back, looking like an eyesore compared to the expensive cars.

"He's in his office," he says, a worried look crosses his face.

"Could you get him for us?" Katie says

The mechanic raises his brows. "Alright."

He walks over to the office. "Trent," he calls out.

I look toward the office window overlooking the bay has its blinds closed.

"What?" Trent says in a muffled voice.

"You got some ladies looking for you."

The door swings open, and I suck in a breath.

"Shit," Katie mutters.

My eyes go wide. "Holy shit. What happened?"

His face is different shades of black and purple, darker around his eyes. His nose looks broken.

With his right eye swollen shut, he gazes at me through the tiny slit in his left eye. He winces from the cuts on his lips when he says, "Hi, Dulce."

I can't stop staring at all the damage. I should feel a wave of satisfaction, but for some reason, I don't.

I'm surprised he doesn't call me by the other slew of names he tossed my way in high school.

"What...happened?"

A door opens, and the sound of footsteps makes me look up at the stairs from the back of the bay. It's Ford, fresh out of a shower. His hair is wet. The black tank top does nothing to hide his muscles or tattoos. The gray sweats he is wearing does nothing to hide...

"Hi, Dulce," Ford says with amusement in his voice.

I look away, hating myself for getting caught staring. *Focus, Dulce.*

I glance at Katie. She raises a brow and then looks at Trent.

"I fell in the shower," Trent finally says.

Ford leans on the red sports car, watching Trent closely.

I know Trent didn't slip to end up with a face like that.

"What were you doing when you slipped?" Katie says it acerbically. "Dropped the soap."

"Very funny," Trent fires back, looking at me.

My eyes cut to Ford when he says, "He'll be alright. Just a little fender bender in the shower."

"That looks like it really hurts," Katie says.

"It's not too bad," Trent says. "You work with Dulce at the bakery."

I roll my eyes. He looks like a swollen pumpkin, and he still has the balls to flirt with Katie.

"Don't worry," Ford says, pushing off the car with a dark look in his light eyes. "He'll be fine." He places his hand on Trent's shoulder, causing him to grimace. "Right, brother?"

"Right," Trent says.

I don't want to be part of whatever is going on. It is obvious Ford kicked his ass.

"You don't have to hide the fact that you kicked his ass," Katie says to Ford.

I clear my throat. "I wanted to ask if you had the estimate ready to fix the van."

"It's fixed," Trent says.

"How... how much?" I stammer, hoping I have enough.

Ford reaches into his pocket and picks up my keys, revealing a small cake on the chain. "It's taken care of," he says.

I look at Trent, and he nods in approval.

"I can't..."

I don't want to owe them anything.

"Dulce," Katie says, reaching for the keys from Ford. She whirls and looks at me. "It's taken care of."

I shake my head and look at my black and white Vans, dirty from the woods.

Ford steps forward. "Can I have a minute with Dulce, Katie?"

Katie looks over her shoulder. "If you promise not to hurt her," she says in a hard tone.

"I would never hurt her, Katie," he says with a hurtful expression like the idea repulses him.

"You have," she says in a stern tone, looking between Ford and Trent. "All of you have. You're all a bunch of pieces of shit."

"I know," Ford admits. "But I'll never hurt her."

"He's right," Trent says, gesturing to his face. "He'll do this again if I so much as look at her."

I grimace at how awful his face looks. Why?" I ask.

"You know why, Dulce." Ford nods at Trent. "That was for the phone. He can't talk through one for a while or see a text."

"You can't beat people up when you were part of it," I tell him.

"I can, and I will. I know you don't understand why, and it might not make much sense to you right now, but all I can tell you is this is only the beginning."

"What the fuck is that supposed to mean?" Katie asks, confused, looking between Ford and Trent.

"If she told you, you know exactly what it means," Ford says, not sure, but I'm assuming he thinks she does because I brought her here with me.

Katie scoffs. "What're you going to go reaping souls or some shit?"

Ford crosses his arms across his chest, making his biceps bulge, and my pulse picks up speed. "If that's what it takes." He glances at me. "I'm not leaving until it's done."

"What's done?" I ask, confused. "What are you going to do? You're not going to jeopardize everything you have worked for."

"I don't care about that, Dulce. I care about you."

Tears slide down my cheeks in frustration. "Don't..."

He cups my cheek, wiping my tears away with his thumb. "Can I talk to you for a second?" He looks at Katie, then at me. "Alone?"

I nod and follow him into Trent's office. When he shuts the door, he wipes the other side of my cheek with his thumb.

"What do you want?"

He closes the space between us. "I'm not leaving until I find out what really happened to you, Dulce. I know you're not going to tell me, and that's okay. I'll find out my way."

"You're wasting your time."

I'm uncertain about his plans, but too much time has already passed. It's too late.

"I don't," he says, looking down at my shoes.

He looks up. "Why are your shoes caked in mud?"

"They're old," I explain. "I've had them for a while."

"Katie's are the same way," he points out, looking at Katie's shoes.

I scoff, not wanting to admit where we were. All that does is leave him with more questions I don't want to answer.

"You're a shoe expert now?"

He smiles. "I'm a lot of things."

"I'm sure."

He gets closer, causing me to lift my chin so I can meet his eyes. I should put distance between us. We should leave, but I can't. His gaze holds me firmly in place.

"Tell me, Dulce. Where were you and Katie before you got here?"

"You're following me now?"

"No, even though I should."

"Why?"

"Because I need to make sure you're safe."

"Bad timing."

Something dark passes through his eyes. "Trust me, I know."

"Do you?"

His lips are a breath away; his eyes trace my lips. "Where, Dulce?"

"Where it happened."

"The road."

I nod.

"Why?"

I close my eyes briefly. "There's a cabin and..."

"And?"

I tell him about old man Moody. I don't know why I tell him. He's the last person I should confide in.

"Are you both crazy?"

"It was my fault. I told her to stop."

"Why?"

I lick my lips, and his gaze darkens confusing me. Every time he takes a breath, my lips tingle when they shouldn't. I should hate this man.

"What?" he says. "What do you need, Dulce?"

Nothing. Telling him what I need is pointless. He would never understand because I would have to tell him everything, and it's something I can't do. Not him. Not anyone.

"So he exposed himself?"

"Yes."

His jaw hardens. "Did you call the police?"

"No. We didn't," I say truthfully.

"He did it while he was still inside his house?" he asks, trying to piece together what happened.

"Yes." I look directly at the tattoo on his throat, trying not to remember what Moody did. "There is no point in calling the cops. We weren't supposed to be there. He could say we were trespassing."

He bends so his eyes meet mine. "He's a crazy, sick old man, and I won't let him or anyone hurt you, Dulce. I know it's hard, but I need you to trust me."

"Why did you hurt Trent?"

"You know why," he says softly, playing with a piece of hair between his fingers.

"Is that what you're going to do—beat people up?"

"I'll do whatever it takes," he whispers like it's a secret. A secret between us.

The tiny hairs on my arms stand up. The strand of my hair is between his fingers like he's memorizing the feel and texture. "Before you leave here, I want to tell you a story," he says.

"What about?" I ask curiously, watching as he struggles with what he is about to tell me.

"My last day of high school, I was supposed to race one last time before I left. I decided to leave at the last minute despite my parents being upset, but I wanted to do things on my own. My way. However, on that particular day, the sky broke apart and began to rain. There was one thing I hadn't done the whole time I was in high school. One thing always lingered in my mind as unfulfilled because I planned to leave. Fate had other plans for me that day, and it wasn't a race. Call it luck. Call it whatever you want. A girl was walking in the rain, and I knew who she was. How could I not? She was always on my mind. I begged her to let me give her a ride home. See, this girl wasn't like the others. She was different. She was the kind of person you could never forget once you saw her. At least I couldn't. It didn't matter how hard I tried. My thoughts would always go back to her. Anyway, it was like God answered my prayers that day. She allowed me to bring her home. I was nervous for the first time in my life around a girl. I didn't know what to say or if she liked me at all. My choices with friends made me a less-than-ideal person. My family. And I didn't do anything to make her think differently. I knew it was my only chance, but I was scared to tell her how I felt." Tingles coat my skin as I watch his thumb and forefinger play with my hair.

"How did you feel?" I ask, my voice betraying the wetness between my thighs.

"I like her," he admits, his thumb and forefinger still playing with the ends of my hair like flint from a lighter. "I thought she was beautiful despite what other people said about her when I first noticed her," he continues, knowing his next words were the spark that would catch the flame. "If I wasn't leaving, I would have asked her to prom."

I'm on fire listening to him. Watching his throat move when he swallows and telling me his story. His thoughts.

"I regret leaving that day, and I think I will for the rest of my life. I know I can't do anything to take it back. To change it. If you ever wondered if I would have asked, the answer would always be yes, Dulce."

If I would wish for one thing, aside from saving the ones I

love from death, it was this. His words when there was nothing else worth wanting for myself.

But the truth was, I couldn't cheat death. I couldn't bring my parents back, and I couldn't save my grandmother from dying. None of those things were possible. There was no such thing as a miracle because, let's face it, those things didn't happen and weren't possible. Four years ago, he was the closest thing to a miracle.

"Why are you telling me this now?"

"Because you need to hear it. You need to know. The same way you need to know who attacked you. The same way I need to know, and I'm the one that is going to find out." He lets go of my hair and rubs his thumb over my bottom lip. "Whatever it takes."

"You can't save me."

He thinks that will fix it—for me. I won't lie and say it wouldn't help because it would. It would give me the closure I need, but it wouldn't change what that person did. The deep scar that changed me forever is visible once you peel away the layers and see the rotten truth underneath.

His face darkens. "I'm not trying to save you... I'm going to do something no one has ever done."

"And what is that?"

With the pad of his thumb, he pushes my bottom lip down. Our eyes lock. My heartbeat triples in speed. Then his gaze slowly falls to my mouth, like he wants nothing more than to taste me.

"Fight for you," he says before lowering his head and taking my lips.

My arms wrap around his neck. He grabs my thighs, lifts me, and walks us toward the wall. My back hits it with a small thud.

"Ford," I whimper when I feel his thick cock between my legs.

"Dulce," he rasps against my lips, grinding his hips.

I arch my back. He sucks my neck, then nibbles my ear. A thousand needles prickle my skin, causing me to gasp, grinding against him, hating that my jeans are in the way. I'm wet, hot, and want nothing more than to feel his skin on mine.

A knock on the door breaks our spell. My feet hit the ground, and his face is still in the crook of my neck when I see Trent at the doorway.

"Get the fuck out," Ford says, taking a deep breath like he's struggling.

Trent walks out without saying a word. A surge of heat flushes my cheeks at being caught.

Ford pulls away slightly and whispers, "Let's get you home."

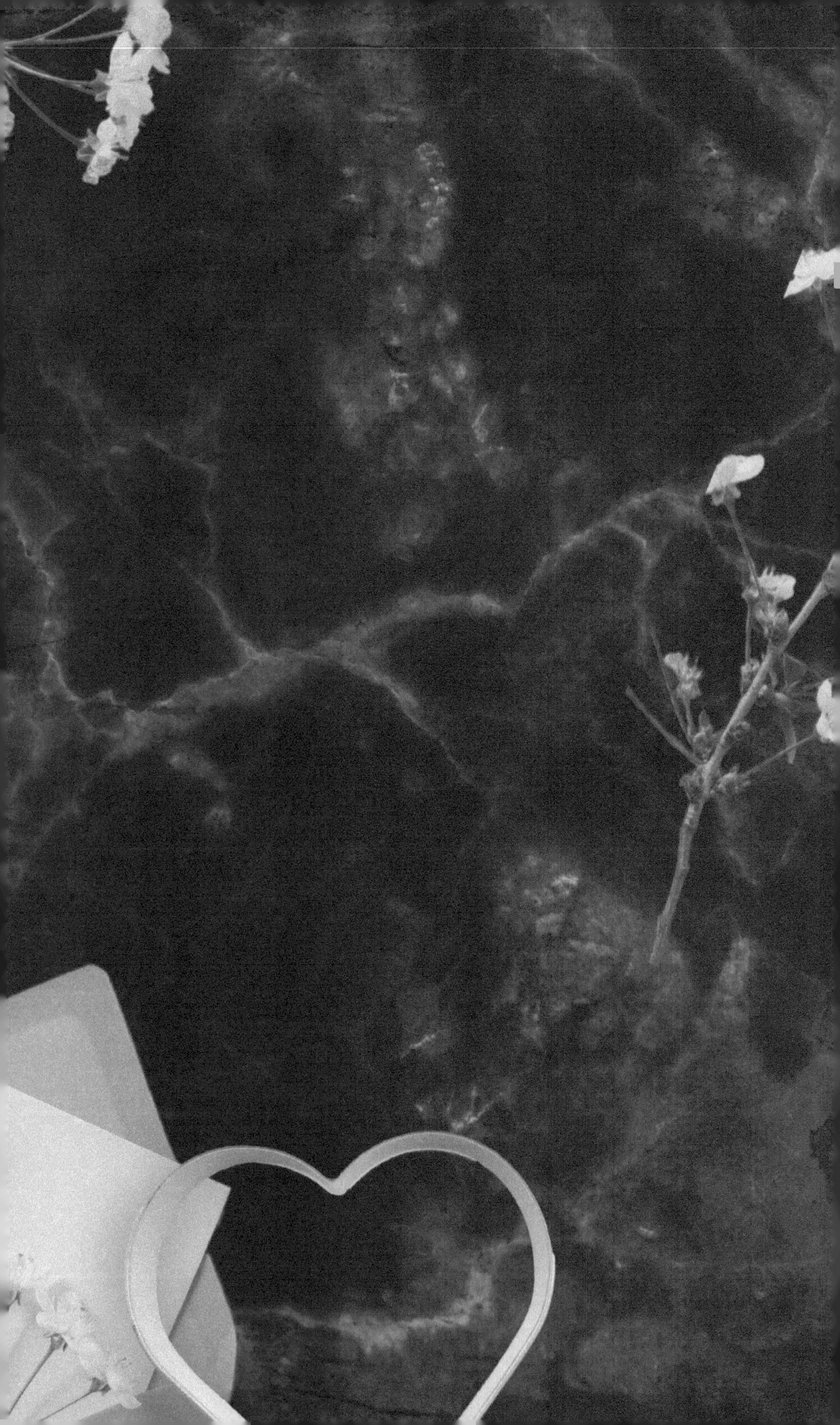

I'm still in a daze of confused emotions for the rest of the day when Katie and I return to the bakery.

Katie and I are preparing to reopen tomorrow. The kitchen and prep area smell like disinfectant, reminding me of a hospital. I didn't have time to find a prep table, so I have to use one near the cooling rack by the sink. At least I have the van and don't have to depend on Katie for a ride.

Katie rinses out the rag in the sink, trying to wipe off the smell. "He said that?"

"Yeah."

I told her about Ford and what he said in Trent's office. I'm still confused about how I feel, or should feel, around him.

"He wants you, Dulce. Don't be surprised to find you're the reason he came back."

"I'm not sure about anything anymore. But for now, I think he wants to be conscious of the past."

She snorts. "There is more he wants to clean, and it's not that," she teases.

I prep the counter with everything, placing fresh supplies. "Is that all you think about?"

"What?"

"Sex."

"No," she says with a smile. "Well, most of the time."

My thoughts drift back to Ford, just as they did in high school. I imagine how he kissed and whether he was gentle or rough when he had sex.

I hated that he was with Summer. I hated it even more when I heard he got her pregnant. I'm not sure if the rumors about him cheating on her with Heather were true. But he messed around. A lot. I wasn't stupid or naive to think he wouldn't. He was good-looking, and he knew it. His friends encouraged him every time they were in the halls and a girl gave him knowing looks or talk about him. I wasn't sure who told the lie or the truth, but someone must have known if he was good in bed or how he looked without his clothes on.

"Are you thinking about it?"

One touch from him has muddled my brain for the rest of the day. "Thinking about what?"

"Him," she says, looking at me with a raised brow. "What you want him to do to you."

"I don't want him to do anything to me."

"Liar."

"I'm not..."

"Your cheeks get red when you lie, and you keep recounting how many pieces of cake go on each tray. You've been on the same tray since we started talking about sex."

She isn't wrong. I've counted the same tray three times.

When it comes to Ford, I can't think. I've tried so hard to forget him. To accept the kiss the other night as a one-off. I'm sure he kisses plenty of women.

The pictures in the tabloids don't lie. All anyone can have for me is pity.

"I think about a lot of things."

Her smile falls, and it's like we almost forgot what happened with old man Moody.

But it did happen.

"You think we should call Danny and tell him?" she asks.

"I'm not sure it matters if we do or don't. We weren't

supposed to be there. If anything, it's like what Ford said—we were on his land, knocking on his front door, and he was inside his house."

"He's disgusting," she says, scrunching her nose. "I hope he rots inside that shithole out there in the woods."

"I agree."

"I think we should report it." She glances at me, revealing her fear. "Not that Moody would seek us out or try anything, but maybe he was involved somehow, and they could investigate. You know," she says like she just thought of something. "Did the police ever say they questioned him or that someone lived close by?"

I shake my head, furrowing my brow. "No. Now that I think of it, no. No one ever mentioned anyone living out there. If it hadn't been for the van leaving me stranded and having to call the tow truck, I would have never found out about him. It's not like he goes out much. I didn't know who he was."

Maybe Danny might know more. He would have told me if Moody had anything to do with it. He would have questioned him that night or the next day, right?

"I think you should ask Danny," she says before leaving.

After Katie leaves and I lock up, I call Danny to meet me outside the bakery before I head home.

After twenty minutes, I hear a car pull up and peer out the window to see the familiar headlights shut off.

I open the door as he gets out of his truck.

"Is everything alright?" he asks, his brows knitting together.

"Are you off today?"

He nods, and I feel guilty for bothering him. "I'm sorry, Danny. I thought you were working." I fidget with my fingers, thinking about what Moody said and how to tell him.

His expression softens. "Don't be sorry, Dulce. You know you can call me anytime, and I'll come."

"Thank you."

I sigh even though I'm conflicted. The concern settles in my stomach, and I tell him what happened.

"Why would you do that, Dulce?" he scolds with a disapproving frown. "Are you insane? With Katie? You could've called me."

This is why I didn't want to tell him. Why I didn't want to call him. He would have talked me out of it, and I needed to see for myself. Deep down, I was tired of being scared and not knowing.

"You could have been hurt or lost."

"But I wasn't. You haven't answered my question. Was Mr. Moody questioned?"

A ball is in my throat. I can feel the quickening of my pulse on my neck as I wait for answer.

He shakes his head, but he doesn't meet my eyes like he is lying and can't look me in the eye. "Not that I know of," he says evasively. "It was four years ago, Dulce."

Confusion clouds my vision. "Yes," I reply. Confusion turns into anger, and I clench my teeth at his response. It's infuriating how he's scolding me like I'm a child. "It was four years ago, and maybe you don't remember, but to me, it feels like yesterday, Officer Mays."

The truth smacks me hard in the stomach. He isn't going to help me. His reaction to Moody doesn't make sense. Something isn't right, and for the first time, I don't trust him.

"Dulce?" His eyes grow soft, but it doesn't stop me from walking away.

"Dulce, wait," he calls out.

Before I open the driver's side door, a loud rumble of an engine comes from down the street. I look behind my van when the front of Ford's Porsche pulls up, rolling down the window and glaring at Danny. "Are you good, Dulce?" Ford asks, still staring at Danny.

"Are you lost?" Danny says. "Don't you have a mansion somewhere and a blonde to screw?"

Ford grins. "I came to check on *my* girl and take her to dinner."

"What do you want, Ford?" Danny sneers.

Ford glances at me and then turns his gaze toward Danny, emphasizing his point. "Well, like I said, I'm not here for you." Ford glances at me. "I'll follow you home."

"That's not necessary," Danny says.

"It's alright," I tell Danny. "He can follow me home. He hasn't broken any laws. It's not like you give a shit about the law."

"That's not fair, Dulce. I've been there for you," Danny says, pleading with his eyes.

I don't believe him.

"I thanked you every day since that night for doing your job." I open the door. "But now it seems like you're not interested in doing your job anymore."

After getting my grandmother to bed and Mary leaves for the night, I couldn't convince Ford to leave. Not after he ordered dinner, and not after he brought a smile to my grandmother's face.

I sit on the couch after a quick shower, not caring if it's from the seventies with tomato-pinned cushions. The TV sits on an old dresser. It's the box kind with a built-in DVD player.

"Did that Dickhead cop say anything to upset you?" Ford asks.

I could tell he had wanted to broach the subject since he followed me home, but probably didn't want to do it in front of Mary or my grandmother, which I'm grateful for.

I slide my damp hair to the side, trying not to sound nervous about the fact that he is sitting right next to me and smells amazing. I want nothing more than to feel his arms around me or for him to kiss me. "No."

"It didn't look or sound like that to me," he says, sliding a piece of hair away from my mouth.

"It's nothing."

"You called him about Moody."

I look away, not wanting to meet his gaze. Afraid that he will think I want Danny. I don't want to lie, so I reply, "Yeah."

"It was the smart thing to do."

I swing my head and look at him in surprise.

"He didn't sound thrilled about it, I guess."

"No," I admit, still trying to process that he isn't upset or thinks it was stupid. "He acted weird. It pissed me off."

"Everyone in this town acts like that when you ask questions."

I tilt my head to the side. "Why is that?"

He gets closer and says slowly, his eyes on my mouth, "Rich people stuff."

"That explains why I don't know much. Because I'm not rich."

"I am," he counters. "It means I can ask questions and get answers."

"Is that how it works? You throw money at it and get answers."

"Sometimes...or..."

His lips brush against mine.

"Or...?"

"I get them my way," he says softly.

"Which way is that?"

My skin buzzes with anticipation, and I wait for him to answer but want his kiss more.

"By force."

"Is that what you're going to do? Get answers by force."

"From them, yes. You, never."

He kisses me softly, his tongue grazing my lips, and then rough. The stubble on his chin is rough on my skin. I moan, fisting his shirt.

When his other hand slides up my bare thigh near the hem of my pajama shorts, my body shudders.

"You taste so fucking sweet, Dulce." He licks the underside of my lips. "Your name is exactly what you are." His tongue snakes over mine. "So fucking sweet and so fucking good," he whispers.

I arch my neck to meet his eyes, biting back the whimper that wants to escape. He gives me a look I have never seen before. Different. Seductive. His eyes eat me alive, burning my clothes off my skin when they trail down my body and stop between my legs.

"Ford," I moan.

He smiles, and then his eyes scan up. He's still cupping my face with one hand, his other on my bare thigh.

"I'm not the same guy you remember from high school, Dulce."

I think the mess between my legs agrees. He isn't the same guy I remember. This is the man who women lose their heads over. The celebrity race car driver they don't think twice about leaving with.

"I see that."

"Do you, beautiful?" He places his lips over the spot on my throat that beats wild for him. "What do you see?" he rasps, dragging his teeth over my skin and lighting me on fire.

My eyes glaze over, and I whisper, "I see... you."

I'm totally wet, wanting nothing more than for him to take me on the couch but knowing it wasn't a good idea with my grandmother in the next room.

I get up, taking his hand. He looks up, and I smile. "Come to my room."

He gets up and follows me, closing the door as I push the stuffed animals off my bed. He comes up behind me, and when I turn around, he is an inch away from touching me. He pushes me on the bed, his knee pressing on the small twin mattress. I instinctively open my legs.

His hand slides under my shorts and finds my wet pussy. I whimper and arch my back, wanting more. I ache for him to go deeper, but he holds his hand, not taking it away but not moving it deeper inside.

"I didn't come here for this. I came here to just be with you, Dulce," he says, rubbing my arousal over my clit.

His eyes dip between my legs, holding his bottom with his teeth.

I grind my hips, and he smiles. "Do you want to come?"

I nod because words have failed me and are stuck in my throat with the moan that wants to escape.

He leans over me, his finger swirling around my clit, flicking it back and forth, causing my climax to build. His other hand is flat on the mattress, muscles bulging beside my head.

"Show me?" he whispers near my ear.

I rub my pussy on his hand, and he matches my rhythm. His eyes watch me lose control until I come on a whimper. Flashing lights explode behind my eyes as I ride the wave. He covers my mouth with the palm of his hand. My eyes fly open, realizing that my grandmother or Mary could hear me and know what is going on in my bedroom.

He chuckles lightly near my ear. "Imagine if I was inside you, gorgeous. Everyone would know."

I walk into Trent's garage after I checked out of the seedy hotel and head upstairs to the spare room he offered, ignoring him as he watches NASCAR reruns.

"Busy night?" he asks, staring at the TV, and then takes a drag of his beer.

I smile. "Wouldn't you like to know?"

He nods, holding his beer in the air by the neck. "Want one?"

"I'm good."

I'm almost to the top by the door when he asks, "You fucked her yet?"

I pause. "Be very careful and specific about who you're referring to, or that mug you have for a face will be a permanent one."

After a long pull, I can hear the smack of his lips. "I didn't mean it like that."

"Well, get used to it. You keep her name and any of your crass bullshit out of your piehole. What I do with her is none of your fucking business."

"I didn't mean it like that. I'm worried you're going a little too fast."

I turn around, taking the steps two at a time, jumping on the last two, and getting in his face. "FAST FOR WHAT?" I grip his shirt in my fist. "You're going all sentimental on me, Trent? Did you consider that when you abandoned her on the side of the road?"

He swallows visibly, then winces. I'm choking him with his shirt, wanting nothing more than to squeeze the life out of him for what he and Chris did. I'm sure if I wasn't a celebrity and didn't have so many eyes on me, I would have killed him, tied him and Chris to the fucking tires of their precious cars, and lit them on fire for what they did to her. But I have to find something—or rather, someone else. Her true attacker.

Leaving her asleep on her bed was one of the hardest things I had to do. Before leaving, I checked her monitor to make sure her grandmother was stable.

I wanted nothing more than to go back to Dulce's room, crawl in her small bed, and fuck her. Eat her pussy like a fucking buffet.

"I-I know, Ford," he stammers. I can see the terror in his eyes. He's afraid of me like he should be.

"You know what?" he says like I care what he thinks only what he did.

My anger builds to the surface when he puts in his invalid two cents, but I have to listen. Analyze every word because something is missing from this puzzle.

"She doesn't trust easily, and you need to be careful, or you'll lose her." He swallows. "Forever."

"You think I don't know that she's terrified, asshole? She has every right to ask questions and not trust anyone. What else do you know about that night?" I press.

Every so often, I drill him for answers. I can't go to Chris's drug-addicted ass for solid information because he's high all the time. I could beat him ten ways from Sunday, and he wouldn't know the difference. Besides, you can't trust a drug addict. He'll say anything for his next hit. Desperate people lie. It doesn't mean that he's off the hook. I let him think that I don't care, and Trent doesn't have the balls to tell him.

A war is never won if the enemy sees you coming.

"I've told you everything I know."

In the morning, I head over to the police station to pay Officer Dickhead a visit. The station is small, and the smell of sawdust and old wood permeates the air. Two wood desks make up the office, and a chocolate-colored shelf has papers stuck on the edge of missing persons across the state. Persons of interest on others who haven't been caught.

"How can I help you?" Officer Dickhead drawls, closing a file on his desk.

I knew he was here today and didn't have road duty. I checked. I threw my last name around, making it seem like my father was checking things out.

I take a seat, not bothering to take off my sunglasses. "I need a copy of the report from that night."

He leans back, making the old chair squeak with a smug smile. He knows I'm asking for Dulce's case specifically. "I'm afraid that isn't possible."

I raise my brows. "Why not?"

"Because it's still an open investigation."

This asshole is lucky he was there to help Dulce, or I would have him fired so I could take him out and beat the shit out of him. Like the ole days when I would fuck around town with my friends. The shit we would get into wasn't talked about. It wasn't reported because someone would disappear or lose their job.

"I can have the preliminary report, and I'm not asking," I say in a stern tone.

His shit-brown eyes grow hard. "Make a phone call. Throw your name around like you rich boys do, but count me out."

"Is there something you're hiding," I ask, looking directly at him, "or don't want me to see?"

I don't trust him, and he knows it. I don't buy the bravado or hero act he puts on around Dulce. Like most people in this town, he's hiding something.

"I'd like to ask you," he volleys back. "Funny." He sits up and leans over his desk. "Don't act like it didn't take you four years to come riding into town on your white horse like some white knight."

He isn't wrong. It did take me four years to come back. To figure out that what was missing would always be her.

"It's also taken you more than four years to find out who attacked Dulce. Any leads?"

He flinches like I punched him.

"None," he admits, but I can't tell he isn't looking into it.

"I find that hard to believe," I fire back, leaning back in the chair and giving him a fake smile. "And frankly, no one in this town gives a fuck, but I do, and it's also obvious you truly don't give a fuck about Dulce."

"That is where you're wrong. I do care about her more than you think."

"I got a different vibe when you took her to dinner," I point out. "You kind of forgot to tell the girl you're fucking that you're interested in someone else."

"Be careful, Keller. You might find yourself in a similar predicament."

"I'm single. I don't do entanglements."

He snorts. "I'm sure Dulce would be impressed by that. And all the women you've screwed since then and the fact that you lack commitment—to your family, friends, or her."

"And you're so great," I say with a menacing smile.

"I'm not a saint, but I have made sure no one else comes near her since it happened."

"Like you did with old man Moody?" I sneer.

When I mention the old man's name, he stiffens slightly and then plays it off like he is arranging something on his desk.

"I'll look into it," he says, but I don't believe him. "He didn't do it," he adds. "That I can assure you."

"He exposed himself to Dulce and Katie and mocked them. Isn't that enough to bring him in? Or how about the fact that he doesn't live too far from where Dulce was attacked?"

His jaw hardens. "I said I'll look into it." I move to get up, and

I'm almost to the door when he calls out, "Ford?" I turn around. He wipes his mouth. "I'm in love with her."

I snort. "You have a funny way of showing her."

I wanted to tell him she didn't feel the same way. She isn't his to love, and if he so much as touches her, he'll end up worse than Trent, but why tell him? It doesn't matter because he will never have her. I'll make sure of it.

The courier hands me a clipboard. "Sign here?"

As the other two men take the table through the back door toward the kitchen, I accept it and sign my name, struggling to comprehend that I have a new prep table I didn't purchase. I scan the packing slip, but it doesn't say who it's from.

"Who ordered this?" I ask.

The man takes the clipboard, tears the top copy of the invoice, and hands it to me. "I don't know. Some company." He strolls to the kitchen to watch the other guys set up.

Katie walks over and smiles. "Why do you bother asking?" She rubs her lips together, trying not to laugh. "You know who bought it."

I do. Only one man in my life right now has money to throw around. I'm sure he owns a pair of sunglasses that cost just as much.

"You're right. I was hoping it wasn't so I wouldn't feel like I owed him."

"He did it because he likes you and—"

"Feels sorry for me?"

"No," she says with a determined look. "No," she repeats. "I think he always had a thing for you but was too chickenshit to do anything about it. Scared or immature. But right now, he is all man, and he has his sights set on you. What he did to Trent is borderline crazy, but I would have done the same if I felt the way he did."

"Like what?" I ask, confused.

I don't know what to feel except that I'm afraid to feel the same way I used to about Ford because look how I ended up. Fucked up and miserable.

"Crazy."

"Crazy?"

She gives me a half shrug and straightens the chair, placing it under the table. "All I can think of is the way he looks at you. He's crazy about you. I know you can't see it, but anyone in the same room with you two can see it." The man is batshit crazy about you."

"I'm not used to it. Besides, a man like Ford doesn't stick around one woman," I admit more to myself than to her. But his smile and good looks were already implanted. The feel of his lips and fingers between my thighs destroyed me for anyone else.

"Crazier things have happened."

Shit isn't wrong, but I don't plan on sticking around, and wherever I go, there is no reason he would follow.

"They have," I say, going along with her way of thinking.

There was no point in telling her differently. There was no point in thinking there would be more between Ford and me. Instead of going against his flirtation or his offer to help me, I was going to enjoy his company.

"Are you sure you're going to be fine here all by yourself?" she asks, snapping me back from my thoughts.

"It's just a couple of hours. I let Mary leave early yesterday, and she told me she would stay so I could catch up."

I hadn't had the time to bake, and since the prep space was limited, I only made the usual items I sell daily. It's like I'm opening the bakery for the first time. Fortunately, I bake all the items fresh daily, but I have orders to fulfill. Like Ford's cookies.

"Alright." She grabs her bag and car keys and clocks out on the register. "Promise me you'll call."

"Promise," I assure her.

"Danny knows?"

I nod, not wanting to tell her that he doesn't. He's the last person I want to call, and I haven't told her I don't trust him anymore.

I set my phone on the back table, hit play on the music app, and smile at the new prep and ingredient combo table, positioned in the center of the kitchen like a shiny new toy, while Lana Del Ray's voice fills the room. It is made of stainless steel with multiple drawers.

I slide each one out and smile at the smooth, seamless way each ingredient drawer slides out.

I start gathering the ingredients to bake Ford's cookies. A tribute to the man who made it possible to put a smile on my face. I owe him that much and the best orgasm the other night in my bedroom.

I'm mixing the cookie batter when I hear a loud knock on the front door and pause the mixing machine. I wipe my hands on a towel.

My stomach does a little flip-flop when I see Ford, dressed in a simple T-shirt and jeans, peering in the window. I unlock and open the door.

When I meet his gorgeous blue eyes, awareness clings to my skin the way it always did.

"Hi." His smile would make any woman swoon.

His citrus scent envelops my nose, making me weak when I kiss his cheek and say softly, "Hi."

He raises a brow after a few seconds when I step back. "Are you going to let me in so I can kiss you properly?"

I flush, embarrassed that I was staring at him like an idiot, and step back. "Oh...Um...come in."

He walks in, then turns to close and lock the door. We stare at each other for a beat. His eyes are on my lips. Mine are locked on his handsome face. The air between us grows thick. My pulse picks up. I'm expecting him to kiss me... or should I be the one to kiss him?

Instead, he asks, breaking the tension. "Busy?"

"How did you know I was here?" I ask instead, trying to remove the sting from him not making the first move.

"Your van is parked out front."

Duh, Dulce. He was driving by, saw your van, and figured you hadn't left.

"Right," I reply awkwardly.

"It smells good."

My nipples harden, and my pulse drops between my legs, reminding me of his words last night. How I smelled. Tasted.

"I was making cookies," I tell him, walking back to the kitchen.

He follows me inside, and I walk around the table, hitting pause on the music.

"How's the table?" he asks.

I'm such an idiot. I didn't thank him for the table. He makes me forget my name when he's around.

I finish mixing the batter. "It's going great," I tell him honestly. "Thank you."

"My pleasure. I asked my manager which table would be the best for a bakery. I hope he didn't disappoint."

I place each cookie on the baking sheet. "Not at all. I'm not sure if he has any experience with bakery equipment, but he did well."

"Are those for me?" he asks, pointing at the cookies. I'm sure he could smell the oatmeal and put two and two together. There was something the way he said it though, an intimacy we shared the day he took me home for the first time. Something we shared between us and not the rest of the world.

I look up. "Huh?"

"The cookies, are those for me?"

I bite my bottom lip. Placing both trays of cookies in the preheated oven. "Yes. Umm…"

I turn around, and he closes the distance between us, causing my words to die in my throat. I can't think when he's this close. My brain ceases to function.

"I asked my manager to do whatever it took and find you the best table, and I'm honored that you're making my favorite the first night since it was delivered."

"It is the best," I breathe.

I'm telling the truth. It's a top-of-the-line prep table, and it must've cost him at least six thousand dollars, maybe more.

"You didn't have to, Ford."

"I did."

"Why?"

He smiles, wiping away the grain of sugar that must have landed on my nose. "Without a prep table, you can't make my cookies." He says this, licks the pad of his thumb, and closes his eyes briefly. *Shit.* "Dulce?"

I swallow hard. "Yeah."

He looks first at the table, then at me. "Can I kiss you now?"

I draw in a breath. "Yes."

He tilts his head slowly, and his lips fuse with mine. I moan. He groans, deepening the kiss. The smell of sugar and citrus wraps around us like a blanket. He turns me so that my back hits the edge of the table and pulls me against him. A moan escapes my throat, drowning in our kiss. I can feel his hard-on pushing against my belly through his jeans. His hands grip my thighs, lifting me onto the table. He pulls back, and our lips make a sucking sound when they break apart.

I want to tell him we can't on the prep table, but as soon as he looks at the two buttons between my breasts on my pink uniform, his gaze slowly shifts between my legs, which are now spread wide. My dress's skirt is bunched up around my upper thighs. Just one movement. A centimeter, and he can see the triangle of my pink panties. I don't want it to end. Whatever is going on between us.

"Are you sweet down there too, Dulce?"

"I don't know," I reply nervously. "Last night, you didn't let me taste myself on your fingers."

I can't believe I said that. The words sound foreign on my tongue.

"You've never tasted yourself?"

I shake my head. I haven't. I've played with myself at the thought of him.

The palms of his hands are hot on my thighs, sliding higher. His thumb presses against my clit. My legs open wider.

His eyes lift. "Let's see... how you taste." He pushes me back. My ass slides across the table as he dips his head. My hands are flat on the metal surface, holding myself up. His lips are between my legs. His eyes fixed on me.

His thumb pushes my wet panties to the side. His tongue swipes my slit. "Ford," I gasp.

He's pressed his face between my thighs, fucking me with his tongue. Goose bumps snake over my skin. My nerves tighten. Sweat drips between my breasts. I grind shamelessly on his face, wanting more. I grip the top of his short hair, pushing my pussy deeper into his face. I need to come.

I moan.

He groans.

"Oh...God. More," I beg him.

His tongue dips and turns. His hands hold me steady on my hips. I ride his face hard, screaming when I come.

The timer on the oven dings. My heart jackhammers in my chest. He pulls out, licking my cum off his mouth.

"The cookies are done," I say, catching my breath.

He smiles and takes my lips, letting me taste myself on his tongue. "I like the way you taste much better," he says between kisses.

"Is that so?" I smile.

"Yes, I believe you think so too, with the way you returned my kiss."

I avert my gaze, feeling the heat rise on my cheeks. Ford has a way of getting what he wants, and I will no longer deny it. He has me. He always did, and I think he always will.

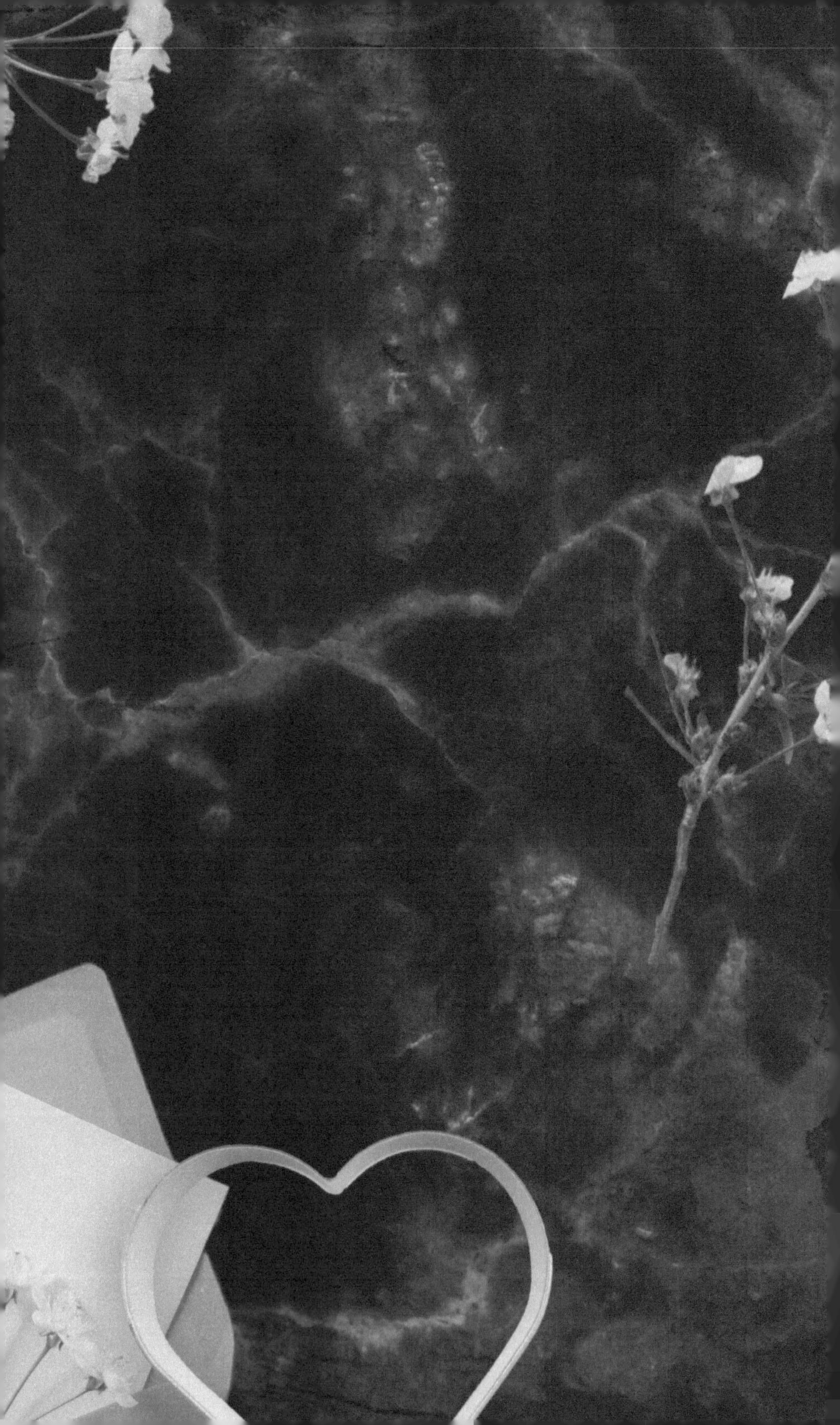

I knock on Chris's door as the sun disappears on the horizon. The blue in the sky is fading to black.

I am still unable to shake the memory of Dulce's moans when I went down on her on Friday. Her name was on my lips when my tongue was inside her, the memory living rent-free in my mind.

It's been three days, and every fiber of my being resists the urge to drag her to the nearest corner and fuck her. Memorize every inch of her body the way my mind has wanted for so long. But that's not how I want her first time with me to go. It shouldn't be in a corner or in a small bed with a thin wall between us and her dying grandmother. It should be romantic and perfect. But all of that has to wait for now.

The door opens. Chris gives me a wide smile as the smell of beer and sweat wafts outside, and I want nothing more than to punch the smile right off his face. Stab him in the eyes and hang him.

"You came back," he says like he expected me.

"I did."

He waves me in.

"Come inside. I'll kick everyone out in a sec."

I walk inside, rubbing my nose, trying to get used to the smell.

Three guys and two girls, both in their underwear, sit on the couch.

Chris taps each of them on the shoulder. "Hey, you all need to get out of here. I have company."

Groans and complaints float across the room as they grab their clothes thrown across the floor, bumping into empty beer bottles and ashtrays as they head out.

When the door closes, Chris plops on the black leather couch.

"What's up?" He nudges his head toward the loveseat. "Have a seat." He lights up the roach. It glows like a beacon between his dirty fingers. "Let's catch up."

I take a seat, careful not to lean back. Who knows what has happened on these couches? I look around at the mismatched furniture. Some looks like it came with the house, while some are new. They're all dirty and need a hose to clean them off.

"What are you up to?" I ask, trying to sound casual like I couldn't care less.

He smiles. "Funny. You should just say what you came to say."

"Like?"

"Man," he says, shaking his head. "I knew you would show up if you found out." He lifts his head and blows out a cloud of smoke.

I play dumb. "Found out about what?"

He grins. "Prom night. I didn't think you still had a thing for her after knocking up Summer." He shrugs. "But who am I to judge?"

"Tell me what happened. Your version."

He smiles like a weasel. His eyes shine brightly like he's telling the best story. "She was the prank. I texted her using your old phone, asking her to prom. She got dressed up all pretty. We picked her up. I don't think the truth sank in yet until I picked her up and she realized you weren't in the car."

He laughs, and I want to burn his eyes out with his little roach so I can hear him scream. "We let her out when she realized you never asked her to prom."

"She was attacked."

He winces. "Dude, I know. It wasn't us, though."

"You two left her there and broke her phone."

He points at me. "Trent broke her phone."

"You should have gone to jail for what you both did."

His reaction grates on my nerves, and I want nothing more than to pummel him to the ground until he stops breathing.

"For a prank?" He taps his temple. "Are you listening to yourself? We pulled pranks all the time. How is it our fault? Let's be honest, Ford. How could she have believed you wanted to take her to prom? Honestly, you never spoke to her, and you didn't care who said anything to her. No one did."

"She got hurt." The words escape my clenched teeth.

He rolls his eyes, and I want to stab him. "Obviously. We didn't run. We spoke to the cops. My parents hired lawyers. Trent's parents did the same. You know how it all works. It's the same thing your parents would have done if you were involved, like you getting Summer pregnant."

"Leave Summer out of this."

He chuckles. "Still got a soft spot for her."

"You know better than that."

He knows I give two shits about Summer.

He shakes his head. Slowly. "Summer loved you, man."

"Well, I didn't."

"So what... You came back here and found out something fucked up happened to the bullied girl from high school you always had a soft spot for? What do you think you are going to accomplish snooping around town, digging for shit that no one can find?"

"The truth."

"I told you the truth. I'm not hiding what I did. Not from you." He takes a drag—"the cops. Trent isn't either, no matter how many times you beat the shit out of him."

He knows I'm not fucking around. I watch his mannerisms. I noticed how different he was from the guy I grew up with. He's different. Something changed him.

"What happened to you, Chris?"

"What do you mean?" he asks like he doesn't know what I'm talking about.

I look around, waving at the room. "Why are you here? What happened at college?"

"It wasn't for me."

"And this is?"

He nods. "I never wanted to go to college. It was my so-called mom's idea."

"You did, but I don't think this is what you had in mind."

"You sound just like her." He leans back and looks around the living room that currently looks like a crack shack. "She said the same thing when she came to visit me."

I had never heard him call his mother like that. Granted, she is like my own mother and every rich woman who married well-off. She lifts her nose when she walks around town as if her shit doesn't stink, but she isn't a bad person. She couldn't have kids, and I bet the last thing she ever thought when she adopted Chris was that he would end up like this. A drug-addicted fuckup who uses.

"What's your plan?" I ask, knowing he doesn't have one.

"What's yours?" he fires back.

"I thought I was going to open a garage with Trent."

"And?"

I sniff, trying not to spit on the wood floor, as the stench of his house clogs my throat. "I changed my mind."

"How long are you staying?"

I get up to leave. "I don't know. Why?" I ask curiously. "Want me to leave town already."

"Nah." He laughs. "I was hoping you would give me an auto-graph," he says sarcastically.

I open the front door, knowing my next visit to Chris won't be in his favor. "Hey, Chris?" I call out when I reach the Porsche.

"Hmm...?"

"Did you visit Dulce to see if she was okay? You know...after it happened?"

He slides his hands into his front pocket, causing the band of his dirty jeans to lower, revealing a toneless stomach and pubic hair. "My lawyer advised against it."

His reply chokes me into rage as I fire up the car. We stare at each other through the windshield until his mouth lifts in a rapacious smile.

I peel out and push the Porsche to the limit, heading back to Trent's garage. When I get there, I apply the e-brake. I ignore the burnt stink from the engine, proof I was driving too fast. The smell of gas and motor oil is comforting, and my rage finally subsides.

"What happened?" Trent says when I walk in. I take the stairs two steps at a time.

I stop and turn around.

The swelling has gone down, but his face still looks like a purple popsicle when it changes colors. "I paid Chris a visit."

"That fucker is crazy and has been strung out since he came back," he says, turning off the TV.

"I know that. Where was he that night, Trent?"

"After we left Dulce, everyone was laughing at prom. Chris ended up going with Summer."

"He went to prom with Summer?"

"I don't know, but she showed up the same way we all did. We didn't do the corsage or any of that shit. It wasn't the same when you left. We all hated it."

I sit on the far end of the couch. "I can tell," I drawl. "Were you with him the entire night?"

"I think so."

I stand, grab him by the throat, and forcefully push him against the wall. "Think, motherfucker."

He raises his arm as dread washes over his face. "It was four years ago, Ford. I don't..." He shuts his eyes. "He was there. We were all there, dancing and having fun. Drinking. Smoking pot. The usual shit. Summer was with him. Heather was there. Vicki. It was all of us."

I let him go. Disgusted with him—with them.

"When you got back, did anyone go missing?" I prompt, already out of patience.

He blinks rapidly, trying to remember. "I don't know. The cops showed up three hours later. They questioned us, and I was scared, man. I was so scared."

"Not for her," I roar. I slam him against the wall, knocking the wind out of him. I pull his head back by his hair. His eyes bulge out of his head. "You were scared to get caught."

"You're right, man," he cries out. "I regret that night." Pathetic tears run down his face. "I wish I could go back and change it." He squeezes his eyes shut. "The look on her face when I left her haunts me every night."

"Good," I spit, letting him go, watching him slide down the wall. "I hope it does. I hope it fucking eats you inside."

"Please," he pleads. "Don't kill me, Ford."

I chuckle. "What makes you think that?"

"I see it in your eyes."

I kneel so we are at eye level. "What do you see?"

With a terrified expression, he says, "I see...it."

I smile.

When I was a kid, I was obsessed with things. In my case, cars. The doctor said it could manifest into other things—like people —if I wasn't careful. He claimed it marked the beginning of borderline personality disorder. Although it was never an issue, my close friends knew about my little problem. Trent. Chris.

Again, no one saw it as a problem. I saw a therapist. Psychologist. A psychiatrist until I was twelve. My parents hated the idea of my obsession with cars and how fast they could go. They called it a phase. I called it my life. I had friends, but there was no one I was crazy about. When I stopped seeing the doctor, he warned my parents and educated them on different types of obsessions and BPD. Honestly, I thought he was full of shit. I didn't check the doors twice. I wasn't a germaphobe. I wasn't violent if I wasn't provoked. Unhinged. Other issues manifested, though, like I didn't fuck women on my bed. I had to do it elsewhere, but many guys do that. It's not uncommon.

The only issue I had was if you fucked with my driving or my car. It's comparable to taking away an iPad from a hyper focused autistic child. You're met with an outburst of someone who's driven to violence.

My father took my car keys after I received my first speeding ticket. I lost it. I kicked his ass. I wasn't proud of it, but he had touched something he shouldn't have. What I loved.

At fifteen, they prescribed medication for me, but I refused to take it. My father threatened me, so I did the same. Eye for an eye and all that. I would inform my mother of the numerous women in town with whom my father had intimate relationships if he were to tell her the things I did.

It was the first time he respected me, or maybe he feared me. He had nothing on me, but I had plenty on him. The scales were tipped. He wanted me to be like him, but I just wanted to race cars. But no one knew I had a secret obsession. A dark one. A secret person.

I made every effort to conceal it.

No one knew. Not my parents. Not my friends.

I wanted a girl who no one would approve of me having, and I knew what that meant. She would end up being the car keys my father tried to take away from me when I did something wrong. I did learn one thing the doctor said: I had to listen some of the time. What does an obsessive or person with BPD do? They do anything to make sure their obsession isn't taken away. If someone tries, they are met with violence. Rage.

My coming back doesn't make sense to some, but sometimes nothing does. If it did, doctors would have answers.

Cures to diseases. Answers to questions no one can easily figure out.

Maybe I was too busy racing my cars and finally got bored, but now that I think about it, Now that I had a taste of what I was missing, I want more, and nothing will stand in my way of keeping her for myself.

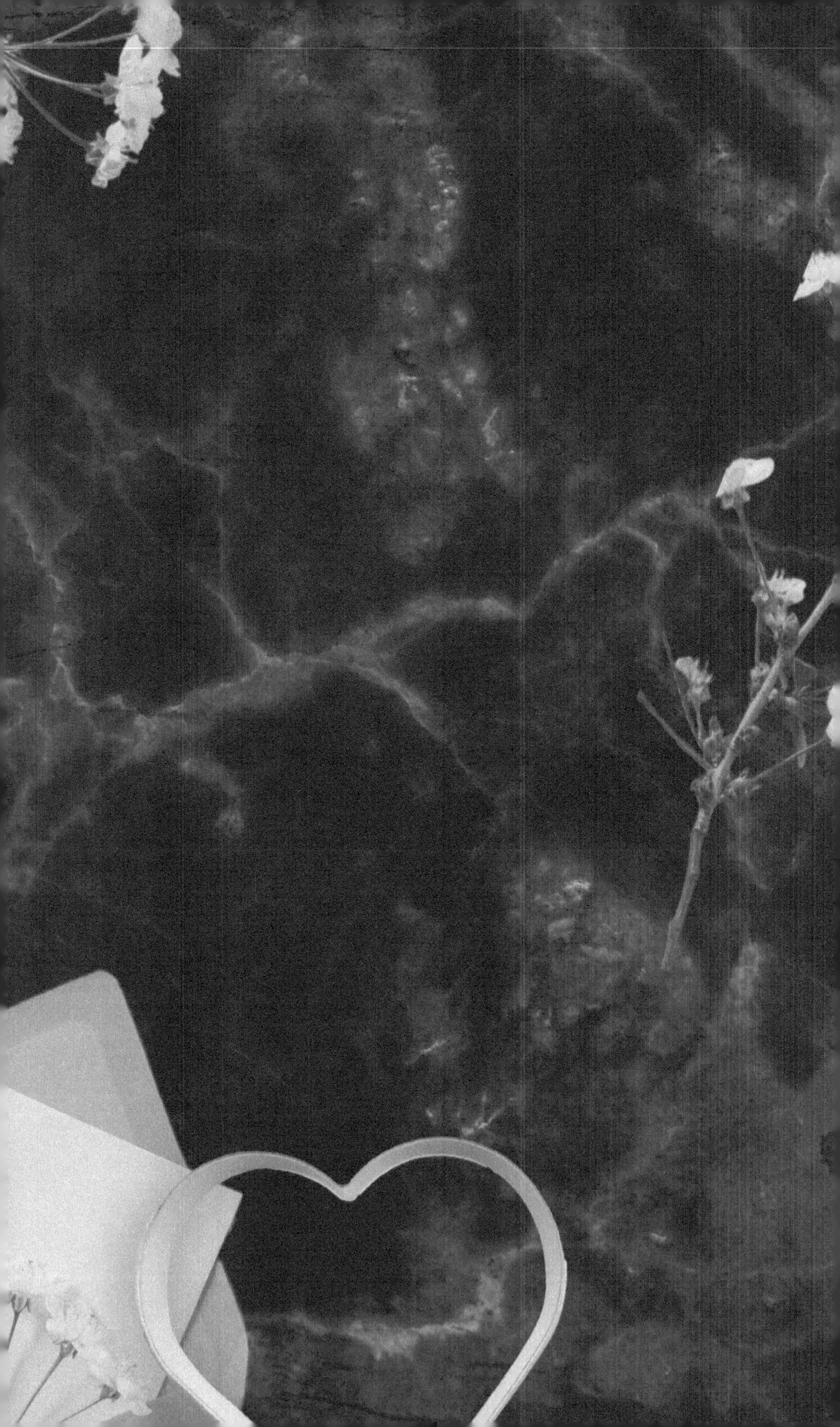

DULCE

I close the register, then hand the older woman with curly red hair her change and slide the box of pastries toward them. "Thank you," I say with a smile.

It's ten in the morning, and it's been nonstop. Closing for two days has customers pouring in like starving children. Not that I'm complaining.

"You look different," Katie says, giving me a once-over.

I look down at the same uniform I wear every day of the week. "How's that?"

Katie looks at me like she is studying a painting. "You have this fresh look on your face."

"Nope."

"Yep, I see it now," she says, her eyes dancing. "You gave him some."

I don't have to ask to know she means Ford.

"Katie!"

"What?" she says, flushing bright red. "You look... you know."
Mental note: never tell her that he showed up last night.

"If I did or didn't, it's none of your business."

"You're right," she says, "but still..."

My eyes widen as another customer enters.

"Fine," she grumbles, turning to help them with their order.

The doorbell dings again. I look up, and my heart drops as

Summer waltzes in like nothing has changed since I last saw her. She is still beautiful despite her stuck-up personality that circles her everywhere she goes, looking beautiful with her perfectly styled blond hair, tailored designer clothes, and expertly applied makeup.

"Oh, hey, Dulce. It's been a long time," she says, giving me a fake smile like we are old friends.

"Not long enough," I mutter to myself. "How can I help you, Summer?"

I'm surprised to see her. She moved out of town after graduation. Is she here because of Ford?

"Still mad?"

I want to throw sand in your eyes.

Instead, I plaster a fake professional smile. "I'm thrilled to see you."

"Are you sure? It was just high school." She waves her hand. "It's supposed to be like that."

"Funny, I don't remember it that way," Katie says, giving her an unfriendly smile.

Summer looks at the menu board above as if she is deciding what to order and ignores Katie's last remark.

She didn't come to eat or order anything.

"What do you want, Summer?" I ask, my restraint running thin.

She sighs. "Fine. I heard..."

"Ford?" I interject.

"Yes," she says with a bubbly smile that I would love nothing more than to smack off her face. "It's why I'm here. I'm having lunch with him."

My heart drops. He wouldn't.

I swallow the hurt rising in my throat and ask, "Then why are you here?"

"I want to apologize for what happened on prom night. I overheard what happened, and I'm sorry. No one thought they would leave you..."

I blink, trying to forget. Her words fading.

Images of blood on my hands. So much blood dripping in a pool at my feet.

I blink the memory away, her face coming back into focus.

"Kind of late. It was four years ago," I tell her, hating her more with every minute she stands in my bakery. I want nothing more than to kick her out, but I can't because her father is the mayor. She could destroy my business.

"Time flies, doesn't it?"

"It does, and there are some things one would rather forget." I glance at her hand, hoping to find a ring, but come up empty. Hoping there's another reason as to why he wants to have lunch with her.

She smooths her salon-dyed blond hair. She is beautiful. Of course, he would have lunch with her.

He didn't stay with me last night. He didn't kiss me goodbye after he drove off after following me home. Her being here is a punch in the gut. A bucket of ice-cold water freezing my heart.

"I guess you should get going," Katie chimes in. "You might be late."

It was closer to eleven, but I couldn't be more grateful for Katie's persistence in getting Summer to leave. She probably came to gloat. She always saw me as a threat for some reason. I never understood why, and it was pointless to ask.

"You're right; he might be waiting." Summer gloats.

When she finally leaves, Katie turns to me. "What a bitch! If it weren't for my job and the fact that she's the mayor's daughter, I would have reached over this counter and punched her in the face."

"I wouldn't have stopped you, but you're right. The only thing saving her right now is her father."

"And the fact that her face was plastered in the local news next to her daddy doesn't help. Do you think she is lying?"

I busy myself cleaning the counters. "No. They have history. I've heard that he got her pregnant before they broke up in high school, and she lost the baby. In high school, everyone pegged them to be a forever thing. Right before prom, I heard he cheated on her, which was why they broke up. I shouldn't be surprised he reached out to her after all this time. They were together."

She scoffs. "And you think he still holds a torch for her or something?"

I shrug in defeat. "I'm not sure what to think anymore."

I need to let him go and accept that whatever we did meant nothing.

"You're going to ghost him, aren't you?" she says like she is reading my mind.

I'm not sure what I'll do, but whatever Ford and I had going was over before it could ever begin.

I toss the rag on the counter. "We're both different. It would never work, Katie. I know that."

Sirens wail from outside, followed by the screeching of tires. Katie and the other small shop owners look out the storefronts.

"Damn," she mutters, peering out the windowpane. "Where did all these cops come from? I thought Airy had four tops."

I look out the window to see four more patrol cars fly down the street with their sirens on. I pull my phone out to see if there is a local alert, but there is nothing. "I wonder what happened."

"Whatever it is, it must be bad," Katie says. The screech of tires and more sirens follow.

Mr. Sheppard from the convenience store next door bursts in out of breath. "Did you hear?"

Mr. Sheppard is an old-timer. He is old and nosy, like most of the people in Airy, and the first to tell everyone when something is going on. Like if they catch someone stealing at the food mart. Or when a couple is getting divorced. No gossip is beneath him to share.

"No, Mr. Sheppard," I reply.

"Old man Moody was attacked." He shakes his head. The sun's glare catches his bald head. "Dead."

"Moody?"

"You probably don't know him. I mean, he was a crazy, sick bastard. I'm sure no one is going to miss him, but he was left for dead." He tries to hide his shaky hand in his pocket.

All the color drains from my face. I can feel Katie's stare, but I don't know if I should feel relieved or scared. "How did he die?" I ask.

"He was attacked is what I heard. Someone found him on the side of the road, bludgeoned to death."

"Shit," Katie whispers.

AFTER I DELIVER A CUSTOM-MADE CAKE, I TURN RIGHT instead of left toward where Mr. Sheppard said they found Moody. I'm assuming it was the same road his house is on.

When I turn onto the road, I see caution tape and about ten police cars surrounding the area. A cop waves his hands like an air traffic controller when he sees my van, signaling for me to turn back, but I ignore him. I scan the police officers, looking for Danny. I see him leaning on the car with a grim expression while another officer tells him something.

I place the van in park and get out, ignoring the officer calling out, "Ma'am, you can't be here. This is an active crime scene."

"Danny!" I call out, ignoring him.

He turns his head at my voice and pushes off the car. When he spots me, he doesn't look pleased to see me.

"What are you doing here, Dulce? You need to go back to the bakery. I'll meet you there when I can."

"I heard—"

He interrupts. "Go, Dulce."

"I'm sorry, Officer Mays. She wouldn't listen," the cop directing the traffic says.

"What happened?" I ask Danny.

"We can't give out any information. Please, Dulce. I'll call you."

"Ma'am..." the traffic cops call out, pointing behind me to leave.

A sports car rumbles behind me. I turn around, and Ford's Porsche pulls up. The driver's and passenger doors open. Ford eyes me in surprise, and then Summer gets out. I glance at Ford and notice he's dressed like he was out on a lunch date. It feels like a kick to the gut.

He looks between me and Summer with a blank expression.

"I guess you're right, Officer Mays. I shouldn't be here," I say and walk back to my van.

"Dulce," Ford calls out, but I ignore him, blinking back the sting of tears and hating myself for thinking she was lying.

I slam the driver's side door and fire up the van. Ford knocks on the window, but I ignore him and back out. There is nothing left for me to say.

The familiar tightness weaves its way into my chest as I drive off with tears streaming down my face. Thick, heavy, full of pain for something so close I could touch, yet so far out of reach it's impossible to keep.

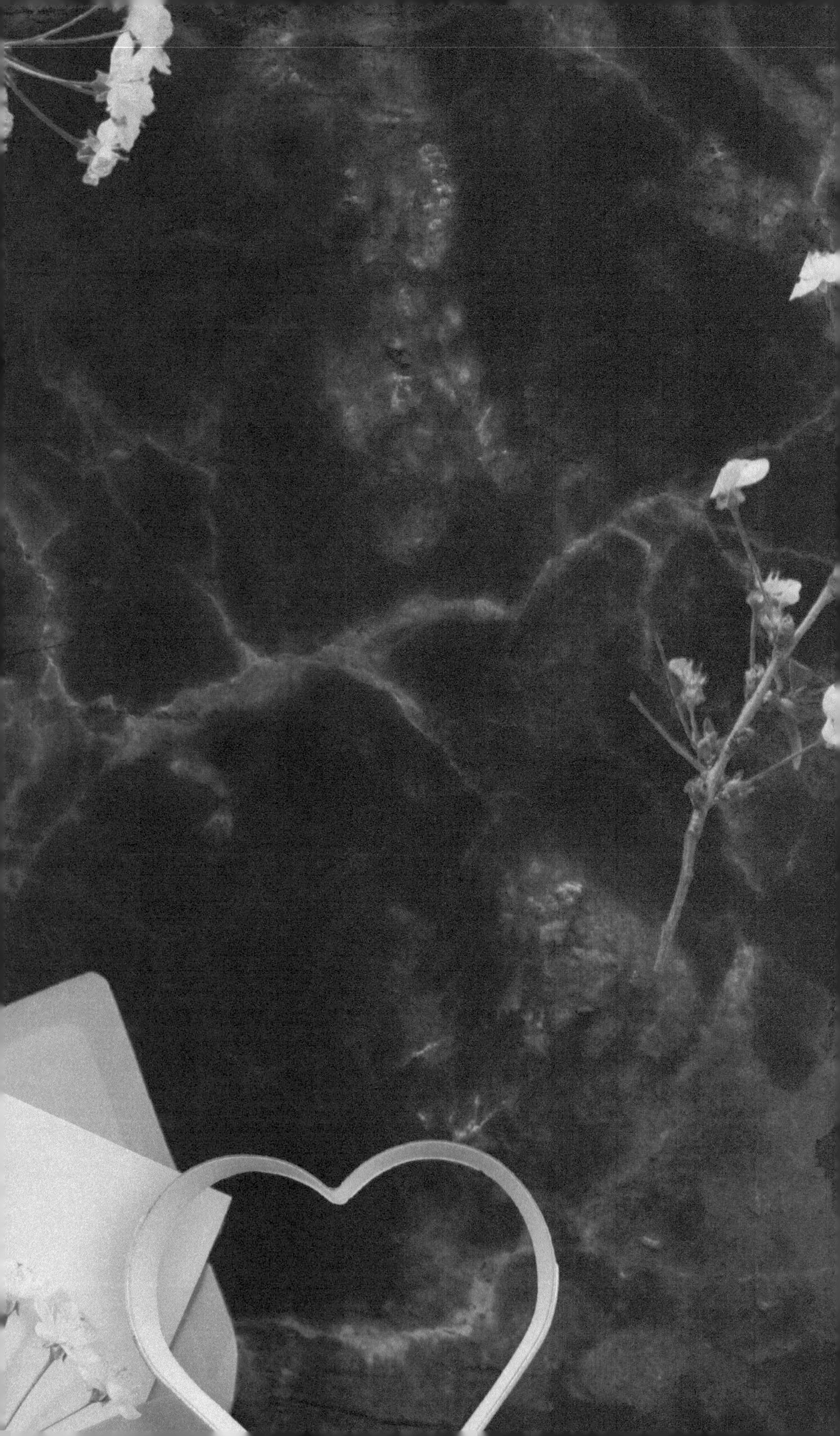

"It was Ford again," Mary says, coming into my grandmother's room with her mouth pulled into a frown.

"Still not speaking to him?" my grandmother says, sounding out of breath while sitting in her wheelchair.

I give her a weak smile. "No."

It's been a week since I saw him with Summer on that godforsaken road. I ignore his calls. I don't answer the door when he stops by.

When he shows up at the bakery, I make sure to remain in the kitchen, making it a point to tell Katie I'm not available. I know I have to talk to him at some point, but I have to accept it.

"You still have feelings for him."

I shake my head. "I do have feelings for him, but I have to accept that he doesn't feel the same way. We're different."

"I think you're not giving him a solid chance to explain himself. He's here for a reason, and that reason has something to do with you. There is no denying that," my grandmother says.

I tell her about Summer.

It was safe to confess that part to her. She knows I could never compete with Summer. They did go out on a date. They were in the car together when they showed up. I don't know why they would. I didn't ask, and frankly, I don't care.

Moody's attacker could have been anyone. Family of the girl

he assaulted. Who knows how many enemies he's gained over the years? That is probably why he lived out there.

Mary leaves the room for a few minutes and then walks back in and says, "Ford is outside wanting to see you."

"Talk to him, Dulce," my grandmother says, trying not to cough.

She's getting worse. I can see it. Not much longer.

Not wanting to cause her stress, I agree, "I'll be right back."

I pat Mary's shoulder on the way out. I open the door reluctantly and find Ford sitting on the old beat-up bench outside with his head in his hands.

He looks up when he hears the groan from the front door as I push it open.

He gets up from the bench, smoothing out his black T-shirt. "Dulce."

I cross my arms over my chest. "What are you doing here, Ford?"

"Why aren't you answering my calls?" he asks like he doesn't already know.

I'm still trying to figure out how he got my number since I changed it four years ago, but he'll lie about it, and I'm sick of the lies. I'm tired of this town and the people in it.

"Because I have nothing to say to you."

He clears his throat. "Is this about Summer?"

"You don't owe me an explanation. For all I know, you have ten women back home waiting for you wherever you live."

It's then I realize that I don't know where he lives or much about his life outside of Airy and what is posted on social media.

"Vegas. I live in Vegas, and the world knows I'm not with anyone exclusively. And I'm telling you, I'm not with anyone else."

"Good to know." I turn away from him. "I have to get back inside."

I pull the door.

"Dulce, wait." He holds the door.

"What?"

"It's not what you think. Summer and me. It's not what it looked like."

I shake my head. "I don't care."

That's a lie, of course. I do care. Ford has the power to rip my heart out of my chest, and I need to save it because that is all that is left.

"But I do," he says.

"Good for you."

I pull the door, but he grips it tighter.

"Tell me what happened that night."

"Why?" I croak. "Why would you ask me that?"

"Because I want to know."

"I can't."

"Why not?"

"I can't tell you here."

"Your grandmother doesn't know, does she?"

I shake my head.

"Come with me."

I can see the determination in his eyes. He isn't going to let this go. Whatever *this* is.

"Why are you doing this?" I ask.

"Because someone needs to."

"It's not going to change what happened or what I think. You're you, and I'm me. We're different."

"Is it because you think I have something going on with Summer?"

"It's none of my business." I shake my head slowly. "You don't owe me an explanation, Ford. We aren't together. We aren't even dating."

It's the truth. We aren't even a thing. I was too busy reading too much into it because he was the boy I had a crush on. The boy I could see giving all my firsts to but all of those firsts were taken. There isn't much left.

"I want to change that. I want to date you."

I ignore the butterflies or the way my subconscious screams at me to say yes.

I laugh like he has lost his mind. "I'm not your type."

He grins. "What is my type?"

"Model type, blond, beautiful."

"I never said I like blondes, and beauty is subjective."

"It's what the tabloids say."

"You've been watching? You googled me? You shouldn't listen to anything on the internet."

I did, but I don't want to admit it. It would make him think I was fangirling him, which I was after the night in my bedroom. Search his name on the internet, and you get hundreds of hits. He has over three million followers, all over the world. He's a sex icon with his commercials alone.

"I don't have to watch or google you; you kind of pop up out of nowhere."

"For the record, I don't like blondes." His eyes fall to my hips. "I prefer curves and women who can bake. Especially cookies."

"I'm sure you could find plenty of women who can bake."

"Why? If there is one right in front of me that I like, and she isn't blond." He lowers his voice. "For the record, I like brunettes who wear sexy retro uniforms to work and stay late to bake my favorite cookies."

"Is this you flirting with me?"

"This is me asking you out for the weekend."

"I have work, and you know I can't leave."

"It is about work. I kind of told my manager Sugar Coated Sweets was sponsoring the event, and at the same time, you're coming as my date."

"You did what?"

He smirks. "You won't take my help so I figured out a way I could help you without you feeling that you owe me. There will be millions of people watching, thousands of fans. It's great publicity, and the fact that your bakery is my favorite is a plus."

I'm speechless. I don't know what to say. He made sure I

wouldn't turn his offer down because all that he just said is true. It's a great opportunity. One that I cannot refuse.

"Alright. I'll go."

He smiles. "You won't regret it, Dulce. I promise to take good care of you." He looks at the front door nervously before asking, "Can I steal you away for an hour?"

"Like right now?"

He nods. "I've missed you, and there is nothing I want more than to spend time with you."

I shouldn't leave with him or believe anything he has to say, but I decide to go because when it comes to Ford, I lose all rational thought, and so far, I feel I can trust him.

AFTER TELLING MARY I'LL BE BACK, I FIND MYSELF IN the car with Ford parked in the back of the diner after two milkshakes.

"Have you ever talked about it?"

I shake my head, playing with the straw in my cup. "Not since the cops, no."

"You know, I may not be a doctor, but if you ever want anyone to listen, I'm right here, Dulce. I can listen."

Tears prickle the back of my throat. No one has ever offered to listen to anything I have to say unless it was forced or required of me.

"I know it doesn't change what happened but sometimes it helps for someone else to know. To understand."

"You won't like to hear what I have to say."

"I won't like it, but I want to understand what you went through."

I tell him everything that happened that night. I stop after I was hit on the head and blacked out.

"You were attacked. Like old man Moody?" he asks, trying to figure out exactly how it happened.

I look at my hands between my thighs and notice they're shaking. He places his warm hand over them let the words I hate tumble out of my mouth. "I was raped." I sniff. "I woke up and knew something wasn't right. Everything hurt. I've never been with anyone before so I had to piece it all in my head quickly what was wrong." Two fat tears slide down my cheeks. "No one did anything. It sounded like they were listening, but they weren't, if that makes sense. I..." I trail off, not ready to tell him the rest. I'm not sure I could ever tell anyone.

"Shh..." He pulls me into his arms, and I breathe in his scent. "I'm so sorry, Dulce. I'm so fucking sorry." I cry in his arms. I don't know how long he holds me, but I feel safe for the first time since it happened.

When he pulls back, there is a grim expression on his face.

"I found out something you're not going to like, but I have to tell you."

With the palm of my hand, I wipe my face. "What is it?"

"Old man Moody is related to Officer Mays."

I feel like I'm drowning. Then a loud ring assaults my ears, but I only catch the last part of what he says next.

"Nephew. Mays's middle name is Moody."

"What the hell?"

"Now what?" she asks when I pull up in front of her house.

I asked around, finding it weird that no family was devastated by the old man's passing. I found out that the closest family member that the old man had was a nephew named Danny Mays. The old man's real name was Hubert Moody Mays.

"I keep digging," I tell her with determination.

"I don't think it's a good idea," she says.

"Well, not doing it is an even worse one," I tell her truthfully. Her opening up to me that she was raped felt like I was stabbed in the chest. What she went through. I don't blame her for not trusting me.

"Who do you think did it?"

"You or the old man?"

"Both."

I'm not sure who attacked you, Dulce. But I'm trying, as for the old man...it could be a message. Something overlooked. Whoever did it will do everything in their power to keep it buried."

"I think you should leave it. It doesn't change what happened. I don't want people to die because of it."

"I can't," I admit.

I can't tell her what I'm capable of. I'm sure whoever it is knows I'm sniffing around.

"I don't want my grandmother to know," she says quietly. "And I don't want her to die knowing I lied to her."

Her grandmother. The picture. She wants her to go peacefully.

"Then we tell her something else,"

"Like?" she asks.

"That we're together. That we're dating."

"That's lying on top of lying."

I give her my best smile. "It doesn't have to be."

"You don't have—"

"I want to." I interject. "I want to go out on dates with you. I want to spend time with you. It will make her happy, and I'm hoping...it will make you happy."

I've wanted you since forever, but I can't tell her that. It would confuse her. Scare her.

"What would Summer think?" she asks, fidgeting with a piece of her hair. I can sense jealousy in her tone.

I find her jealousy cute.

"I'm not with Summer, Dulce. I'm not interested in Summer. I asked her to come down so she could tell me about that night. She was at prom with Chris and Trent. I was taking her back to her car when I saw you drive off. I heard about Moody and knew where you went, so she jumped in mine."

"Oh..."

My phone dings, cutting her off.

It's an incoming text from Derek.

Derek: You need to make it here in two days.

I have to meet my sponsors at the Charlotte Motor Speedway.

I clear my throat. "Could you come with me to Charlotte and stay overnight? I'll pay Mary double her fee."

She hesitates, opening and closing her mouth. "I don't know."

"I know it's short notice, but it will be beneficial for your business."

I want to take her to dinner. I want to spend time with her alone, away from Airy.

"If I leave, how will I make it to the event with all the food?"

"How many cakes and cookies can you make in two days? I'll help."

She lets out a puff of air. "Depends on the event."

"Alright, make as many cakes as you can in different flavors. I'll send a courier to have them shipped to Charlotte. I have sponsors waiting for me at the Charlotte Motor Speedway. There will be press, paparazzi, screaming fans and loud cars. It's not far from here. It would be good to get away for a bit. You'll be back by Sunday. I can hire someone to help Mary if she needs to leave."

"Alright," she agrees, and the pressure I felt in my chest quickly dissipates. "I'll be ready."

TWO DAYS LATER, I WAIT IN THE MEET AND GREET before the race begins. The sun is out, the trees swaying in the wind. My car is in the back trailer, and I'm waiting outside Dulce's house for her to come out.

After a few minutes, my heart jumps in my throat, and my palms sweat as I watch Dulce walk down the broken path wearing leggings and an off-the-shoulder T-shirt. Her long hair blows to the side, and she has never looked more gorgeous.

"If you keep staring at her, the sponsors might think you're too distracted to race," Derek says from behind me.

"They better get used to it. Is everything ready for tonight?"

"Have I ever let you down?" he replies in a Southern twang.

"If there is ever a time when I need you to come through for me, it's now."

"I never pegged you to have a soft spot for a woman."

"If it only was a spot," I mutter before she reaches me.

"Hi," Dulce says nervously, looking back and forth between Derek and me.

"Derek, Dulce Webster. The owner of Sugar Coated Sweets."

"It's a pleasure," Derek says, taking her bag.

"Nice to meet you," she replies softly.

I take the bag from Derek, earning a surprised look. "Well, that's a first," Derek mutters.

"First of many," I tell him, leaning close to place a peck on her lips. "Hi."

"Hi," she says right back.

"Good morning," I whisper.

"Good morning," she says shyly. The blush on her cheeks spreads to her neck.

Derek clears his throat. "We need to get going, Ford."

When we arrive at the event, I had Derek arrange for Sugar Coated Secrets to have a tent with a banner made with her logo to market the bakery. I also made copies of her menu and QR code so people can place orders remotely.

"You didn't have to do all this, Ford," she says, watching from the suite above the track in awe.

"It's my pleasure. Everyone will know where they can buy my favorite cookies from."

"Ford," Derek calls from the door.

I turn. "I'll be right out."

Sponsors are waiting for me to make an appearance, but I want to make sure she is comfortable.

"Is it like this all the time?" she asks, looking out at the crowds of fans with my number painted on their faces. Some with signs with my name on them. People scream and cheer in the stands. Some with their phones out. They even rolled out a red carpet. It is a full PR event. Thousands of fans have come out to watch me race.

"Depends on the race. Formula 1 is more of a show. More money. In Italy, it is a bigger show for sure. Huge parties after the race. Executives from every car manufacturer."

"Full of celebrities?" she asks, but I can tell she's nervous

"Yeah. Drinking, dancing..."

"Hotel rooms," she says, looking at the woman flirting with the drivers below. Women wearing short skirts and T-shirts tight under their breasts. Some wear shorts so short they should be arrested.

It's no secret I end up sleeping with some of them. The tabloids love to show that part.

I take a pull from my water bottle. "Yeah, good thing this time I came with someone I don't have to escape from the following morning."

"Is that supposed to make me feel better?"

"You'd be the first."

"The first?"

"Yeah, the first." I grin, loving the fact that she is jealous. "How many girls do you think I bring to watch me race?"

"I don't know. There are a lot of things I don't know about you."

"Whatever it is you want to know, all you have to do is ask."

"What is the real Ford Keller like?"

I place a peck on her cheek. "You're gonna be the first to find out."

Derek walks back in. "Ford?"

I turn around. "Tell them to wait."

"Why?" Derek stammers.

I look back at Dulce. "I have a date with my girlfriend."

DULCE

A DRIVER PICKS US UP IN A BLACK SUV OUT BACK, which is full of security.

We arrive at a well-known Italian restaurant in the city, and I instantly feel like I should have changed. Ford can wear a plain shirt and jeans but manages to pull it off like he's wearing a suit. It also helps that he's Ford Keller, and no one would say anything to him about what he wears. On the other hand, me with my simple dress and boutique no-brand wedge heels stick out in a restaurant that takes reservations only.

The hostess takes us out back to a table that is dimly lit and intimate. A few couples are having lunch, oblivious to the fact that Ford Keller is having lunch a few tables over. We get a few curious looks aimed our way as he takes a seat next to me instead of across each other.

"I hope this is okay." He gets comfortable, his pant leg rubbing against my thigh and causing havoc between my legs.

And then it hits me. I'm on a date with Ford. A real date.

"It's fine," I chirp, grateful as the server fills two glasses of ice water.

Ford picks up the menu, scanning it like this is normal. Like we've had hundreds of lunches like this before a race.

"Are you supposed to be eating before a race?" I ask.

He cocks his head. "No."

"Won't you get in trouble?"

"As long as I don't drink alcohol before I get behind the wheel, I think I'll be fine. Besides, I'm going to win. I can do whatever I want."

"Cocky."

"I'm trying to impress you."

"I think it's working."

He laughs loud. "How's that?"

"I'm here with you."

"You are, and that makes me happy."

"How's that?" I ask, not able to look away from his gorgeous mouth, remembering it between my legs. I want nothing more than for him to do more and for this day not to end.

"I like being around you, Dulce. I've expressed this before, and I wasn't lying when I said it."

He orders for us both when the server returns and then moves close and whispers in my ear. "The truth is, Dulce, I've always wanted you."

I swallow, not knowing how to respond. Not knowing what to say to that. I turn my head, searching his gaze for a crack in his words. To see if there is a lie or a motive behind them, yet all I see is desire, want, and possession.

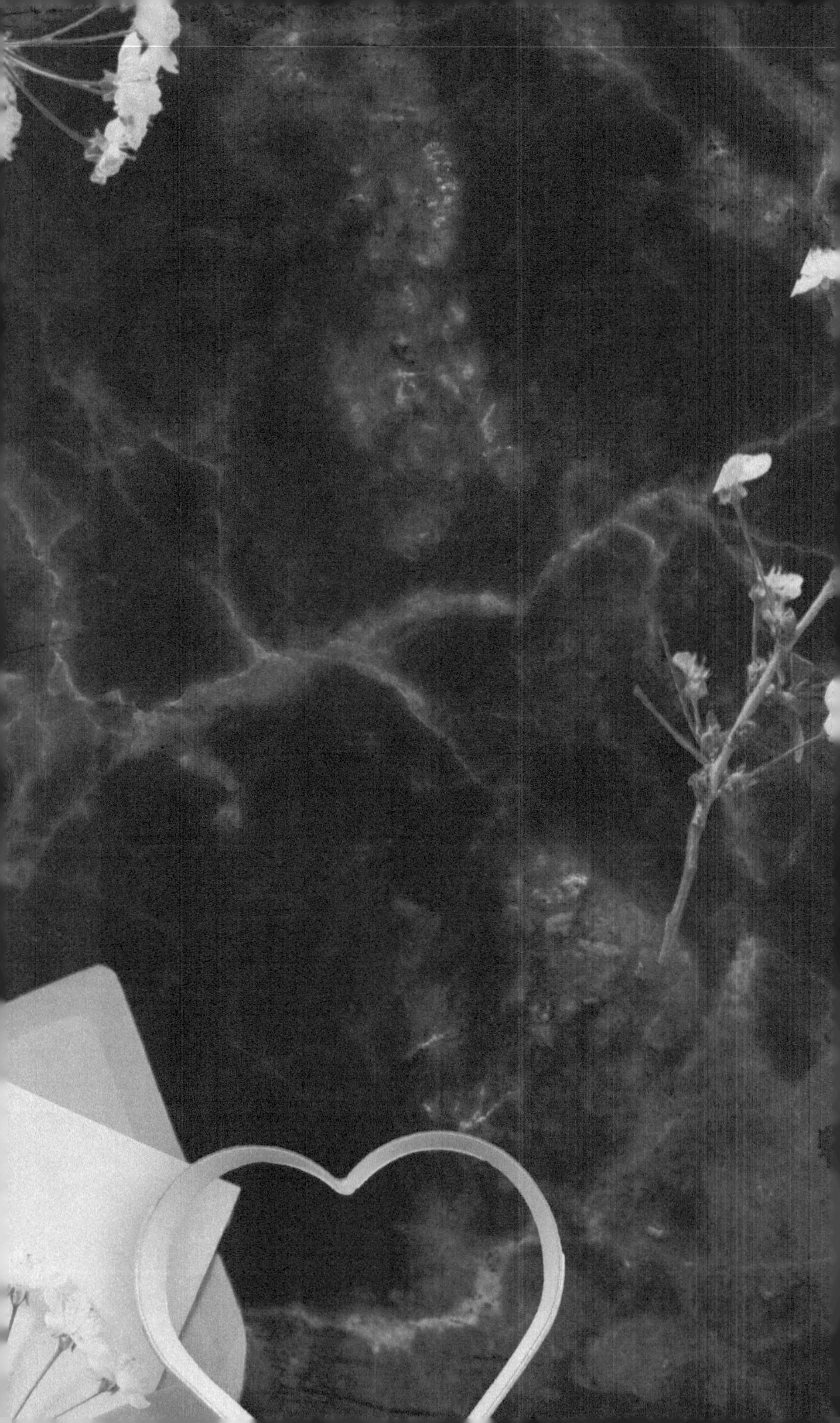

After the race, Katie called me to tell me we would need to hire more people to help with the influx of orders. Apparently, Ford Keller eating cookies from Sugar Coated Secrets is a big deal. I have to order more supplies. Hell, after delivering all the orders, I can afford to cover all my expenses and buy a new van.

The suite Ford's team booked is lavish. It's the nicest hotel room I have ever been in. A king-sized bed with Italian bed sheets and designer flute glasses. Champagne bottles on ice that I can't even pronounce. Thinking about our lunch date earlier has my thoughts turning to sex. It's all I can think about since we came back when he said he's always wanted me.

The suite at the track is just as nice, with an incredible view and more champagne. Food. Water bottles that cost more than an average meal at a restaurant. Sponsors is what he said, making me feel my paltry cakes bland in comparison.

The crowd is going wild on the track. There is a knock on the door of the private suite before the door opens.

"Dulce," Derek calls out.

"Hi, Derek." Derek has been nice to me since Ford left to go interview. He keeps asking me if I need anything, and I can tell he cares what I think about him. I wonder if Ford told him to make sure I was okay at all times.

"He's waiting for you."

I swallow nervously. "Ford?"

He nods with a grin. "That's the one."

I look out the window at the massive crowd. I spot Ford smiling at the cameras. Thousands of women taking selfies with him. "Down there?" Imagine being in the center of the massive crowd. What would people say? Am I pretty enough to be with Ford? Would he tell them that we're dating, or will he brush it off? I don't think I have ever been around so many people before. The most was in the gym for the school's pep rally before the football game.

"Umm..."

"Come on. He really wants you down there to celebrate. He won first place. I don't think anyone has ever seen him drive like that. It was impressive." His eyes light up with excitement. "It's like you're his good luck charm."

He was awesome. He beat a record. I look at the smile on his face and have never seen him so happy before. No wonder he couldn't wait to leave Airy. This is his dream.

I turn around. "Are you sure it's a good idea, Derek?"

"It is. It means a lot to him if you're down there."

I follow Derek through the throng of bodies. The crowd screams louder as we approach the main stage. It's hot in the midafternoon, but I'm sweating for a different reason. I'm nervous to be in front of thousands of people watching me with Ford. This is his element, and I'm way over my head with all the attention from fans and the paparazzi.

When the crowd breaks apart, giving me a clear view of Ford, my stomach does a familiar little flip. His eyes lock on mine, causing heads to turn in my direction.

He walks over with an exhilarated smile. "Hi."

"Hi," I say right back, wanting nothing more than to kiss him. He's gorgeous in his racing suit. It's zipped down, revealing a white T-shirt underneath, showcasing his ripped chest and abs, with his hair disheveled.

He slides his hand around my waist and brings me close to his side, giving me a peck on the lips.

A woman sticks a microphone in front of his face. "Who's the lucky lady, Ford?"

"I'm the lucky one," he says, squeezing me tight. The crowd fades away in the background. Our eyes lock, the beat of my heart in my ears. "Will you go out with me tonight, Dulce?"

I smile, wanting nothing more than to share this moment with him. "I would love to."

RUMMAGING IN MY BAG, I WANT TO KICK MYSELF FOR not thinking of bringing anything nice to wear for an evening out.

I honestly didn't think we were going to go out for dinner or that he would ask me out anywhere else. I thought I was here to see him race, promote the bakery, and serve the cakes and cookies I baked into the wee hours of the morning the night before the courier showed up.

I ended up watching the race and not having to hand out anything. Ford had Derek hire an entire team with the bakery's logo and banner. There was a gorgeous pink-and-black tent I have never seen before all made up like I had an entire marketing team at my disposal.

There is a knock on the door. I check the time on my phone. Ford said he'd pick me up at seven, but that's three hours from now. My anxiety is running high as I open the door, not knowing what to expect. He hasn't called.

"Are you Dulce Webster?" a woman asks, surrounded by another women about my age and a man with green hair.

"Yes," I reply tentatively. "Who are you?"

"I'm Jermaine, and this is Tina and Britney. We are here to help you get ready for dinner. Hair, makeup, and..." He pauses, assessing me. "Don't worry. Mr. Keller said to take good care of you. You won't have to worry about a thing," he says animatedly.

"Mr. Keller gave us strict instructions." Jermaine speaks to the women like I'm not in the room, and I'm a doll they have to dress. "He said not to cut or dye her hair. He doesn't want to change her; he only wants to enhance her," he tells Tina and Britney, then turns to me with a smile.

I glance at Tina and notice the garment bag with a box I'm assuming are shoes. Ford thought things through when he asked me to come.

After checking in with Mary and the nurse Ford hired, I let them do their thing and glam me up. I've never been to a salon or had my nails professionally done, but a girl can get used to this. It's one night.

I just hope it doesn't turn out the way prom night did.

FORD

I knock on the door to Dulce's suite. I didn't want her in a separate room, but I have to take things slow after she told me what happened that night.

She probably has no idea, but I have security monitoring this floor. I'm not planning on sleeping here tonight. It's why I decided we have dinner in my penthouse suite so we can have more privacy. I want her all to myself.

When the door opens, my throat goes dry. She's wearing the black cocktail dress with a high slit. Her natural hair is silky straight, the way I like it. There is nothing I want to change about her, but I sent a glam team to pamper her. Her short nails are painted a red to match the red suede five-inch heels I don't plan on taking off.

I make it obvious I like what I see the way my eyes slide over her. Slowly. Deliberately undressing her.

"You look gorgeous, Dulce."

"You look nice too, Ford."

I give her my arm. "Shall we?"

She rubs her glossy lips together, and all I can think about is her mouth wrapped around me. "Just a sec." She walks back in the room and comes out with her phone and the designer evening bag I picked out. "I'm ready."

We take the elevator up to my floor. If she's nervous when we step into the penthouse suite, she doesn't show it. Her eyes take in the luxury of the room. It's more of an apartment with the marble floors and tall windows with the view of the city.

"Wow," she breathes. "Is this how you've been living since you left?"

I smile. "This is nothing but yes. This is my life. Hotel rooms in different cities, parties, and endless people."

"A far cry from Airy."

"I've done okay for myself, I think."

"Yes, you have," she says, looking out at the city lights. "Is there anything you regret?"

"I think everyone has regrets in some way or another. As for me, I have one. How about you? Any regrets about staying?"

"No," she says, but I can tell she isn't telling me the truth.

It would make perfect sense for her to want to leave town. It's obvious her grandmother is too sick to move anywhere else. Money is another issue.

"What about school? I know you had the grades. I'm sure you could have gotten into the best culinary school in the country. You still can."

She sighs. "That shipped sailed a long time ago. I don't regret staying. I hate Airy, but my grandmother is the only family I have left. I wouldn't trade her for some fancy culinary school when she has taught me everything she knows."

"What are your plans?"

She shrugs. "I don't know. I haven't thought about it yet."

She's leaving. I can see it in her eyes and the way her cheeks go red under her foundation. She plans to leave and not look back. That just won't do. I could never let her go.

There is a knock on the door. It's room service. The hotel staff wheels in a cart with champagne and a meal for two expertly selected. I wanted the best for her.

When they leave, I pull out her chair. Then I uncork the bottle of champagne and pour her a glass.

"How about you?" she asks when I take a seat across from her.

"Are you planning to settle down, or will you continue to live your life dangerously?"

I smile. "Both."

"Who's the lucky woman?"

"I think you know."

"Do I?"

"By the time the night is over, you'll leave here without any doubts."

"Real smooth."

I cut into my steak and give her a wink. "You should see me drive."

"I have, and you were great, by the way," she praises, taking a sip of her champagne.

Her approval strokes my ego. Being here with her and having dinner after a race feels normal. Like we have been doing this for years. There is no awkward conversation. She isn't giggling or texting on her phone, telling the world she is with me. I have her full attention, and fuck if she doesn't have mine.

I can't wait to have her.

After the table is cleared, I look at her champagne glass and notice it's half full.

"I'm not much of a drinker."

"It's not that. I'm making sure you're not tipsy."

"How come?" she asks innocently. "I noticed you haven't touched yours."

"Another first. I want to be of sound mind when I'm with you. It's been a while. I don't wake up..."

"In a hotel room with a random blonde," she finishes for me.

"You read up on me?"

"Only the juicy stuff."

I chuckle. "Oh, there's plenty of that, but I'm not interested in you to be part of that kind of story."

"I appreciate that. It's bad for business."

"Hm, that depends."

She raises a brow. "On?"

"How you're a part of it."

I want you so much.

"And how do you want me to be a part of it?" She angles her head, her silky straight hair sliding to the side.

She's flirting with me, and I like it. I like it a lot.

I look around the penthouse and then at her. "Well, you're the first to be invited to my room. I usually reserve a separate room."

"Like the one I'm in?"

"It wasn't for the same purpose. It was so you felt you had space to think. To choose."

"To have sex?" she says with a challenge in her voice.

"No. That's up to you."

She swallows, fingering the edge of her glass. "Do you want to have sex with me?"

"You know I do, but I would never force you. I would never make you feel uncomfortable."

She shifts in her seat, causing the slit from her dress to open, showing the skin of her thigh almost to her hip. She tries to pull the dress, but she would have to move her leg, and if she does, if she moves an inch, I'll see all of her.

I don't move an inch, holding my breath.

"Is this why you chose this dress for me to wear?"

My nostrils flare. I chose it so I can fuck her out of it, but also so she can feel beautiful. So she would never doubt that she isn't.

My eyes zero in on the spot. I relax in my chair. "What do you think?"

She moves her leg, and I get a perfect view of her pussy. I look up to see the challenge in her gaze. All the blood in my head rushes to my cock.

"I'm not sure what to think."

"That depends on what you want, Dulce."

"What do you want, Ford?"

"I think you have a good idea of what I want." I call her over with my finger. "Come here, beautiful."

She gets up and walks over, stopping between my legs. I look up when I cup her bare pussy. "Can I have you, Dulce?"

She licks her lips timidly. "Yes."

My fingers slowly slide between her folds. A whimper escapes her throat, and I have to adjust myself to keep from bending her over the table. "I'll go slow, and if you want me to stop, I'll stop. Understood?"

"Okay."

I get up, moving my hand between her legs. She sucks in a breath. I find the zip on the back. The dress gives way, pooling between us on the floor, leaving her naked before me in just the red heels. "Don't take your shoes off," I demand as my fingers slide deeper, feeling how wet she is. I want to drown in her. "Is this for me, Dulce?"

"Yes," she says breathlessly, her hair falling to the side like a curtain. Her nipples pebble over upthrust breasts. High and perfect.

"You're gorgeous, Dulce," I say hoarsely, pressing my face on her lower belly. Her skin familiar and sweet. "Don't ever think otherwise."

I'm struggling. If I take her the way I want, she'll be frightened. Her fingers slide through my hair like she is testing out the strands as I lick and suck, holding her by her hips. My tongue finds her slit.

"I liked your hair longer," she confesses.

"It's not practical when I have to wear a helmet."

"Oh..."

She is still nervous, and without much thought, I ask, "Have you ever been with someone, Dulce...like this?"

She shakes her head. "Not like—"

"I understand." I interrupt, not wanting to ruin the moment, but I had to ask.

It makes my blood burn at the implication of what that means. I have to make this good for her.

I push her back gently so I can get up and carry her bridal

style to the main bedroom. I place her on the mattress. She holds herself up on her elbows, watching me undo my dress shirt.

My cock is so hard in my pants, I'm not going to last.

"Place your feet on the edge of the bed and open your legs."

She hesitates. For a second, I think she might not do it and run, but she does it. I remove my pants, socks, and shoes, kicking them off to the side. Her eyes fall to my cock. It's hard, hot, and leaking. I fist myself as I step closer to the edge of the bed and stand between her thighs.

"Have you seen a man's cock before?" I clear my throat. "Like this?"

She shakes her head slowly, and her innocence pours off her, creating havoc within me.

Fuck me. She was a...when...I close my eyes, removing that thought. This is about her and what I want to give her. "Dulce?"

"Ford," she says softly.

My hand jerks my cock, hot and heavy. Her eyes are on me as I fuck myself.

"Spread your pussy lips, Dulce." She does, and it's like fireworks have gone off behind my eyes. I let out a groan as thick ropes of cum paint her pussy and lower belly. Her thighs tremble. "Show me how you play with yourself, baby. Play with my cum." Her eyes close, and her fingers rub her clit. It's so fucking hot watching her.

She arches her back, and I can't take it. I line up with her entrance, pushing her hand away. Her eyes snap open. The head of my cock full of cum rubs her slit.

"Ford," she gasps, but I don't stop.

The friction causes heat. Wet sounds.

"You want me inside you, Dulce?" She nods. "Open your pussy for me."

She spreads her lips, and I push.

Her eyes widen.

She's tight. Her lips grip the head of my cock like a vise. Like a fucking clamp, and it makes my pulse jackhammer. I ease into her bit by bit. It takes everything in me to keep from plunging into her and fucking her the way I want. Hard and unapologetically.

I bite the inside of my cheek, trying to hold back. Praying I can when she grinds her hips.

"I want more," she begs.

I close my eyes. "I'm trying to hold back. I don't want to hurt you. I never will."

"Please," she mewls, grinding her pussy with my cock halfway inside her. "Don't hold back. Not for me. You feel too good for it to hurt."

I grab her thighs and plunge the rest of the way, pumping into her savagely. I expected her to cry out and tell me to pull out and get the fuck off. I didn't expect the smile of pure pleasure that paints her lips. So I fuck her. I fuck her hard. Our skin slaps. Her red heels dig into my lower back as her tits bounce with each thrust.

"Fuck," I growl into her neck, nipping on her skin. "I'm going to fuck you, again...and again...until I'm all you think about.'"

"Yes, oh...God...yes," she cries out. "Ford, I'm going to come."

I can feel her pussy clenching. Her thighs shake. Sweat drips down my torso to where we are joined. My balls slap against her.

"Come," I demand, pressing my lips to hers. "Come all over my dick." She cries out.

I slide my hands under her ass, pressing into her deep as I come for the second time. So fucking deep. I wanted to make sure she never forgets this moment. The moment she became mine in every sense.

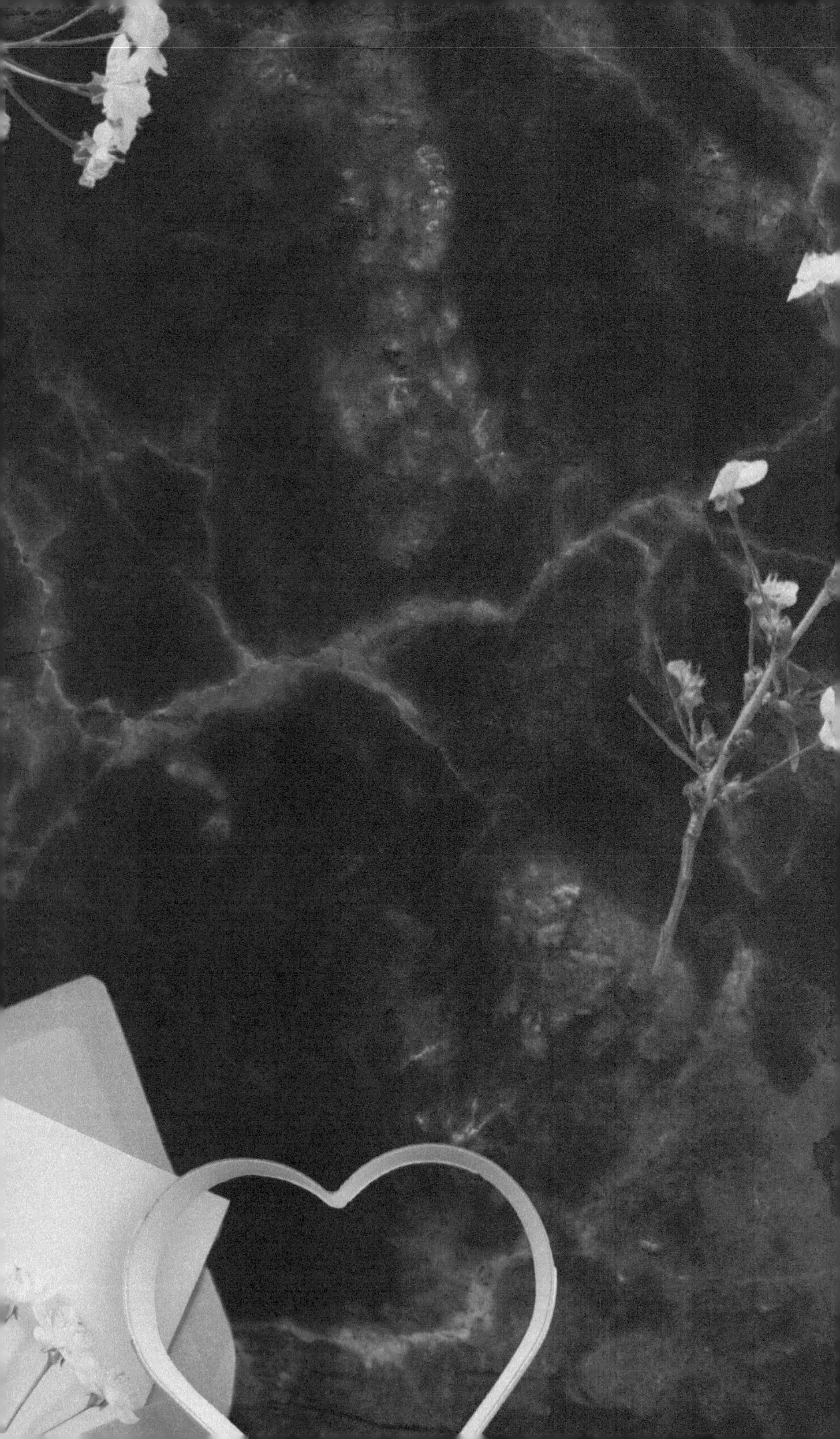

I wake up sore all over in the most delicious way. My skin tingles. Butterflies float low in my stomach. Worried about morning breath, I look over but find his side empty. The closet is open on the other side, and then there is a door that must be the bathroom.

I slide naked out from between the sheets and walk inside. There's a freestanding tub, like something out of a magazine. Smiling with anticipation, I turn on the water, checking the temperature as the tub fills. On the side table are sundries like a shower cap, face bar, body wash, and lotion. After opening a few and inhaling their delicious scents, I move over to the sink, where I find a toothbrush and paste to help me get rid of that morning breath.

When the tub is about halfway, I step inside and almost groan at how relaxing the water feels on my sore muscles. I lean back, closing my eyes for a few seconds.

My hand slides lower over my stomach until my fingers find my swollen clit. I wince and then sit up. Suddenly, I'm in my bathtub at home.

A scream clogs my throat. There is blood everywhere, but I feel no pain. I raise my arms and see the red rivulets of water drip over my skin. It smells like rust. The water in the tub is bright red and is slowly rising.

I stand, panic gripping my throat. No, no, no, no! Not again.

I run my hand over my stomach, and it's still flat. The swollen flesh I remember is long gone. *It's not there, Dulce. It died.*

What's happening? I look around, screaming Ford's name, but nothing comes out. I'm met with silence. I try again and nothing.

I reach between my legs. Surrounded by a glob of blood is a tiny baby. An alien creature with huge round eyes like a bee.

It blinks. "Mommy," it says in a little voice echoing in my head.

"Dulce!" Ford calls out.

My eyes pop open, and I take in a lungful of air, trying not to suffocate. I blink repeatedly and tuck my knees under my chin, shaking my head.

He's holding me in his strong arms. Safe. Comforting. Attentive. I look around, and I'm shaking on the bed.

"You were dreaming," he whispers.

I turn toward him, taking in his wide eyes. He's shirtless, and the light from the morning sun shines through the edge of the curtains.

It was a nightmare.

"I'm sorry," I choked out. My heart pounds inside my chest, hating that I ruined the most beautiful night.

"There is nothing to be sorry about," he says, gently caressing my cheek with the back of his fingers. What did you dream about?"

"I'm sorry. It's nothing. It happens sometimes," I lie. It happens all the time but admitting that to him would be opening the door to the past.

"How often does it happen?"

I shrug. "A few times a week. It's no big deal."

"If this happens that many times, I think you need to talk to someone."

I shake my head. "I can't."

"Why not?"

"Because doctors cost money."

I've googled my symptoms. It's some type of PTSD from trauma. Therapy is recommended, but that isn't an option. I don't have the money for a therapist, and the ones in town can't be trusted, but I don't tell him that.

There is a knock on the door.

He grabs a shirt and pants off the chair on the corner and gets dressed. He moves to his bag, digs inside, and hands me a T-shirt. "Here, put this on."

I pinch my brows. "Who is it?"

"I called my manager and told him to call the doctor assigned to my team to come check on you."

"Why?"

"The truth? I was scared when I heard you thrashing in the tub, and you wouldn't wake up. I didn't know what to do."

I should be mad at him, but he was worried. I can see the worry etched in his face. Only one person in this world worries about me, so it's nice that someone else does. I slide my legs down, place my feet on the plush carpet, take the T-shirt, and put it on.

When I'm done, he moves to the door and opens it.

A man in his late fifties walks in with a bag. "Hi, I'm Dr. Long," he says, shaking hands with Ford. "Derek said you needed me to see someone in your room."

"Yes," Ford says and gestures to me. "This is Dulce. She was in the bath having a nightmare, and I couldn't wake her. I didn't know what to do," Ford says helplessly. "She was screaming for me, but I couldn't get her to wake up,"

I feel my cheeks flush. I can't make eye contact with Ford. He gives me the best first time, and I screw it up by having a nightmare and freaking him out. I have the worst luck in all of humanity. I try to make myself look smaller by sinking my butt into the mattress.

Dr. Long asks me basic questions, and I answer until he gets to the more personal ones, like if I have any ongoing conditions he should know about. Been to the emergency room. I glance at Ford, sitting in the accent chair near the window.

Dr. Long pauses. He glances at Ford and then at me. "If you would prefer..."

"He can stay."

"Alright. I'll make this part quick. Last time you've seen a doctor? Are you on any medications? Do you suffer from panic attacks?"

I tear my gaze from Ford and look out the window at the bright blue sky. "The last time I saw a doctor was in the emergency room."

"For?"

It's like all the air is sucked out of the room. While the doctor enters information on his tablet, I feel Ford's gaze on me and hear him shift in his seat.

All the air leaves from my lungs. I haven't been asked that question since I was placed on birth control during the follow-up with my gynecologist to avoid getting pregnant.

Seconds tick by.

Ford's eyes are glued to my mouth. He's waiting for me to answer. So is Dr. Long, who's watching me with a raised brow. The glow from the tablet reflects off his reading spectacles.

"Miss Webster?"

My heart rate slows, and I let out a deep breath.

I clear my throat and cross my arms. "I had a miscarriage at home when I was in the shower. There was a lot of blood, and no one could drive me to the hospital. My grandmother's nurse called the ambulance, and I was treated at the ER. "

He nods, taking notes on his iPad. I can feel the heat of Ford's stare on the side of my face.

"How long ago was that?"

I look down at my hands. "Almost four years ago."

"Have you been diagnosed with PTSD or having panic attacks?"

I shake my head. "No."

"Medications or pills you take daily?"

"Just birth control," I reply, avoiding Ford's gaze.

The doctor's finger hovers over the screen. "Did the nightmares or panic attacks start after the miscarriage?"

"Something like that," I reply, feeling a heavy weight pressing down on my chest. It's not the only reason. My mind races, playing what happened over and over.

"I see," he says, but he doesn't see because that isn't the whole story.

Dr. Long places the tablet on the side table. He reaches inside his bag for his stethoscope and blood pressure cuff, then walks over to take my vitals.

I glance at Ford. His jaw is set. A hostile stare aimed at the wall. I'm wondering what is going through his head. Is he disgusted? Does he regret sleeping with me?

The sound of the Velcro as the blood pressure cuff comes off my arm pulls my attention back to Dr. Long.

"Have you seen a therapist or a doctor about the episodes?"

"No."

"Alright," Dr. Long says, "I'm going to give you a prescription for a medication to help you sleep. I sent the script to the nearest pharmacy. If you are interested in therapy sessions, I will leave a number of a good one with Ford. I recommend you call and make an appointment. Do you have any questions for me?"

"No, thank you."

He probably thinks I'm stupid for not getting help, but Chris's and Trent's lawyers warned me not to. They told me not to speak to anyone.

Ford gets up. "Is there anything you need from me?" he asks Dr. Long.

"No. I'm done here." Dr. Long turns to me, handing me his card. "Call my office. The appointments for refills can be done virtually."

"Thank you," I say gratefully.

Ford waits until Dr. Long leaves the room before facing me as he scrolls through his phone. "Your medication will be delivered shortly," he says like he didn't just hear another part of my fucked-up life. Like he doesn't see how I'm breaking inside.

He waits, watching me with an unreadable expression.

Tears clog my throat, making it impossible to speak. I know this changes everything between us. There is no way it couldn't. There must be a ton of questions running through his mind. I want to ask what he's thinking, but I'm afraid to hear the truth.

I lie in bed while he scrolls through his phone. His fingers fly across the screen, and we sit in silence. The tension in the air stretches like a rubber band.

When the sun rises across the horizon, there is a knock on the door.

Ford quickly gets up and opens the door. "I have a package for Dulce Webster," the man says.

"Yes," Ford replies. I hear the door close.

Ford walks to my side of the bed and hands me a small paper bag containing the medication the doctor prescribed with a bottle of water.

I take the medication, hoping we could talk before the medication kicks in to help me sleep. His phone rings, and the moment to talk vanishes as he walks into the bathroom to take the call. After fifteen minutes, my eyes start to get heavy. The last thing I remember is Ford saying hello behind the bathroom door.

I look out the window, watch people moving on with their lives while mine is constantly breaking at the seams as tears stream down my cheeks.

When I wake up six hours later, Ford is gone. There is no point in calling him. If he wanted to talk, he would have stayed. He would have called.

My hands tremble when I place the phone on my ear, listening to it ring. "Hey, what's wrong?" Katie asks in a worried tone.

I sniff and wipe my face. "Can you come and get me, Katie?"

"Oh, no…Let me guess, he left."

I nod like she can see me. "Yeah."

"You said he would."

Deep down, I knew there was no future. One night was all I would have with him.

"I did. It's what he does."

I hear her grab her keys in the background. "I'm walking out the door. Was it worth it?"

I glance at the rumpled white sheets and then at the red heels at the foot of the bed and smile. "Yeah, I finally know what it's like to forget and feel something for once."

"It's his loss, Dulce. You know that, right?"

"Yeah," I lie.

"I got the address to the hotel you sent me last night."

I look out the window at the tiny café. People walk in and out. Cars turn into the hotel. "I'll meet you across the street. There is a little café."

"I'll be there in a few hours."

"Thank you, and drive safe."

I walk over to the desk and grab the notepad and pen. I write him a note. I grab the red heels and dress, placing them neatly on the bed.

I close my eyes, and a memory of last night comes rushing back. My eyes lift when he finally pushes inside me. I see myself in the reflection of his gaze. He doesn't move for a fraction of a second, and at that moment I'm his, and he's mine. One fleeting moment when all is forgotten, and there is nothing but us in the room. There is no past. No future. Just the moment when we fit perfectly for the first time even though I knew it would never happen again. Not with him. Not for a girl like me.

I place the note on top of the black dress where he can see it.

I'm sorry about last night. I should've never stayed.
Dulce

DULCE

"So how did it go?" my grandmother asks. Katie dropped me off after I told her what happened, leaving out the part of the miscarriage. I keep telling myself it's for the best. The sun hadn't come up and it was already over.

"It was perfect. I have more orders than Katie and I can handle," I tell her with a smile. "I can finally get a van for deliveries."

"That's great," she says and then coughs up blood. My heart sinks. "I'm sorry." She folds the napkin, hiding the truth. "It's nothing."

"It's...something, Grandma." She gives me a wan smile like she isn't bleeding from the inside the way my heart is bleeding out as I lose her.

I STAYED UP WITH HER UNTIL MY EYES COULDN'T STAY open. We talked. I laughed. We cried. More blood came up from her lungs. I cuddled next to her, holding her hand like a child with its mother.

She was the only person I had, and she was leaving me.

"He'll be good for you, Dulce," she says weakly. "I know it. Ford...he'll take care of you."

I sniff.

"Yes, Grandma," I say in a small voice. "I love you so much."

"And I love you, Dulce. You go live your dream, baby girl. You don't have to worry about me anymore."

Her life was slipping through my fingers, and all I could do was hold on.

"Don't go," I whisper. "Please... don't leave me." I close my eyes as hot tears run down my cheeks.

Mary walks in at six o'clock the following morning. I don't realize I've been talking to my grandma for so long, holding her hand frozen in place. Holding on to the last moment. The last time she took a breath.

"I made the call," Mary says. "They should be here any minute."

The monitors begin to go off. Her O2 starts dropping, and I know this is the last time I'll hear my grandmother speak. Hear her last breath.

"I love you, Grandma." I bury my nose in her shirt. "You rest now with Mom and Dad."

The ambulance came ten minutes later.

While she died in my arms, I don't regret any of the lies I told her.

She passes on peacefully, with no worries about me, and that's all I wanted. She's held on for me for so long, and it's time for her to go.

"Time of death, seven twenty-three a.m.," the Mary says.

I hear the gurney as they wheel her out with a white sheet covering her body.

I turn around, not wanting that to be the last image of her. Mary squeezes my hand. "I'm so sorry, Dulce."

I nod, but my heart is breaking.

"She was a wonderful lady."

I try to speak past the lump of grief in my throat. "She was.

I'm going to miss her so much." I look at her through a blur of tears. "Thank you, Mary. For everything."

"It's not every day I get to spend time and take care of my best friend. Thank you for welcoming me into your home and giving me the best years with her. Do you need anything?" Mary asks.

My grandmother wanted to be cremated. She didn't want to be worm food. She wanted her resting place to be in an urn next to my parents.

"No. I'm going to get some sleep."

She nods. "I'll call Katie and tell her."

"Thank you."

I HEAR LOUD BANGING COMING FROM THE FRONT DOOR. "Dulce!"

Hearing Katie's voice, I look at my phone on my grandmother's nightstand and see that it's dead.

I drag my feet, rubbing sleep from my eyes as I open the door.

"Whoa!" Katie says in surprise, rushing inside. "Shit, I don't know what to say because anything I can say won't change it, but you look like shit."

I turn around, not caring that I look like shit but knowing she is just trying to cheer me up.

She shuts the door. "When's the last time you took a shower?" she asks cautiously.

I don't remember. I crawl into my grandmother's bed, where I've slept since they took her three days ago.

"I don't know."

She points at my phone with the black screen. "Are you planning on charging that?"

"No."

She sits on the edge while I lie on my side, staring mindlessly at the wall.

"Do you want me to pick you up something to eat?"

I shake my head. "No."

"You have to eat," she says quietly.

I shrug.

"The bakery needs you. I tried to make the cakes, but they suck. I mean, they taste okay, I guess, but it's not the same." I remain quiet, and she continues, "Ford called this morning. He said he wanted to talk to you and that you were not answering your phone. I hope it's okay that I told him. He said he was coming. He had to get track time or whatever that means, but he's coming."

I sigh. "I don't care."

When you have no one left, you kind of stop caring.

"Trust me, I wanted to tell him where to stick it, but I figured you wanted to do the honors."

"I don't want to see him, Katie. If he comes, I won't answer. I plan to change my number."

"That bad?"

"It's not like I have a big contact list," I mutter.

Sad but true. I only had her number, Mary, Danny, Ford, and my grandmother. That list has gotten smaller. It's only Katie and Mary.

When I leave Airy, it will be none. Katie and Mary will have moved on, leaving me with no one to call. No one to come home to. No one to listen.

I have to move on now that I've sorted my grandmother's remains. It was pointless to hold a service. It wasn't like many people visited her.

"Is everything set up?" I drop the car in third, the Lamborghini roaring down the street.

"Are you going to tell me what's going on?" Trent says.

"Answer the question," I grit.

"Yeah, it's a party."

"Good."

"Do you think this is a good idea, Ford?"

I can't think of anything better.

My phone beeps from an incoming call. I pull the phone away from my ear and see Derek's name flashing on the screen.

"I have to call you back," I tell Trent and press the green button.

"Oh, thank God," Dereck says, relief pouring from his voice. "Ford, I know you hired me, and I'm pushing the limit right now, but...are you out of your goddamn mind? You have to be in Italy in four hours."

I thought I would be able to take this race, but I never thought coming back to see her she would need me.

"I'm not going. I have to take care of something first."

"Like you did when you walked out on that poor girl. Don't think I didn't notice."

"I know it was fucked move on my part, but I have my reasons, and it has everything to do with her. Trust me, she's important to me, Derek. That part isn't a lie. I thought opening a racing shop back here was what I wanted, but it's not. That was a pipe dream when I was a teenager."

He sighs. "Look, I don't mean to be a dick, but ever since you went back to your hometown, everything has been falling to shit. Now, what is it about this girl?"

"She's mine," I growl, gripping the steering wheel and shifting into fourth.

"Then why the fuck did you leave her there in the penthouse?" he asks cuttingly. "She had a nightmare, for God's sake."

All I can think about is killing someone for what they did to her. The moment the words miscarriage left her lips, I felt like grabbing the tablet from Dr. Long's hands and breaking it into pieces so he wouldn't enter it in her file.

Then regret burned like hot coals for leaving her in Airy and not taking her with me, but I couldn't. I had a problem I couldn't subject her to. There was no fixing my obsession with her. There wasn't a magic pill that would make me forget her. She was engraved in my head.

The only option four years ago was to leave. It was a mistake. Not leaving, but not taking her with me.

I walked out of the hotel room because I was ashamed. I couldn't look at her and tell her it was going to be alright because how could I? It wasn't alright. She was suffering, and I couldn't do anything to take her pain away. All I could do was avenge her, and I didn't want her to see it in my eyes. I didn't want her to see what I was capable of, or for her to tell me to stop. Because the truth was, I would never stop. Not for her.

"Her grandmother just died."

"Oh...Jesus. That girl has some luck, huh?"

"Be careful, Derek," I warn.

He says it like she is bad luck. Race car drivers are superstitious but not me. I'm the best at what I do, and she isn't bad luck. She just needed me.

"I'm sorry. I didn't mean it that way."

"Since I have you on the phone and you're going to call me in a few hours anyway, I'm on my way now to her. I can't be in Italy. Make an announcement to the media that there is a death in the family, and I'm needed back home."

"You do know she isn't your family, right?" he points out.

"She will be very soon."

He lets out a frustrated sigh. "Fine. I'll do it. Are you sure you can't make it to the race?"

I roll my eyes. "I gotta go."

I hang up and take the car out of sport shift mode and stop at a red light near Main Street with a perfect view of the bakery.

I left her sleeping on the bed. She needed rest, and I was too busy planning. The less she is involved, the better. Frightening her away would do me no good. I admit I was angry. Not with her but of what she went through. At that moment, I wanted to take her with me and never bring her back, but I knew that would be impossible. She had her grandmother to look after, but now, she is going to need me more than ever.

After I left the hotel room, I dealt with my anger the only way I knew how—on the track. I was a madman behind the wheel, wanting to destroy and kill everyone responsible, but it wasn't that simple. I had to plan before coming back to Airy.

I grip the steering wheel to keep them from turning the wheel around and going to her. The note she left me imprinted on my mind like the tattoos on my skin. Permanent. Unable to wash off.

I turn left and head to the church.

I find a spot in the back, where I told Trent to leave the rented Toyota Camry. It's inconspicuous and blends in. No one would look for me in it.

I get out and walk into the small church weathered with age. The grass is slightly burnt near the pathway.

The handle to the entrance is rusted with age. The heavy door is darkened by years of sunlight and use. There is a loud click when I open the door, followed by a loud creak.

A breeze floats through the air before the door shuts behind me with a loud clank. The air is stuffy, with a strong smell of incense and flowers. There is no air-conditioning.

"Can I help you?" a man's voice says with a gravelly undertone. I turn and find the priest dabbing his weathered face with a napkin, giving me a once-over.

"I would like to pray for someone who just passed away," I reply.

He nods and motions me over. He opens the Bible, and I follow him in prayer.

Looking up at the man himself nailed to the cross, I silently repent for the things I've done. I ask for forgiveness.

When I'm done, I silently pray for Dulce. For what she went through alone. I ask Him to give me life so I can make hers better.

I walk out sweating profusely, not feeling better, but like a sinner begging for forgiveness and not finding any.

I don't think there is a God who would forgive me for what I plan to do. After leaving her in the hotel room, it all clicked into place. I knew who it was. I knew who did it. He may have fooled everyone else, but I saw it when I left his house that night. Not even the drugs could take what he had done to her from his eyes.

It was Chris.

I drive back to the bakery, hoping to catch Dulce. She hasn't answered any of my calls, and I can't say I blame her.

I don't deserve her. I don't deserve my fame or fortune while hers was full of struggle, nightmares, and death.

I walk into the bakery, taking a deep breath at the familiar smell of her delicious cookies. I can smell the oatmeal and hint of cinnamon.

I catch Katie at the register. When she senses me standing at the counter, she looks up and rolls her eyes.

"Is she here?" I ask softly, sliding my hands inside the front pockets of my jeans.

"She doesn't want to see you," she says with an edge to her voice.

"Look, I'm not the bad guy. I know whatever it is she might

have told you looks bad, but I'm not the bad guy." I close my eyes briefly. I'm struggling to stay calm and not barge into the kitchen and frighten her. "I really need to speak to her."

She swallows hard. "I need to tell you something." She looks at the camera, at me, then pulls out her phone, and I watch her fingers fly across the keyboard.

My phone buzzes in my pocket. I open the text and look at the picture.

It shows three dead rats in front of what I recognize as the bakery's back door.

"WHICH RAT WILL WIN THE RACE?" is written in red on the white concrete before the step. It looks like blood.

"When was this?" I ask, anger surging like a tidal wave. I'm surprised the screen doesn't crack under my grip.

"Two days ago," she replies.

"Has anything like this happened before?"

Her lips flatten as she shakes her head nervously. "No."

I can tell she's lying, and there's more. She types on her phone and looks up.

A message goes through, and my nose flares in anger. My blood boils when I see a dead rat on the kitchen prep table with a sinister message written in the same fashion. Her needing a new table starts to make sense.

"I'm sorry," she says, "for lying."

"I'm not mad at you, Katie. You didn't do this to her. Just be there for her, alright?"

She nods. "I will."

I pocket my phone. "Thank you for telling me. If you hear or see anything else, let me know. Day or night."

I need Katie on my side, but Dulce needs a friend right now, and Katie isn't a bad person. She just hangs around bad people.

Trent told me about her. How he knows her from the next town over with a bad rep. I didn't push, but I know there is something there. I could sense it that day between them in the garage. Hate, resentment, sexual frustration. Feelings I know all too well.

She nods, but I can see the guilt in her expression. She feels torn that she is betraying Dulce by telling me things without consulting with her first. Dulce probably told her not to tell me about the rat and the messages.

"Is she in the kitchen?" I ask, determined to talk to Dulce. "Don't worry, I'll tell her I forced my way in."

"She's heartbroken," she says softly. "She needs you right now, Ford. She needs someone. I'm not sure what is going on between you two, but she is hurt that you left her."

"I'm here, and I'm not going anywhere without her," I assure her before walking around the front counter.

I push the door to the kitchen, and I catch Dulce's wide-eyed gaze when she spots me with her hand wrapped around a whisk. Her other holds a large mixing bowl. Her eyes have dark circles and are puffy, like she's been crying.

"Hey," I say delicately. "How are you doing?"

"How do you think?" she says sarcastically.

"I've been worried."

"I bet," she says, anger vibrating in her voice whisking away, the metal making a squishing noise. "What do you want, Ford?"

"I want you."

She snorts. "I bet you do," she says and then lets out a frustrating sigh. "If you came to pay your respects. Thank you. She was very fond of you; I appreciate you keeping your word. She died thinking you took me to prom, and I had a great time."

"Is that what you think I'm worried about?" I say slowly. "You think I don't care what you must be feeling right now?"

"I wouldn't know what you care about. I'm kind of confused with your motives, but your actions are clear, and I'm no different from the women you screw in a separate hotel room and leave without a backward glance come morning?"

"That's not..."

She raises her brows. "True? I guess the tabloids made it up, and those pictures posted online are fabricated, and all those women are liars."

"Not with you."

"Oh…that's right. I didn't make it to morning. I'm not that lucky. I don't get an answer from a simple text either."

"Dulce?"

She drops the whisk, splashing batter on the table. "What?"

"That's not why I left."

She averts her gaze, blinking back tears. "I know why you left, and I don't blame you." Her voice cracks on the last part.

"That's not why," I admit. "I would never judge you."

Tears run down her beautiful face. "What was it, then?" she croaks. Regret?"

"Never. I could never regret you, Dulce. I'm here. For you. I didn't leave because I don't want you. I left because I had to do something."

I close the distance, causing her to face me.

"We would never work," she says, fighting a sob that wants to escape. "I'm not like those women."

I whisper in her ear, "I don't want you to be, Dulce. Trust me, I like the way you are just fine." I cup her face gently in my hands so she can look into my eyes. "I'm here because I'm ready to make it work, Dulce. I'm here because I want you the way you are. Broken, beautiful, and all mine."

She laughs, and I'm not sure if she is crying or not. She sniffs, looking up at the ceiling. "You should be dating a model. Married to someone famous. Have gorgeous kids with. A wedding in Italy, for God's sake."

I press my lips on her forehead. "I want all those things but not with a model or someone famous. I want that with you." I dip my finger in the bowl and scoop up some batter, then suck it off my finger. "I like my future wife's cookies. Always have. Her cakes." I dip for some more, spreading it on her lips, and bend my head so my tongue can lick it off. "The way she tastes. So sweet like sugar."

Her tongue licks mine, and she lets out a small whimper.

"Her babies that look like both of us vacationing in our villa in Italy. Replacing bad memories with the ones with us. If she has a nightmare, I'm there holding her, whispering in her ear that I will fight for her. Every fucking day if she'll let me."

"You're crazy."

I smile, taking her wrists and feeling her pulse points. "Besides, I made a promise to an old woman on her deathbed when she looked at me like I was the sun because I put a smile on her granddaughter's face. I promised her that I would love her granddaughter, and I do. I fucking love you more than anything in my life. Call it an obsession. Call it whatever you want, but I loved you the moment I smelled your skin for the first time. Tasted what you made with your hands. I fell in love with every part of you, and I'll do anything to make it right. I know more than you think, Dulce. But the truth is...I came back for you."

"That doesn't make sense. You've been gone for four years."

"It does if you let it. If you can remember the little things from the past."

"Remember what?" she says, confused.

"Let's just say you weren't crazy if you ever thought I wasn't watching you when we were in school."

Katie walks in and looks back and forth between us. "Are you two good now?"

"I'm not going to kidnap her?" I say sarcastically.

"I said I was going to look out for her and that meant from you too," she confesses.

I knew she would tell her sooner or later.

Dulce glances at Katie. "What are you talking about, Katie?"

"He told me to watch over you," Katie admits. "Basically, call him to tell him where you were and what you were doing at all times of the day," Katie confesses. "Everything I told you was true about my past except who my ex-boyfriend was. It was Trent. Trent's the asshole who broke my heart. He cheated on me with Summer. When Ford wanted to make sure you were okay, he knew I hated Trent and asked me for a favor after that day in the garage when you took me with you to see Trent."

I pull out the wrapper she gave me that day four years ago from my back pocket. Dulce gasps when she sees it covering her mouth.

"I've always kept it," I profess, looking at it. "It's my good luck charm. I never race without it."

"Is that why you ordered the cookies every week since then?" Dulce asks curiously, staring at the paper. "Under a company name."

"That's part of it."

You're my sweet obsession, and I don't plan on letting go. Ever.

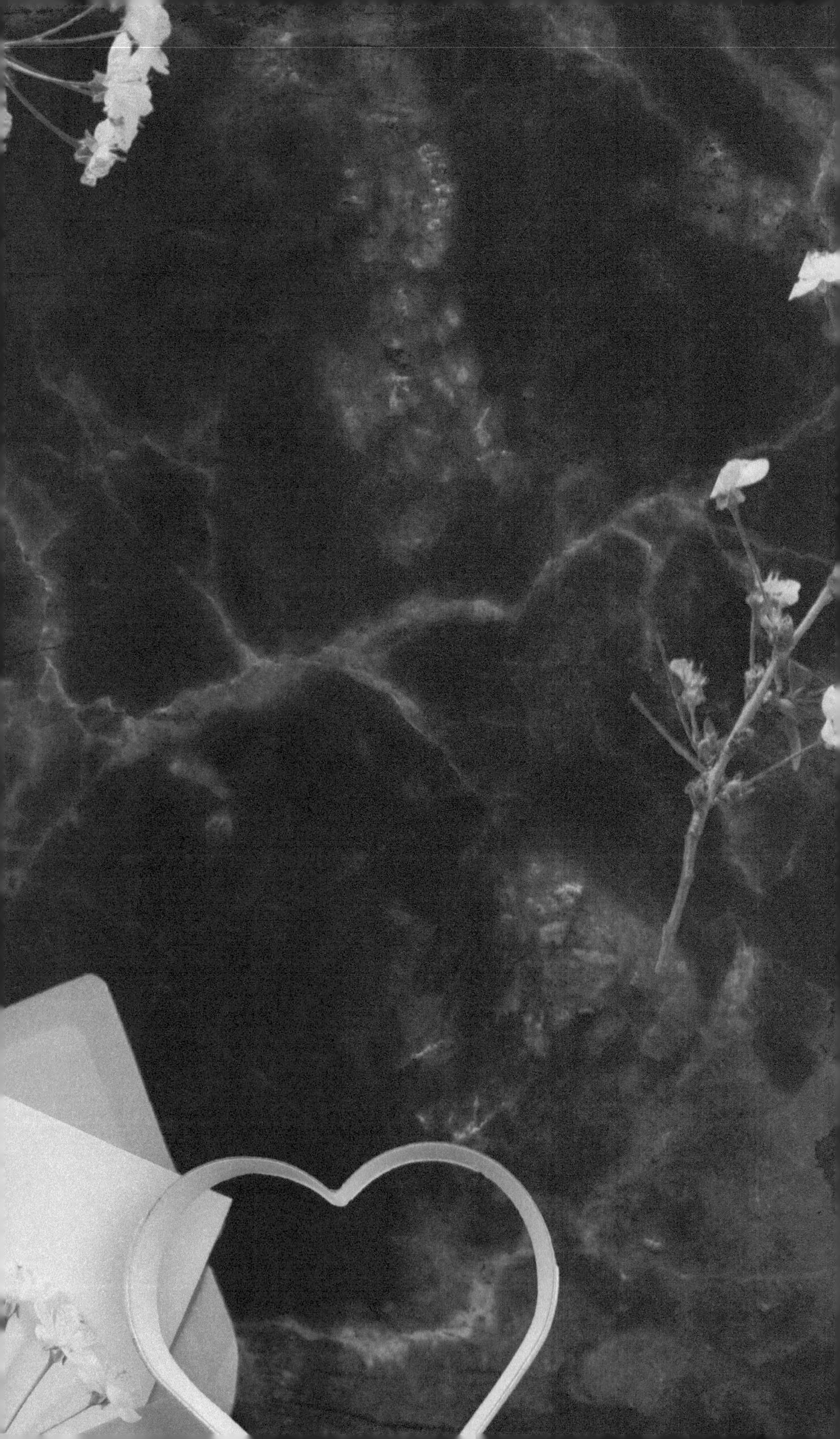

Flashes of his face go off behind my eyes like a camera snapping pictures. White light. Hot breaths. His hair through my fingers. Heat between my thighs. Moans. His voice.

"You're perfect."

It's what he said to me the night in the hotel before it turned into a nightmare when I took a bath in the infinity tub.

I back away. "Ford?"

"Yeah?"

"The other night...."

"I'll be out front," Katie says, taking it as her cue to leave the kitchen.

"When we had sex," I finish for her after the door swings shut. "We didn't use a condom."

The thought that we didn't takes root. We didn't use protection. We didn't even discuss it. It's not like I have to worry since I'm on birth control, but I don't remember taking it the night my grandmother died.

"I'm aware."

Dread takes root in how he will react when I tell him. My stomach clenches, voicing what I don't want to admit. "I'm on birth control, but the night my grandmother..."

"What?" He looks at me, perplexed.

"I forgot to take it." I look away, ashamed of how stupid I am for being irresponsible. "It doesn't mean…"

"It's okay." He pulls me close. "We'll deal with it. I'll take care of you if you are."

I look up and meet his sexy blue gaze. "Who are you, Ford Keller?"

"The boy from high school who was secretly in love with a girl he didn't think he deserved."

"I've been in love with you since I was a teenager," I confess.

"I believe that, but I knew if I stayed all those years ago, my parents…It would have been impossible."

"I understand."

He's right. There was no way we could have been together. It would have been us against the whole town, but now he is different. Older.

"When I heard you were still here, I knew the reason. I knew your grandmother was alive. Selfishly, I hoped no one swept you off your feet, and I was too late, but I never knew what happened or what they did. I would have come back."

"Why did you leave the other night?" I ask, searching his gaze for the truth.

"Because I had to know who hurt you," he says honestly. "Because I was angry that they think they got away with it." He caresses my lips with the tips of his fingers. "I'm not going to stop until I do, but I need you to trust me."

"What do you need from me?" I ask darkly. "How do you plan on finding out the truth?"

"I was kind of hoping you could help me out with that."

I swallow. "You want me to try to remember."

"It could be a smell. A trigger."

"You know," I say, pulling away and continuing to mix the batter. "I think you're right."

"About?" he asks, leaning on the prep table.

"The triggers. I knew it wasn't old man Moody because I didn't get flashbacks. Granted, I was scared. Terrified. Disgusted.

But the memories didn't come. They come in like flashes of a camera going off. Nightmares. Dreams."

"Tell me."

I look up, hoping he would find out. I want more than anything to catch the son of a bitch who ruined my life. "Can you take me out to the woods?" I pause and lick my lips, hoping he will say yes. "Where it happened?"

"Are you sure?" he asks, and I see the determined look in his gaze. He would.

"Now that you're here, yes. I'm sure. I want to try. I want to know. And then, I want to leave Airy for good."

AFTER I FINISHED CATCHING UP ON ORDERS AND THE cakes Katie attempted to bake but looked like they belonged in a bad episode of Gordon Ramsey, Ford drives me home and tells me about the rats Katie found this morning before I arrived.

"You think whoever is behind it knows I'm with you," I ask.

"Whoever it is, lives in Airy and never left," he says like he's positive.

"That narrows it down."

When I unlock the door to my house, I blink back the tears when the silence reaches me mixed with the smell of damp wood and my grandmother's powder. The antiseptic smell is gone. The beeping from the machines silent.

The medical supply company took everything the next day like it didn't matter someone died using it until their last breath was taken.

"She was a wonderful lady," Ford says, picking up a photo of her when she was better. "She loved you."

"She was my mother and father since I was ten years old."

He places the small picture frame back on the table. "Do you remember them? Your parents."

"I try, but as time passes, you start to forget. My mother's scent. My father's cologne. The sound of their voices. Their laughter. It fades piece by piece. Sometimes I have to look at a picture to remember exactly what they looked like."

"I'm sorry," he says, picking up the prom night picture. "I wanted to ask; do you still have this dress?"

I shake my head. "I woke up naked. My clothes were missing."

"All of them."

"Yeah. Why?"

"I wanted you to wear it for me one day so I can take a new picture."

"You could keep it." He looks at me, confused. "The picture. You can have it."

"I think I will. It was for me you dressed up for, and I wish more than anything to have been the one to pick you up."

"Then none of it would have happened."

"That and I would have told our kid the night I took their mother to prom."

"My grandmother was right about you."

"She wanted me to remind you to tell our family stories." I pinch my brows. "I had a long conversation with the woman who raised you. I made her a promise, and I intend to keep it."

"What promise is that?"

"Meet me in your bedroom and find out."

A blush rushes my cheeks. Memories flash like a movie. My back arched, him behind me wrapping his hand around my long hair, taking me from behind while his hand muffles my moans over my mouth. The delicious burn between my thighs as he thrust inside me.

"You're remembering."

"Huh?"

I close my eyes, listening to his words. "When I fucked you on your twin bed muffling your screams while you choked my cock." I can feel his breath against the back of my neck. "Was it good the other night or the first, Dulce?"

"Why don't you remind me?"

He chuckles. "There it is. That mouth I like so much. The way it surprised me that day in your bedroom when you wanted me to fuck you. One night when I would have given you more."

I arch my neck, resting the back of my head against his chest. "What are you waiting for, Ford?"

His hands rub over my hard nipples, fumbling with the buttons holding my uniform together. He pulls, and the buttons pop off, hitting the wall, the rest bouncing off the floor. He turns me around and pushes me against the wall near the staircase. His eyes fall on my thin bra, then lower to my white panties, where my thighs are squeezed together.

He pulls himself out of his jeans, stroking his cock like an exhibitionist. "Is that for me?" I ask playfully.

He presses the head of his cock over the wet spot on my panties. "This is always for you."

I'm on fire. My clit is pulsing against his hard cock. I grind my hips, and he groans, pulling my panties. I hear the tear before he rips them off. He picks me up, and my legs wrap around his hips.

"I missed you," he says right before he slides inside and fucks me against the wall. His eyes never leave mine as he thrusts repeatedly hard and fast. His mouth falls to the crook of my neck. I raise my hands above my head and hold the wood rails from the stairs.

"More," I moan, loving the way he feels inside.

He licks the skin on my neck and lips. "So sweet."

My climax builds fast as he goes harder. I gasp when I'm about to come.

"Ford."

"You're close, Dulce. Don't wait for me. Come."

My insides clench when I can't hold it anymore. I scream when I come. The sweat drips down the middle of my back. My hands, slick with sweat, almost slip off the wood.

I can feel that he is close because he doesn't stop. Sweat drips down the side of his face and his neck.

His eyes grip me, holding me in their depths. My gut tells me this was all planned—All of it. Him here at the right time isn't a coincidence.

"Marry me," he says, with his cock still inside me.

"Are you proposing to me?"

"Yes. I am."

I'm stunned. I stare into his blue eyes, trying to figure out if this is real or some kind of joke. Ford proposing to me is the last thing I expected while having sex. He's still inside me, and I don't know what to say or what to do.

He finally pulls out of me, and then, everything happens so fast. He puts himself away and picks me up, taking me to my room and placing me on my bed.

He turns around, giving me his back, and I sit half naked, stunned, trying to process everything.

I lean to the side, trying to see his face. "Ford?"

"Um, can you give me a minute," he says, digging in his pocket.

"Okay," I say, trying to cover myself.

When he finally turns around, he goes down on one knee with the most gorgeous engagement ring set in a black velvet box. The solitaire is big and looks expensive.

"I know it's too soon, and you might think I'm crazy, but I am. I'm crazy about you, and I know we don't know each other like we should, but we can. We have the rest of our lives to do that, but I was thinking...I was hoping." He looks into my eyes, holding the box up like an offering, and continues, "That you would say yes, and we could do that as husband and wife. There is no reason I can think of to wait. I think you've waited for the right person to come along, and I'm that person, Dulce. I'm right here, and I want to give you everything you have ever dreamed of."

My heart beats so fast I don't think I can find my voice. Ford is both my dream and my past wrapped into one.

I look at the diamond shining like a beacon under the warm light of my bedroom. How many times have I dreamed of him in this very room hoping one day he would know I existed?

"I promise to love you and protect you. And I don't care if you fall pregnant. It would make me happy if you did. As long as you're happy."

I lift my hand and place my finger over the large emerald diamond. "It's beautiful," I whisper with tears in my eyes.

"I asked a special lady one night if an emerald diamond was the best, and she told me it symbolized true love."

He's talking about my grandmother. She is the only person I know who had an engagement ring that was an emerald.

A tear slides down my cheek. "Yes," I whisper.

He leans his head slightly like he can't hear me. "What? What was that?"

I laugh. "Yes, I'll marry you."

He plucks it from the box and slowly slides the diamond ring on my finger. "It's perfect."

"How did you know my size?" I ask, looking at the way the diamond sparkles.

"This lady I know made sure I got it right."

My bottom lip trembles, remembering what she said. Ford will take care of me. She waited all this time because, for whatever reason, she knew he would come back.

"Are you ready?" he asks.

We were supposed to go to the woods before it got dark. I almost forgot.

I nod. "Yeah, let me take a quick shower."

I grab the bag with flashlights, battery packs, and two long sweaters from the trunk.

"Are you sure we shouldn't do this in the morning?" Dulce asks, looking at the sun as it sets.

"I think if you are closer to the time of day it happened, it would trigger a memory," I tell her, pointing at the tree line.

She looks down the road. "Remembering the rocks digging under the pads of my bare feet. The stinging pain..." She closes her eyes like she is in pain.

There is nothing I want more than to take it away.

"Danny found me right about here." She points at the middle of the road and then looks to the right by the embankment, where it isn't as steep. I always wondered why he was driving down this road."

"I don't think it was fate or luck," I tell her.

"You think he was part of it? That he was involved somehow?"

"They never caught the bastard, and he is a cop. He made it seem like he was your hero. Checking up on you for the last four years."

"You have a point."

I hand her a flashlight and one of the batteries for her phone.

"Here. So you don't get lost or lose power on your phone." I look over at the tree line. "Where do you think it happened?"

She walks toward the embankment, and before I can stop her, she slides down, thankful she is wearing jeans. "I think it was here. Well, where I ran from." She looks back up and then to her left deeper in the woods."

I slide down the same way she did and walk ahead. Letting her follow. "Here?"

She looks around like she is trying to find a clue or anything that she can remember. She steps forward, and I give her a minute because she needs this. Closure.

"Take your time," I assure her softly.

She turns her head and then nods. I wait and watch her, her Vans crunching over the thick brown leaves with every step. Every so often, she looks back as if she is measuring the distance from the road to where it happened.

She takes about ten steps and then stops. Looks at the trees, then at the road, and back.

"I think it was here." She closes her eyes and continues, "I heard screaming. Like something was being attacked and it was being mutilated... it was dark, and I was stupid for running in the woods instead of following the road, but I turned after they left and thought I saw someone following me."

"Who?" I ask, holding on to her every word, trying to keep calm even though my heart is beating hard inside my chest.

As much as I want her to have closure, I want to finish this.

"I don't know. I thought it was my mind playing tricks on me because it was dark. I was alone and scared. I was so scared, Ford. There was someone, and he was following me. They knew I would be out here. They knew. There is no one for miles. I have driven down this road and except for Moody's cabin, there is no one."

She looks around, and I lean on a tree, watching her.

A breeze causes the leaves to move. A twig snaps, and Dulce jolts. "I'm right here," I assure her.

She wraps her hands around herself, and I want to go to her, but this needs to play out. My phone goes off in my pocket from an incoming text.

> Trent: It's all set in place. I see her.

I pocket my phone before she turns around.

The sky is bathed in twilight. Her eyes stare at the ground when the screams start.

She jolts, and I come up behind, pulling her to my chest. "What was that?" She muffles against my chest.

Silence, and then a man screams louder like he's in pain.

"HELP! HELP! OH GOD!"

Dulce grips my shirt. "Ford?" she cries out.

I stare at her, not moving an inch. Our gazes lock, and I can see the confusion swirling in her eyes.

"Ford, what is going on?"

"Do you trust me?" I ask softly.

Her eyes go wide. She looks scared shitless.

"Do you?" I ask a little louder.

She nods. "Yeah, but..."

Another piercing scream. She grips tighter.

"It's okay," I soothe, rubbing her back.

"How. Who's out there screaming?"

"Who do you think?" I tell her, removing her hand from my shirt and walking deeper in the woods, following the markers I left behind.

"Where are you going?" she asks frantically.

"To find out who's screaming?" I say calmly. "Don't you want to know who it is?"

"But..."

I raise a brow. "I'm here. Nothing is going to happen. You can call Officer Mays." I smile. "I'm sure he would come."

She glances at her phone and then looks up. "There's no signal."

"Out here, no."

"Ford, you're scaring me," she says in a shaky voice.

Another pathetic scream.

"I think someone is terrified." I nudge my chin for her to follow. "Let's go investigate."

She follows me for ten minutes until it's dark, and we have no choice but to turn on the flashlights. This wouldn't have worked during the day.

The scream gets louder until we reach the source all dressed in white, hanging from a tree by his pathetic limbs.

"Oh my God?" She looks left and right and then lets out a piercing scream when Trent comes out from behind a tree. "You scared me. What the hell?"

"Sorry," Trent says apologetically.

Dulce looks up. "Why is he up there?"

"I think you should ask him that yourself, Dulce?" I reply.

Chris kicks out his legs like that is going to get him out of the shit he is in.

"It hurts," he cries out in pain.

"It should; your guts are hanging out. I'm sure the drugs in your system have worn off by now."

"I think I'm going to throw up," Dulce says, placing her hands above her knees.

"He's ugly, isn't he?" Trent says with a smile.

"Nice handiwork," I praise. "I couldn't have done better myself."

He's naked like he left her with his intestines hanging out. His face smashed on, and his cock half off.

"It was him?" she asks and then closes her eyes.

"You son of a bitch. I'll kill you, Ford," he says, gurgling on the blood pouring from his mouth.

"I think you would have to get down first, and I don't see that happening. Why don't you start by telling her the truth? Start there."

"It was... me," he admits, "I did it. I did it. Christ," he moans. "It hurts."

Dulce runs behind a tree to throw up. I walk over and hold her hair out of her face as she retches.

"There he goes," Chris says between gasps, "we all knew she was your crazy obsession..." He gurgles. "But I had to know...I had to know how good her pussy was and damn..." He gurgles, coughs, and continues while Dulce throws up, "It was good."

"Shut the fuck up, Chris," Trent growls. "How long, Ford?"

"Until he gets here," I reply.

Dulce takes a breath. "Who?"

Footsteps approach. We turn our heads.

"Well, well. The plot thickens," Trent says in a surprised tone.

"What the hell is going on?" Officer Dickhead says, looking at Dulce and Chris hanging from the tree. "What the fuck?"

"Danny," Chris says, "you see... they are my friends."

"What's going on?" Dulce says, perplexed.

I shine the flashlight on Mays and then on Chris, "Tell her," I demand.

Mays pulls out his .9 mm and aims it directly at Chris.

"What are you doing, Danny?" Dulce says, looking between Mays and Chris.

"Yeah, what are you doing, Danny?" Trent mocks.

"Not a fucking word, Chris," Dickhead warns. "You open your mouth, and I'll put a bullet in you to match the gaping hole in your stomach."

"Damn, bro. That's how it's going to be. You try to move in on my girl, and now you're going to kill me for telling her the truth?" Chris whines, blood dripping down his chin.

"This goes one of two ways. They kill, or I will," Dickhead tells Chris, moving closer.

"I'll take liar for two hundred, Alex," Chris singsongs, then his voice goes gravelly like sandpaper. "Tell them what you did, Danny."

"Who are you?" Dulce asks Danny with tears in her eyes.

I shine the flashlight on his stupid face so she can see how much of a lying piece of shit he is.

He squints and steps back from the light. "His family threatened me. I have a dark past, and this was my fresh start. My uncle is Moody. He was out here with him that night," he admits, lowering his weapon in defeat.

"Moody?" she says in disbelief, and the Dickhead nods with a painful expression.

"It's why I came back when he asked me…"

"To come and help him with me," she says, my hand tightens on the flashlight.

Danny nods.

"Motherfucker," Trent says. "You're related to that sick old fuck Moody, and you helped this piece of shit rape her?" he bellows.

"I wanted Dulce…but she wanted you, Ford," Chris says through the pain. "She wouldn't look at me the way she looked at you," Chris says like that's an excuse. "I wanted a family. She was perfect, but she didn't want me."

"So raping and leaving her to die was the answer?" I thunder. "Do you know what you've done? What she went through. She could have died."

"I've been inside your girl…" Chris spits. "Both of them so that must count for something."

"Shoot him, or you'll go down. You'll be up there with him. Disembowelment was a form of capital punishment, and God knows you deserve it," I warn Danny.

Mays points the gun at Chris. He won't shoot all of us. Maybe Trent and me, but not Dulce. I can tell by the way he looked at her, he wouldn't.

Chris is a dead man hanging. He'll bleed out and die anyway. I made sure of it, but I'm not sure what I'm going to do about this lying piece of shit in front of me.

"You lied to me, Danny," Dulce says with disgust and hot tears streaming down her cheeks. "You knew it was him," she says, her voice shaking in anger. "That is why you were driving on the street. You were looking for me."

"I know, and I'm sorry, but I didn't let him go near you after that," the Dickhead says.

"The rats?" she questions, glancing at Chris.

"That was me," Chris says like it's a game.

"This is all a game to you," she whimpers.

"Dulce, come here," I call to her softly.

A sense of relief washes over me when she practically runs over and wraps her arms around me.

"I knew it was only a matter of time before Ford would piece everything together. I thought he didn't care, and I would've made it right. I would have taken care of you. Protected you." Mays tries to convince her, but it falls on deaf ears.

She glances toward him, gripping me tight like I'm her anchor.

"Like you did for him," she says, pointing at Chris.

"We all have secrets, Dulce," Chris says, and my blood turns cold. Chris glances at me, his eyes half open. The drugs are wearing off, and he continues, "Ford has been keeping one from you. One he begged for no one to tell."

Dulce loosens her grip and glances at me. "What is he talking about, Ford?" she says, taking a breath after a sob.

"Tell her, man," Trent urges.

I hold her hand. "I have a problem."

Chris gurgles on a laugh.

Danny's hand is shaking, but he doesn't loosen his grip on the gun. "I can't," he says.

Silence. I look at Trent, and he gives me a signal with his eyes.

"You bastard," Dulce finally says.

"I'm sorry," Danny says in defeat, closing his eyes.

I move swiftly and tackle Danny to the ground. I take the gun from his hand and point it at his head. He raises his hands in surrender.

"Get up," I demand.

He gets up, and I motion with the gun for him to move toward Chris.

Chris's head is rolling to the side. He's lost a lot of blood and will bleed out soon enough.

"What do you plan on doing, Ford? You'll end your career. And for what, a girl from Airy," Danny taunts. "You could have any woman on the planet. Why her?"

"Shut up and kneel," I demand in a hard tone, pointing the gun at his head.

"He laughs. You'll end up in jail, and her business won't last a month. How do you think she's stayed in business this long? She pays the least amount in rent."

"You never wanted her to leave for fear she would remember and tell the truth about what Chris did," I point out, piecing everything together.

He needed help.

"We couldn't tell," Trent says, standing behind him.

"The nice guy act is a ruse. It was so they would adopt him and get the money we needed to survive. I became a cop, but the pay sucks. I needed more," Danny adds.

"But why Dulce?"

"We all hated you, Ford. Hell, I hated you. There was something about the way you looked at her." Chris turns to Dulce. "Do you know he is sick, Dulce?"

Dulce glances at me with a confused expression, wiping her mouth.

"We all wanted to fuck you," Chris says, above a whisper. "I did, and that makes me your first. You never forget your first, Dulce. We could have been good together— better than Ford. He's crazy. Obsessed. He knew where you lived, what you ate. He made sure you stayed a virgin."

"Could you just die already?" Trent cuts in. "You always talked too much."

I hesitate for a moment, not knowing what is going through her head right now.

"I wasn't the only one there that night," Chris says.

Hot fury burns in my gut. I press the tip of the gun to Danny's forehead. "Speak!"

"I-I was there," Danny stammers, earning a look of betrayal from Dulce. "I helped him rape her," Danny confesses.

I pull the trigger. Dulce screams, and Danny slumps over. I wipe my prints off the gun and hand it to Trent. "Take care of it."

Dulce watches stunned at Danny's body lying on the thick leaves. His blank eyes open.

"Get her out of here," Trent calls out as he walks closer to Chris.

I grab her hand. She is shaking uncontrollably. Most likely from the shock. "Shh," I say in a hushed tone. "I got you. No one will ever hurt you again, but I wanted you to see for yourself."

Another gunshot. Chris's body slumps, dangling from the rope. I light the path following the red markers nailed to the tree, finding our way back to the road.

I help her up the embankment. When we reach the road, she sobs into my chest. "They all knew. They all lied."

I wrap her in my arms. "I know, baby. It's over. It's all over. You're safe."

"You knew I wouldn't remember what happened when you brought me here."

I wasn't sure, but I wasn't going to let this go. Danny's involvement made it a huge complication. I had to pin Chris's death on him. I couldn't take Chris out and leave Danny to go free and risk him telling anyone. He had to pay, and killing a cop is hard to cover up.

"I love you, Dulce," I breathe in her hair as I wait for Trent. "Always remember that."

A gunshot goes off from Trent pulling the trigger, making it look like Danny shot Chris.

"I love you, too," she says through tears. "What now?"

Katie pulls up in the rented Camry as Trent dashes out of the woods. "Let's go. We don't have much time," she says.

Trent opens the passenger side, and Dulce and I slide in the back. "Where are we going?" Dulce asks.

Katie glances at her through the rearview mirror as she drives us to the airport. "To Italy."

She looks up at me. "Italy?"

I smile. "Remember that villa we talked about?"

"You have one of those?" she asks, dumbfounded.

"I do," I tell her.

"Lucky," Katie says, then glances at Trent, "You don't have a villa."

"I don't live in Italy," he says like she's an idiot.

"Oh...that's right. You live in a warehouse in the middle of nowhere." She smiles sarcastically. "How romantic."

"I like it hard and fast. Like my car."

"You finish fast, like your car," she fires back.

He leans back in his seat. "I've had no complaints." He shifts in his seat. "You didn't."

She scoffs. "Not to your face. You didn't stick around long enough."

"I lose interest fast."

I sigh. "Will you guys just fuck already," I cut in.

"Hell no," they both say in unison.

I can tell this is going to be a long ride.

"Are you okay?" I say softly near Dulce's ear as she looks out the window, oblivious to Trent and Katie bickering like teenagers.

"Yeah," she says, squeezing my hand.

She hasn't let my hand go since we got in the car. The Tiffany engagement ring on her finger digs into my hand. A stark reminder that she said yes, and that, finally, she's mine.

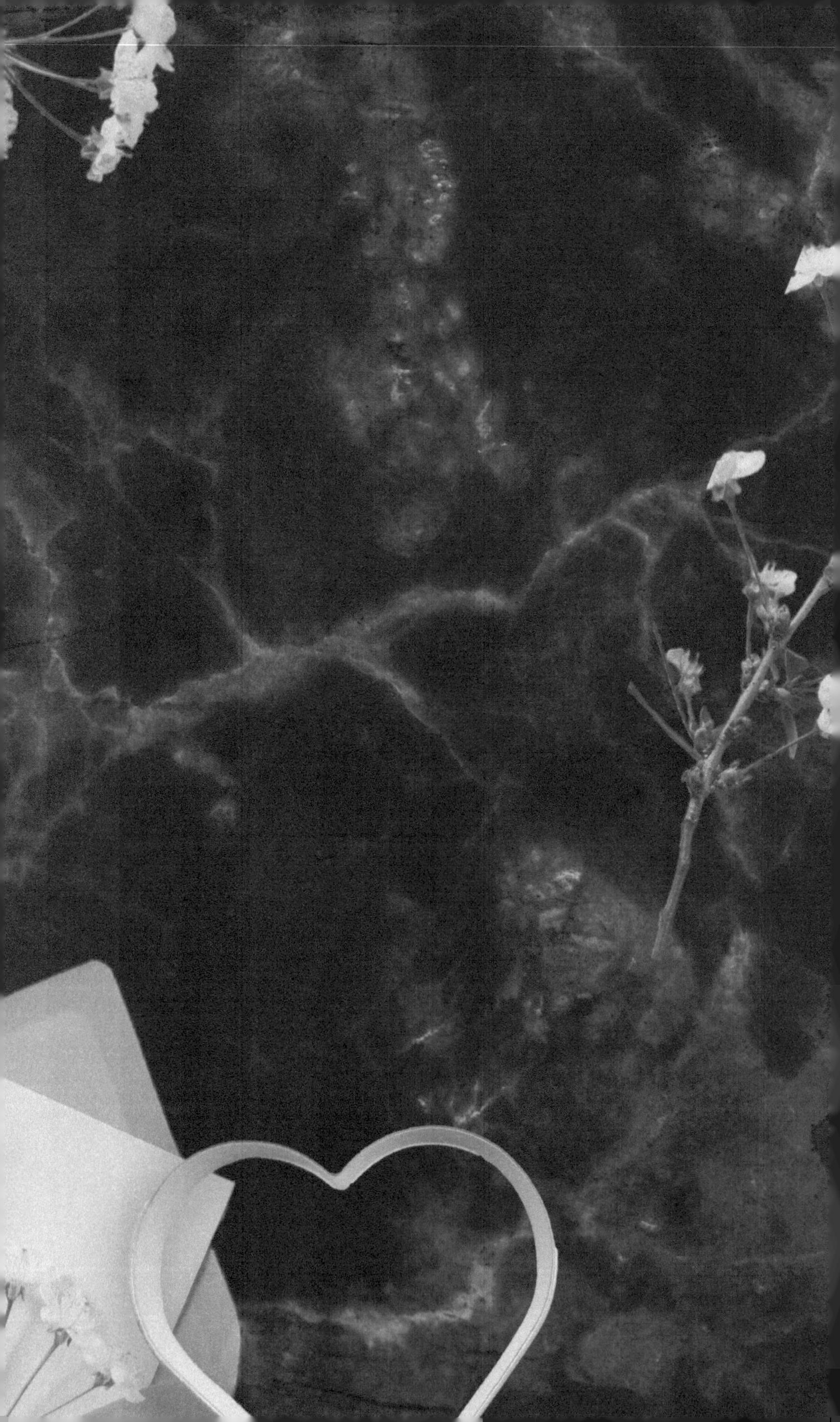

DULCE

One Year Later

I glance at Ford as he squeezes my hand. His smile is calm and controlled, but something is unsettling about it—something that never quite goes away. I've learned to ignore it because of the attention he gives me. He's gentle, attentive, and caring. His house in Vegas and in Italy were stocked with clothes in my exact size. The chef's kitchen mirrored the same equipment in the bakery.

But now, as Dr. Jordan looks between the two of us, a nagging feeling creeps into my mind. His words keep repeating in my head. *"How did you think your husband knew who to call that night at the hotel room? Or why he ordered the same cookies every week for the past four years?"*

My mind spins as I blink. I remember that night—when Ford called Dr. Long from the hotel and asked specific questions. But he knew. He always knew. I never questioned it—not really. I chalked it up to coincidence, to Ford just being... Ford.

But now, I can't shake the unease.

"Ford..." I speak softly, my voice suddenly tightening in my throat. "Why did you call Dr. Long at the hotel that night?" Did you know about my nightmares?

Ford's eyes flicker for the briefest second, and then his smile widens, but it's no longer reassuring. If anything, it feels... predatory.

He leans in slightly, his hand gripping mine tighter, and my heart skips a beat. "Because, Dulce," he says slowly, his voice like velvet wrapping around my throat, "I've always known where you were. But they weren't supposed to do what they did. And for that, I'm sorry."

A cold shiver runs down my spine. I try to pull my hand away, but his grip only tightens.

"What do you mean, Ford?" I ask, my voice barely above a whisper.

Ford leans back casually as if we're discussing the weather. "Everything I've done... was for you, but you're mine. Always."

My breath hitches. *Always?*

Dr. Jordan clears his throat, but I can't look at him. My eyes are locked on Ford, and suddenly, everything—every coincidence, every moment that seemed too perfect—starts to fall into place. The bakery sponsorship. The day he took me home on my birthday. The way he always showed up when I needed him. Months before my grandmother passed away.

Oh my God.

"You've been... waiting?" I ask, the words trembling on my lips.

Ford's smile remains unwavering. "Of course, Dulce. How could I not? I couldn't take any chances. Not with you. But I never knew about that night. I was on a plane, and Chris took what was mine."

I stand abruptly, my heart racing, but there's nowhere to go. Ford stands, too, stepping closer. Too close. I can feel his presence, towering, suffocating.

"Ford..." I say, my voice breaking. "You... you planned all of this, didn't you?"

He tilts his head, his eyes dark and piercing. "I did what I had to do, Dulce. For us. For our future."

I stumble back, but my legs feel weak, like they won't hold

me. I glance at Dr. Jordan, searching for some kind of help, but all I see is his calm, knowing expression. Like he knew this would happen. Like he *expected* it.

I shake my head, panic clawing at my chest. "No, no, this isn't right. This isn't... love."

Ford steps closer, his eyes locking onto mine. "Love?" He laughs softly, darkly. "This is the only kind of love, Dulce. The only kind that matters. You're mine. And you always will be."

His words wrap around me like chains, tightening with every second. My heart pounds in my ears, my breath coming in shallow gasps. I want to run, to scream, but I can't. I'm trapped. Trapped in a life I thought was mine but was never really mine at all.

Ford smiles, his hand brushing my cheek, and I flinch. "Don't worry, Dulce," he murmurs, his voice soothing but filled with a darkness I never fully saw before. "I'll always take care of you. Always."

I look into his eyes, and all I see is obsession. Control. Possession. Mixed with love that is dark.

If I ever thought I would leave Airy, I was alluding myself. Ford will never let me go. And I don't think I will ever want him to.

THE END

ABOUT THE
AUTHOR

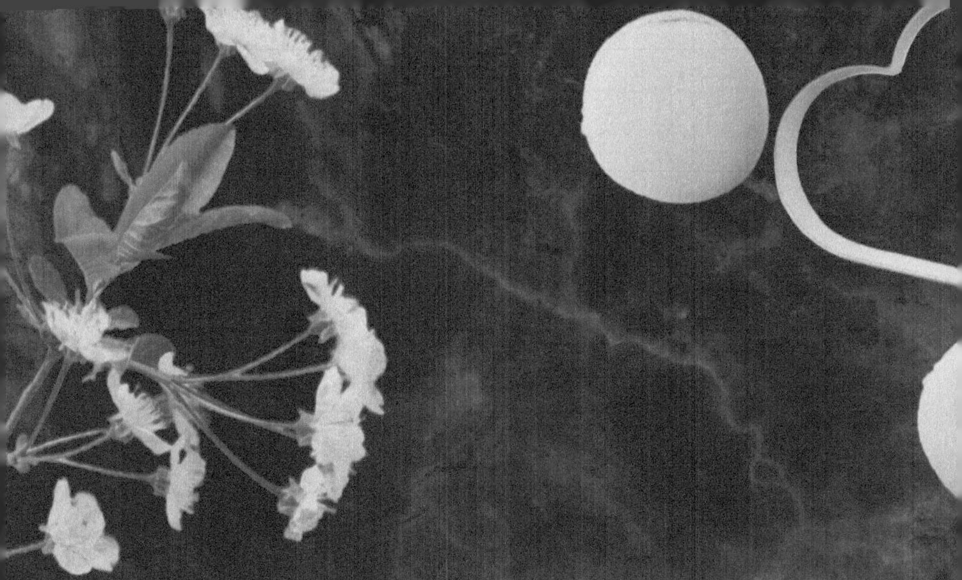

Carmen Rosales is a best-selling Dark Romance and Latinx author. She loves to write in different genres of Romance and erotic horror under her alter ego, Delilah Croww. Beyond her writing, Carmen is a devoted wife and mother who loves spending time with her loved ones. Join her VIP list and Newsletter- www.-carmenrosales.com

    Follow her on Social Media and stay up to date with her new releases: